P9-DUH-282

THE HORTON TWINS

THE
HORTON TWINS

BY

FANNIE KILBOURNE

Short Story Index Reprint Series

 BOOKS FOR LIBRARIES PRESS
FREEPORT, NEW YORK

First Published 1926
Reprinted 1970

INTERNATIONAL STANDARD BOOK NUMBER:
0-8369-3750-3

LIBRARY OF CONGRESS CATALOG CARD NUMBER:
74-142266

PRINTED IN THE UNITED STATES OF AMERICA

TO
CHARLES
AGAIN, OF COURSE

CONTENTS

THE HORTON TWINS

I

TWINS

HAVING your first baby is like taking a long trip in a sleeper. You suddenly wake up in new and unfamiliar country and you can hardly believe that in such a short time you've traveled such a long distance. It isn't a bit like walking somewhere leisurely with lots of time to get used to the change. There you are, all in a minute so to speak. And you're more than likely to have a whole trunkful of your old ideas that are just like clothes bought for another climate and that you can see aren't going to be an earthly bit of good to you here.

Of course, all this was particularly true for Will and me on account of our having twins. Why, now as I look at a girl pushing a mere single baby carriage, she seems like a care-free amateur with nothing on her mind but her permanent wave. Still, the expectation of having just one baby was enough to scare me into making a lot of resolutions.

This was partly because I was living in the very midst of horrible examples. Rosemary Merton has three babies, Mrs. Frank Kirsted one, Corinne Smith two. And as I looked about at them, I decided that I wasn't going to take the chances with my husband that they were taking with theirs. You see lots of movies of baby hands drawing husband and wife together and they don't write any

stories about those that wedge them apart. But I just
looked about me and realized that if having a baby made
me as near a total loss as it had some girls, it would be
asking a lot to expect Will to like me any the better for it.

Take Rosemary Merton, for instance. When I think
of the game of bridge that girl used to play and then
look at her now, it makes my blood run cold. She'll
stop right in the midst of playing three spades, doubled,
and say, "Do you know, I've had to increase the dextri
maltose in Sister's food again?" Or worse still, she'll
keep right on playing absently with that "listening" look
on her face that all girls with babies seem to get. Being
at the table with her while she's trying to decide whether
it's a door squeaking or Junior waking up is just like
playing double dummy. She who used to finesse down
to the nine spot now can't be depended upon not to trump
your good king! She and Mrs. Frank Kirsted kept talking one night about "Dr. Holt's book says this" and "Dr.
Holt thinks that—" till Roger Lane threw down his hand
and said, "Girls, have a heart! Are we playing bridge
according to Hoyle or according to Holt?" I don't
think that was original, but all the men, particularly
those who hadn't any babies themselves, laughed most
sympathetically.

And there is simply no holding any conversation with
Mrs. Ted Winters since she's had her baby. In the
very midst of discussing the row in the Water Street
church or whether bobbed hair is really going to stay
in, or anything interesting, she will suddenly turn to the
baby carriage and say:

"And what does oo think about it, pessus?"

Considering how it bores me to have a three-months-old baby constantly being included in the conversation, I could see what a fearful thing it must be for Ted Winters to hear that sort of talk all the time.

I could tell, by things he'd say now and then, that Will was a little apprehensive, himself.

"Let me give you a tip, Dotty," he said one evening as he enameled a blue stripe around the bassinet we were making. "When any man asks you how the baby is, don't tell him."

"Don't tell him?" I echoed, puzzled.

"No," said Will firmly. "He doesn't want to be told; he's just asking to be polite. Oh, of course, if a kid's sick or something, but not ordinarily. Now for instance, when I meet Howard Morton, I say, 'Well, how's tricks?' and when I meet Rosie, I say, 'Well, how're the kids?' Howard says, 'Oh, fine!' or 'Going strong' or something of the sort and lets it go at that. But not Rosie. She'll keep me standing on Water Street there for fifteen minutes and tell me every ounce that each one of her three has gained or lost during the last week. It's all lost on me. Gosh, I don't know within *ten pounds* what a baby ought to weigh, so what's a couple of ounces more or less to me?"

It was a lot of things like this, horrible examples and so on, that made me make such strong resolutions. I simply would not get like other mothers. I would not turn all my conversation into baby talk, I would not turn our whole home into a nursery like Corinne's, where the baby carriage stands in the middle of the living-room floor and the kiddie car in the dining room; where the bathroom is always full of bottles and every time you sit down in a chair without looking, some doll collapses under you, squeaking "Mamma."

No man likes a house like that and no man likes to see a snappy young wife get baby-ridden and worried and dowdy. No, sir! And I wasn't going to do it. I would never—so help me, John Hancock!—get to be the kind of woman that people look pityingly at their husbands and then say, "Oh, well, she's a good mother to his children."

I said something along this line to Mother one day, and she said comfortably:

"Don't worry. You'll get along all right. Will's a good man and he's fond of you. That's the main thing. If you have a good husband who loves you, there's always some way to manage." I said nothing to that. Mother always places a great deal of faith in virtue, which is all right in its way, of course, but everybody sees a lot of situations where just being good butters no parsnips. Mother smiled reminiscently. "My," she said, "it doesn't seem yesterday that Kathie was tugging at my skirts, and you were crying in your carriage. You were an awful cry-baby. Many a night your father used to walk the floor three and four hours with you."

Mother seemed so pleased over this memory that I didn't tell her how deplorable it was. As every modern mother knows, walking the floor with a baby is about the worst thing any father can do.

And I was going to be a modern mother. I was going to do the way all the best baby books tell you: feed the baby regularly, just so much, and then lay it down and forget it. None of this floor-walking business for my husband. Will is just as good a man as Father, but I believe that goodness can be pushed too far.

And I was going to run my own time by a budget. I found that idea in a magazine while I was getting ready for the baby and I knew the instant I saw it that it was the right dope. The article said you should budget your time as well as your money, not just spend it helter-skelter on whatever comes along first and then have none left for the things you really want it most for. Will and I have always stuck to a budget and I know it works with money, so why wouldn't it with time, I asked myself.

Long before the baby was due to arrive, I had my daily budget all made out. I found out from Rosie and Corinne just how long it takes to do everything for a baby so that there should be nothing amateurish about my plan. And it worked out beautifully. Ten minutes to wash the breakfast dishes, twenty to bathe the baby, half an hour to go marketing, and so on. When it's properly planned, there is a great deal of time in twenty-four hours. My budget left loads for reading and for manicuring my nails and doing all such improving things.

It worked out so simply and beautifully that I was eager to pass the idea on to the girls who had never heard of it. Goodness knows, I was trying to be helpful, but there are an awful lot of people who haven't got a progressive bone in their heads. When I showed my carefully worked out budget to Rosemary and Corinne, they *laughed*. In fact, as they read on down to some of my smaller items, such as "Chat with Will—ten minutes, glance in to see that Baby is O.K. ten times at one-half

minute—five minutes, use ice on complexion—three minutes," they simply went into hysterics.

"But isn't this sort of inefficient?" Rosie fairly choked
with giggles, ironing a little bonnet briskly all the time.
"Couldn't you economize a little more, chat with Will
while you're using the ice, for instance? You'd save
seven minutes a day right there."

But in spite of their joking, I believe to this day it
would have worked all right if I'd had just one baby.
Not that I regret the twins one instant, though. I'd
rather have my pair than a dozen mere single babies.
But there is no use denying that there is something staggering about twins. Why, Will was so awed that for two
days after they were born, he wasn't able to do a thing
but send telegrams. He wired to all his relatives and all
his college friends; when these ran out, he began on mere
acquaintances and I'm not sure he didn't work down to
total strangers before the fit wore off. A boy and a
girl! Two perfect, healthy babies.

Corinne lent me her bassinet, and Rosemary and Mrs.
Frank Kirsted practically outfitted the extra baby with
clothes that theirs had outgrown. We named the girl
Katherine after my sister, and the boy John after Will's
father, which set Father Horton up so that he paid the
doctor bill. Everything seemed to be working out like
magic.

There was one gorgeous week after I came home from
the hospital. Father said he'd treat me to the trained
nurse for that extra week, the two mothers ran the house.
I didn't have a thing to do but see callers, get flowers,
look at the babies and enjoy Will's treating me with such

awed respect, just as though he didn't realize that even assorted twins like ours were more good luck than good management.

But at last, of course, it was over. I was feeling perfectly fine again, both the mothers went home, glad to get at their spring cleaning. The trained nurse packed her bag and departed. After so much confusion and excitement, it seemed strangely quiet to sit down in the living room, just Will and I.

Will stretched his legs comfortably and grinned at me. "Well, Ma?" he said.

"Well, Pa?" I answered, grinning back. It really seemed just the gayest sort of joke in the world. Will suggested that we get Roger and Dulcie to come over and play Five Hundred for a while and I agreed, and decided to go and put on my pink dress.

Suddenly, from the sewing room we'd turned into the nursery, came a "Weh! Weh!" One of the twins was crying.

I paid but little attention to this, waiting unconsciously, from force of habit, for the nurse or Mother or Mother Horton to go to it. But as I heard no hurrying footsteps, the wail rose louder. And then it came to me that there was nobody but me to go. I suppose every woman who has been through that moment knows the feeling, and there's no use trying to explain it to anybody who hasn't. I felt suddenly all weak and wobbly.

I was alone in the house with those babies.

"I guess I'd better go and see what's the trouble," I said, and my very voice sounded faint and scared.

It was little John who was crying and by the shaded

night light I could see his face all screwed up and simply scarlet. I stood there, looking at him, not knowing what on earth to do and every moment I stood there, he cried louder and I felt more apprehensive. It didn't seem natural for any human face to be so red, perhaps he had a fever. Then suddenly at the top of a cry he stopped as though he were holding his breath. Suppose he should choke!

I had to do something. My hands shook so that I could hardly do anything, but I did manage to pick him up the way I had seen the nurse do, holding his head, and feeling as scared as though he were a lighted bomb. He caught his breath all right—looking back on that moment I realize now that he had never been holding it at all— and when I laid him down on his other side, he stopped crying instantly. As quickly as that the crisis was over.

I drew a shaky breath of relief and turned to the door to go out. But before I had opened it, I felt something ominous in the utter silence from Katherine's bassinet. Anxiously, I tiptoed over. She was lying perfectly still. Too still to look right! I bent clear down over her and to my horror, I couldn't see her breathe.

Cold fear clutched at my heart and I grabbed her shoulder. At the first touch, I knew that my fears had been groundless, the little shoulder was soft and warm. Instantly her eyes flew open, she stared straight up a moment, then pursed up her mouth and gave a howl, compared to which John's had been as nothing.

It may not have been more than three minutes more before I had her turned over, too, and quiet. Perhaps I hadn't been in the sewing room more than five minutes altogether. Some of the most harrowing experiences of life, though, can be crowded into five minutes. I went back to the living room feeling weak and shaken. And there sat Will, looking just as he had when I left him, for all the world as though nothing had happened.

He looked up at me cheerfully.

"Roge and Dulcie aren't home," he said. "How about getting the Vans?"

For a moment I just stared at him, unable to recall what on earth he was talking about, when at last I realized that he was still thinking about Five Hundred.

"I scarcely think I could play cards to-night," I said with hurt surprise, "after what I've been through."

Will looked startled.

"What you've been through?" he exclaimed. "Was anything wrong?"

I opened my lips for a reproachful reply, but I closed them again without speaking. What was the use? In that very instant, I saw the first crack of a great chasm widening between Will and me. Will did not understand. And all I could say could never make him understand.

If I repeated exactly what had happened, I realized myself it would sound simply silly. I had no words to describe that feeling of frightful, crushing responsibility that had fallen on me like a load of brick, with no warning. All the months I had been waiting counted for nothing, nor the time in the hospital, not even all the gay exulting since the babies had come. It was as though without a moment's warning, in that ten minutes in the sewing room, I had become a mother.

I rose the next morning and began what was without any exception the hardest time of my life. No human being who hasn't tried it knows what it means to do your own housework and take care of twins.

The first morning I thought about getting out my time budget and then decided not to. The budget made for one baby would be no good for twins. I thought that later in the day when I got my work done, I would make out another budget. But I didn't make out any budget because I never got my work done. Not that day nor any other day. From the time the alarm went off at six in the morning till I'd finish the supper dishes around seven, I kept going like a two-mile runner, my tongue simply hanging out. And after that there was still the ten o'clock feeding and the two A.M.

I was so tired all the time that any time I'd sit down a minute, I'd drop off to sleep. I never slept for more than a minute or two, though, coming to with a frightened start, dreaming I'd lost one of the babies or something. For a million times harder than the work was the terrible feeling of responsibility, the constantly having them on my mind.

And there wasn't a soul I could turn to. Will would offer kind of helplessly, "Isn't there something I can do to help you?" and was awfully nice about bringing in baby clothes off the line or something menial like that, but he didn't understand.

My own mother who would have been wonderful had had to go up to Minneapolis because Kathie was expecting her second baby any day, and Mother Horton was just nothing but a worry to me. She had no sympathy with modern science. She came in the first morning while I was getting the bathtub ready, the bath thermometer in one hand, my baby book in the other.

"The bath must be given for the first few weeks at 100 F.," I read, "during infancy at 98 F., after six months at 95 F., during the second year from 85 to 90."

"Good heavens!" she said impatiently, "you'll never last out to the second year if you pay any attention to that book! You don't need any thermometer for a baby's bath. Just test it with your elbow."

She thought feeding babies regularly was the silliest thing in the world, because that meant you sometimes had to wake them out of a sound sleep at feeding time. She said that was downright abnormal.

Sterilizing everything, too, she thought was stuff and nonsense.

"I wonder Dot lets you in the house," she'd joke to Will, "until you've been placed in cold water and brought slowly to a boil."

And she confessed to me, absolutely without shame, that she had always let Will suck on a pacifier to keep him quiet!

"Oh, the book says that's the worst thing in the world!" I exclaimed, horrified. "It ruins a baby's digestion besides making it nervous. The book says a human being's health for an entire lifetime depends upon the way you treat it as a baby."

Mother Horton just sniffed, glancing at Will, who chanced at the moment to be eating his tenth waffle.

"Well, if I've made a nervous wreck and a dyspeptic out of Will," she said, "may I never have to buy groceries for a strong man."

Honestly, there were times when I almost wished Will had turned out to be an epileptic or something, so that she couldn't settle any argument by just pointing to him. He must have been as strong as a horse or he'd never have pulled through a mere half of the things that were done to him. But, of course, I could never prove anything by quoting the best baby books ever written.

"By Dr. William Paul Van Alstyne," she'd say scornfully. "And has Dr. William Paul Van Alstyne ever been a mother?"

The worst of it all was that, in spite of her terrible ideas, she was so wonderful when it came to handling a baby. She could get both those twins dressed in the time it would take me to get one's band pinned on tight enough. This gave her such an unfair advantage. She'd say:

"Heavens, Dotty, you can't put a sleeve on like that! You're bending that child's elbow the wrong way." Then she'd slip the sleeve on as easy as nothing at all and smile at me so triumphantly that I knew she was thinking that proved there was no sense in sterilizing the bottles.

No, take it altogether, Mother Horton wasn't much of a help. All the girls, Rosie and Corinne and Mrs. Frank Kirsted went by the books, I knew, but someway, I didn't like to go to them. I would keep remembering the way they had laughed at my time budget.

But as the days went on, one dead-tired day after another, the thing that kept me unhappy, that ran along underneath my thoughts no matter what I was doing, was not the hard work nor the getting tired, nor even the feeling so responsible. It was the belief, growing upon me steadily and surely, that Will didn't care a whoop about the babies.

He was proud of them, of course, but that was all. As far as he was concerned, they were just a kind of a stunt. He would try to pretend a keen affection, but you can't fool a mother. I knew he was just doing it to please me. He'd come in and watch me bathe them Sunday mornings and say:

"Husky little beggar, isn't he?" or "I wonder if she'll be as good looking as you are."

But just as often, he'd merely pick them to pieces. Say:

"Isn't her stomach all out of proportion to her body?" Or, "What makes him keep his mouth open like that? It makes him look kind of simple-minded."

And in a few minutes, he'd get bored and go outside and talk to Roger.

Those babies never bored me. When one of them would take hold of my finger or drop its little bald head down in my neck, the strangest feeling would come over me. A feeling so strong that it made my tonsils ache and gave me a queer all-gone feeling in the pit of my stomach. I suppose it's what is called mother love. And there was no use pretending that Will felt like anything like it.

If he had, he could never have been so reasonable.

"Why can't you get in a little nap this afternoon?" he would ask, "and then get Ella Crowninshield to come and stay till ten so that we can go to the movies with the crowd?"

It would sound reasonable enough. But some way or other, I never once got the nap. One of the babies would sneeze during the morning or refuse its food or break out with prickly heat and even if I lay down, I'd be too worried to go to sleep. And then if I did get to the movies, I never saw a thing on the screen. I'd suddenly recall that I had told Ella to give the babies a little water in a bottle if they cried and hadn't told her to warm it. Heavens, for all I knew she might at that very minute be feeding them ice water!

Or Will and I would be sitting out on our porch and I'd say, "If John hasn't gained any when I weigh him in the morning, I'm going to call up the doctor." And would realize too late with a guilty start that Will had been in the very midst of telling me about selling the Dusenthal place and that I hadn't been listening to a word he was saying.

And to think that I'd ever criticized Rosie's bridge just because she trumped my good king! The once I tried to play, the only thing that kept me from trumping my partner's ace was that I couldn't remember what was trump.

I could see that all these things annoyed Will. And I couldn't blame him. It was reasonable enough. But someway, feeling as I did about the babies, I couldn't seem to be reasonable. If Will only loved them, too! He'd understand then why I was afraid to leave them a minute, why I couldn't seem to help thinking about them all the time.

But he didn't understand and there were times when I'd feel that he was restless and impatient, times—though I wouldn't breathe this even to myself—when perhaps he wished we hadn't had any babies at all.

I would urge him to go down to Howard's to fool with sleight of hand of an evening and was glad to have him go on over to the Verblen Pavilion to watch the bowling tournament without me. But even so, we'd always been free to have company or go out any old time we wanted to before the babies came and I could see that Will felt tied down. So did I, of course, but being so crazy about the babies, they pretty much made up for this to me. But I could see that they didn't to Will.

The day that Roger Lane had his uncle's big twin-six sport roadster to use and invited us to drive into the city in the evening with him and Dulcie, I made up my mind that I would go, come what might.

It was one of those wiltingly hot days when even if you haven't anything to do you feel too tired to do it. But I just forced myself along with my work so that I'd have time to get in a little nap and be fresh for the evening. Of course, I didn't get the nap, but I determined to be fresh just the same. Will came home from the office a little early in high spirits and put on his white trousers and blue coat. All through supper he joked and was so gay and seemed so pleased over our going out together that I realized with a little regretful pang how much he had missed not having any fun at all.

I was so tired that I couldn't eat anything, but I drank a lot of iced tea, which is always bracing. Ella Crowninshield was coming to stay with the babies and

I had told her every little thing to do for them, and determined I wouldn't think of them once while I was gone. She was going to do the supper dishes which would give me time to dress. I hadn't had a minute before. It was a half-hour before time to start and I decided to take a cold bath, which would pep me up still further.

"You beat it and start to dress," Will said. "I'll put the butter and stuff in the ice box. Hasn't to-day been a wilter, though! I'll bet the office has been a hundred and ten." He looked out the window at the long low car without any top, standing at Dulcie's curb, and heaved a grateful sigh. "Some boat!" he said.

I echoed his sigh of relief and anticipation. I could just feel the cool breeze blowing through my hair.

While I was sighing, the telephone rang. It was Ella Crowninshield. Her mother was sick and she couldn't come.

I looked at Will in utter consternation.

"Isn't there somebody else you can get?" he asked anxiously.

"Who?" I asked. Mother was still away, Mother Horton was staying overnight with her sister in Verblen.

"Couldn't you hire America?"

"Leave my babies with that ignorant washwoman! She always leaves the ice-box door wide open and if I don't watch her, she'll go off leaving gas escaping from every burner in the kitchen stove. She's afraid of the telephone—she wouldn't know enough to call up the doctor if one of them should be sick."

"There surely must be somebody we can get," Will

urged. It was just disappointment, of course, that made his voice sharp, and it was mostly ignorance that made him suggest leaving the babies with America. But I was so hot and so terribly tired, so disappointed, too, that I felt like sitting down and crying.

And at that moment, Roger and Dulcie came in the door. Roger was all spic and span like Will in white trousers and blue coat, and Dulcie in a new silk broadcloth sports dress looked like a million dollars, her hair all water waved, her white slippers simply immaculate, with new jet buckles. The gingham dress I still had on was as limp as a rag, my hair hadn't been touched since six o'clock in the morning. Dulcie moved one hand and I noticed her shining nails and recalled that I hadn't cleaned my white shoes. It was just too much.

I couldn't think of anybody we could get to stay with the babies and I was too tired and discouraged to try very hard.

"It's a perfect shame," Dulcie was saying sympathetically. "I suppose there's just no way you can go, then."

"I guess not," I answered.

"How about you, Wilhelm?" Roger asked. "Couldn't you go?"

"Oh, no," said Will hastily. "I won't go if Dot can't."

In spite of his quick answer, I know Will so well that I could see he was crazy to go.

"Oh, go on anyhow, Will," I heard my own voice saying. "There's no use in our both sticking at home just because I have to."

He protested that that didn't seem fair and I heard

myself keep right on urging him to go. My own voice
came to my ears, the way it does sometimes when you're
awfully tired, as though it were somebody else's. And
that somebody else kept saying things I didn't mean at
all. It might be selfish and dog-in-the-manger-ish and
everything else, but I didn't honestly want Will to go.
It seemed to me that I couldn't stand it if he did go.

And yet I kept right on urging him to. And little by
little he was yielding.

"Oh, come on," Roger urged him, too. "Dotty
wouldn't care just this once. We'll bring her back some
ice cream."

"Well, if you're dead sure you don't mind," Will said
doubtfully to me.

"Not a particle. I'll get into something cool and read,"
the voice over which I seemed to have no control, said
lightly.

So lightly, so naturally, that Will was persuaded.

"Well, if you're dead sure," he repeated.

And in a minute the three of them were gone. The
two men in their flannel suits looking like a pair of care-
free college boys, Dulcie, looking just as young and care-
free and so dainty and gay. They waved back at me as
the car swung around the corner and away. I went back
into the house. It was hot, the dirty dishes stood on the
supper table, my limp old dress stuck hotly to my shoulders. I felt old and shabby and left out of everything.
One of the babies cried and I went in to the sewing room.
They were fussy, too, with the heat.

I gave the baby some water and turned him over. Then
I sat down by the window and faced the utter failure I

had made. I, who had started out with such gallant plans. Who had vowed to keep fresh and good-looking and gay and interested in everything, to be a companion that my husband could both enjoy and be proud of— here I sat, in a faded gingham dress, too tired with tending house and babies to do anything else.

The house, too, after the trim, nifty way I had meant to keep it! The table full of dirty dishes, a stack of baby clothes on the living-room davenport—I had been bringing them in from the line when the telephone rang and had forgotten even to pick them up. Things simply couldn't go on like this! I recalled Will's going away without me, first to Howard's, then to the bowling tournament, protesting a little less each time, honestly glad to get away from the house. Would he some time, perhaps, be glad to get away from me, too? I thought of him striding along beside Dulcie to-night. With the world full of fresh, dainty, pretty girls, could I expect him to keep on preferring me, in my wilted gingham dress, too tired even to listen to him when he talked to me?

Oh, there must be some way—there simply had to be! With a sudden feeling of panic, I got out the time budget I had made before the babies came. The time budget that had left me so much leisure for everything.

Slowly I read through the items. No wonder the girls had laughed at it. "Read two books a month, one-half hour a day." I swallowed bitterly over that item. It had been days since I'd had time to look at the morning paper. "Ice for complexion—three minutes!" Ice for complexion—it was all I could do to find time to brush my teeth!

With an aching lump in my throat, I started in to try to change that budget to fit twins. Twice as much washing, twice as many bottles, twice the baths and so on. I put down only the things I absolutely had to do each day, and for every necessary item, I cut out enough time from some unnecessary. In no time, it got to where the only items left to cut were sleep and the reading-and-complexion sort. I cut sleep to seven hours and a half and didn't dare go any farther than that. Then one by one the other items went. The items I had counted on to keep Will loving me.

And as I drew a line through one after another, I felt I was giving up Will. And I couldn't help it. The babies were here and mine—the work couldn't be cut. There was the twenty-four hours a day that had once seemed so long, and there was what absolutely had to be done. I looked down at the hopeless figures and I thought of Will, trim and handsome in his flannel suit, riding away with Roger and Dulcie. The lump in my throat seemed to sweep all over me, hot and choking.

Little John whimpered and I dragged myself across the room to look at him. His two fat little hands above his head, that dear funny little bald head. The faint hope that maybe I could forget the babies just a little, maybe even neglect them a tiny bit, vanished in a sick drop of my heart. That helpless little mite lying there, not able to speak or move no matter what happened to him, sick or frightened maybe, crying out for help and nobody even to hear him—I felt against the feeling of a tiny baby in my arms, soft, limp, warm—

I dropped my head on the edge of the bassinet and

cried hot, scalding tears. The babies were so frighten-ingly dear to me and life was so hard.

I was crying so abandonedly that I didn't hear the door. Suddenly I heard steps at the sewing-room door. Fright-ened, I looked up to see Will.

"—got out at Verblen and came back by street car," he was saying. "Just couldn't go off and leave you alone a deathly night like this—don't know why I ever started —oh, honey girl, what's the matter?"

He gathered me up in his arms and carried me back to the window. Hot as it was, it seemed to me that all the comfort in the world was there tight in his arms.

"What's the trouble, sweetheart? Are you just hot and tired or is it something else?"

"Oh, Will, it's my budget," I choked out. "There isn't any use—I can't make one out that will work—"

"Your budget?" Will picked up the page I had been working on, peered at it in the twilight. There they were, all the one-baby items changed to fit two, all the items I had started out so blithely with drawn through with heavy lead pencil, scratched right out of my life.

"'Change dress for supper—ten minutes,'" he read. "'Ice for complexion—three, Chat with Will—ten min-utes'"—all the things I had meant to do to keep him for my lover scratched out! Will read on down the list. For a moment I thought he was going to laugh. Then, suddenly, his eyes filled with tears.

"Oh, Doll," he said, "you funny, *funny* darling!"

"That isn't the worst of it, either," I said hopelessly. "I've cut out everything but just the absolutely neces-saries and it won't work out. I've added them up and added them and—and they come to twenty-five hours and twenty minutes every day!"

"Good Lord!" said Will.

He took the list and read down it, item for item.

"Honey, why in the name of Heaven, haven't you told me?"

"Well, I didn't know what could be done—they're my babies and—"

"They're my babies, too," said Will, "and I'll tell you what can be done. Here I've thought I was doing all my share because I worked in an office nine hours a day. Nine hours, and you working twenty-five hours and twenty minutes out of every twenty-four! Why haven't you told me?"

"But what can we do?"

"Do? We can even up this budget."

"But it's all housework and baby-tending—you don't know how to take care of a baby."

"Neither did you till you learned. I'm just as smart as you are and a darn sight stronger. Now let's see those items."

Slowly he went down the list, stopping every now and then to say, "Now I can do this when I'm home for dinner," and "we'll both get up at six and you can do some of these while I'm getting breakfast."

"It doesn't seem right for you to have to get breakfast," I protested.

"Did it all the time we were camping, funny thing if I can't do it to help out with my own babies."

And "I'll wring out the clothes and hang 'em out while you're getting dinner."

"Oh, Will, you *can't* do baby washing!"

"Can't I?" Will grinned. "Watch me!"

His voice sounded so big and strong and dear and dependable. It was all very modern and scientific, putting down items like "sterilizing" and "make formula" with so many minutes after each one, yet someway it made me think of Mother being young and worried and Father walking the floor at night with me. Bad as it is to walk the floor with a baby, I felt I never really appreciated Father before.

And one by one, I saw time coming back for some of the items I thought I had scratched out of my life forever. Not all of them, but plenty. Some of these Will laughed at just as the girls had, but I didn't care. Because he'd stop and rub the back of his hand against my cheek and say:

"Oh, Dotty, you nut! You dear, funny, darling little nut!"

And then, "Well, here's two we can double up on. You can chat with Will while we're folding the diapers." And he laughed again and rumpled up my hair and I felt as though, after all, life wasn't quite so real and earnest and depressing.

"And here's item number one, young lady. You go and get your cold bath and go to bed. I feed these babies to-night."

I opened my mouth to tell him he couldn't, he didn't know how, he might hurt the babies. But something inside me told me in time to shut it again and I did, without saying a word. Will had watched me lots of times, he knew more about it than I did when I started. And if I pushed him aside and took it out of his hands, he'd lose all interest and feel the way I do when Mother Horton laughs at my ideas. I choked back all my natural instincts, said, "Oh, Will, you peach!" And walked out of the sewing room!

I glanced in at the door fifteen minutes later all cool and ready for bed. Will was fussing with the bottle warmer and didn't hear me and I just stood and watched him. I might not have understood the peculiar look he had on his face so well if I hadn't been all through it, myself. He looked willing and eager, but serious and scared. As though the responsibility of the universe had fallen on him like a ton of brick. I was just going to tell him to cheer up, that that awful first feeling does wear off, when he looked up and saw me. He beckoned mysteriously, led me over to Katherine's bassinet.

"Look," he whispered. "I was just going to go after you. There, she did it again! Dot, that kid is smiling!"

I looked down at little Katherine and then up at Will. And I knew that I wasn't alone in the world with those babies any longer. The look on Will's face was responsible and scared and silly and proud. The unmistakable parent look.

"Just wait," said Will in an awed tone, "till I tell Frank Kirsted that!"

I glanced up at Will in surprise. But he wasn't even smiling, and I didn't smile either. Just slipped my hand into his and looked down at the baby, too. She was too cunning for words. And Will was so tickled with her. I wouldn't have said a word to spoil it. Not for worlds would I have told him that the books all say when a child under three months old apparently smiles, it is just gas on the stomach.   Science is all right in its way, but Will was taking on enough of the work and responsibility of being a parent to be entitled to all the fun there is in it.

II

GOLF AND THE SERPENT

THERE seems to be a serpent in every garden of Eden but it is really strange that it should always be Dulcie. Not just for me alone—it seems to have been decided by fate that she should be the serpent for the entire town of Montrose.

Before any of us girls were married, of course, this was natural enough. Dulcie was awfully pretty and such a flirt that she could keep any town in the world from being exactly a restful place for other girls. We had all got used to Dulcie, though, and, as our husbands were used to her, too, nobody minded her flirting with all of them any more than we minded the silly rowdy things Marge Kitteridge was always doing. Marge never could go to a party without dropping a spoonful of ice cream down somebody's back or telling each of two people privately that the other one had suddenly got deaf but was sensitive about it so please not to mention it but just shout at him. Everybody to his own idea of a good time, we used to say, and let it go at that.

Dulcie had been, in fact, my rather special chum. Living next door, we always used to be going back and forth to dinner, and sewing together afternoons, and so on. This was quite natural as so many of our old crowd weren't married, which made them seem too hopelessly immature to be any company for an adult person. And those that were married were always having babies, which made them worse still.

Why, one day when some of the girls in our old high school were having a reunion luncheon, Dulcie started right out by saying:

"Well, I give my baby spinach water and orange juice. What do you give yours?"

Everybody looked up in surprise, knowing that Dulcie had no baby. Then all those that did have laughed kind of sheepishly, realizing that they undoubtedly must have made bores of themselves. Dulcie and I often used to speak confidentially of Rosemary or Corinne and say what a shame it was they were dropping out of everything so and not paying so much attention to their clothes and things like that. There is nothing that makes you feel quite so close to another person as speaking in confidential criticism of some mutual friend. Yes, Dulcie and I were really quite intimate.

And then my own twin babies came and all changed. One of the first things I noticed was that Dulcie didn't seem nearly so congenial as she had. Actually, she didn't seem to know anything. Why, one day I went upstairs to get a handkerchief and when I came back she said, "Did you feed the babies?" As though you could feed two babies in two minutes! And she was so flippant about the twins. She always called them Nip and Tuck till one day she came in when they were both howling their heads off at once and then she started calling them Rack and Ruin. Rosemary and Mrs. Frank Kirsted and I used to discuss her sometimes, wonder if she and Roger weren't

ever going to have any babies and say it would be a
shame. A baby would make her so much more human.

It was at about this time that I began to get the first
faint glimpses of the fact that Dulcie was going to be
the serpent in our garden of Eden. The trouble was that
Will admired her. I don't mean in the least that he was
a particle interested in her sentimentally or that there was
the faintest thing the most jealous wife in the world
would object to. But he thought she was pretty and
clever and smart-looking, all of which there was no denying she was. And goodness knows, I didn't mind Will
thinking so, too. But there is no denying that, after
my babies came, it was sometimes a strain to have Dulcie
childless and living right next door.

Many a time when I've been so dead tired at five o'clock
I wanted to sit right still in my bungalow apron and
never move again, I've glanced out of the window to see
Dulcie in a periwinkle-blue voile opening up her gate-
leg table out on the porch, and known she was going
to serve supper out there. And once I'd seen her, I'd
realize I just couldn't let Will in for seeing such a contrast. I'd make myself take a cold bath and put on my
own rose dotted swiss and set our supper table out on
the porch, too. A cold bath, of course, always does pep
you up a lot if you can just make yourself take it.

Dulcie never seemed to realize that it was any harder
for me to do things than it was for her. She'd say:

"Oh, come on and go to the movies. You know Will
wants to go. Get Ella Crowninshield to stay with the
babies. Oh, of course, they'll be *all right*, won't they,
Will?" Or, "I've got a pattern for the niftiest sports

dress and it only takes three yards—why don't you get some of that wash silk from your dad's store and make one, too?" Or, having whole afternoons to waste, she'd read up the fine points of Mah Jong and then kid me for playing it about like dominos.

I used to simply run a fever trying to keep up with her. Once in a while, I'd surprise her, too. I'll never forget the satisfaction I got out of going Mah Jong on all pairs. I'd stuck the Mah Jong book up over the ironing board that afternoon and studied it by snatches while I was ironing the babies' dresses. And that evening when Dulcie looked in amazement at my seven pairs of tiles and started to say I wasn't Mah Jong, the solid satisfaction I had in saying in a superior tone:

"Why, Dulcie, haven't you ever heard of the Heavenly Twins?" And showing her the place in the book that proved my hand was very unusual and doubled my score three times.

Still, in spite of bright moments like that, occasionally, Dulcie was a terrible strain. I didn't realize how much of one she was till she went away on a summer visit. The heavenly peace that settled over our little house! I stopped feeling all the time like a child that is being jerked along by the hand of an older person who is walking too fast. We spent most of our spare time with Howard and Rosie Merton and the Kirsteds and Scott and Corinne, people who had babies of their own and, therefore, some sense. When any of them came over of an evening, they didn't stick around till eleven o'clock—they knew that ten is feeding time. Once in a while those girls wouldn't get around to doll up for supper, either, and they thought it was stupid to try to play Mah Jong as conscientiously as though you had to make your living at it.

During that peace I actually managed to get my life systematized, even with twins, in a way I never in the world could have done it with Dulcie right next door, starting something new to worry you just the minute you got the old one settled. Will helped me a lot with the babies and we got things to running as smooth as clockwork.

We decided not to go away anywhere for a vacation, but to spend the money in the "vacation" part of our budget box on other things. Will took half of it and joined the new golf club the Harvester crowd has started out toward Verblen. Half our money wasn't enough but Father Horton paid the rest because he thought it would be a good thing for their real estate business for Will to be able to take prospective customers out there. The other half of the vacation money I took to spend having Ella Crowninshield in once in a while to stay with the babies.

It was a glorious scheme. I began getting out to bridge parties afternoons again now and then. I even read a new book once in a while and felt pretty satisfied because I kept myself up better in general than Rosie or Corinne and just as well as Mrs. Kirsted. Saturday afternoons Will put in learning to play golf. The Harvester Company closes Saturday afternoons, so does the bank, of course, which left Frank Kirsted and Roger free then, so Father Horton gave Will the time off, too.

Will and I had always used to do something together

week-ends, but Will was so crazy to learn golf that I didn't have the heart to object. I knew he really needed the exercise and I had to admit that by having Ella once in a while, I really had more time for fun than he did. He was so dear about helping me a lot with the babies that I felt it was only fair. Besides, he was very careful about getting home to supper on time.

Oh, everything had got to running like a well-oiled clock. Mrs. Collier, who is a perfect wiz about keeping house and who has her children so well trained you feel they can't be healthy, actually complimented me on the way I was managing.

"It's all in system," she said. "System—and being firm. I tell Mr. Collier and the boys that I am not running a restaurant. They know the mealtimes and any one who is late, has no meal. That's all."

I had to laugh at the idea of running Will like that. But fortunately, I thought, I didn't have to. Will wanted to help me make things go smoothly and I wanted him to be happy, too. So we got along beautifully.

Till Dulcie got home!

Actually, Dulcie hadn't been home two days before all my peaceful, satisfied feeling of life going smoothly had vanished. To begin with, we all went on a picnic out to Lake Winneposocket and went swimming. Dulcie wears a black bathing suit and there's no use pretending she doesn't look simply gorgeous in it. I had brought my old suit and, to my horror, I found I could scarcely get into it.

Not that I was fat in the least, goodness knows. Rosie had twice my trouble getting into her suit and even Mrs.

Frank Kirsted, who used to have a better figure than Dulcie, appeared a little broad. Looking about at the other
girls who had babies, I should have been very well pleased
with myself, but seeing Dulcie looking like an ad for a
summer resort was annoying.

And to cap the climax, while we were riding home,
Will actually hinted that I was putting on weight.

"Everybody does after they have children, Will," I
said a shade coolly. Rosie and Corinne and Mrs. Frank
Kirsted and I had spoken of that, only that afternoon. It
had satisfied us all perfectly but it didn't seem to satisfy
Will.

"I suppose the stuff you eat at those bridge parties
afternoons is fattening," he hazarded.

I said nothing to this, the fact that we are quite likely
to have salads with lots of whipped cream and mousses
and such things making any good answer rather difficult;
but I realized right then that with Dulcie's return all my
peace of the last two months was imperiled. Already, I
began to see glimmerings of unrest ahead.

But that was as nothing to the glimmering I got the
first Saturday afternoon after her return home. Will
and Roger and Frank Kirsted and Howard had gone out
to play golf, as usual. Rosie and Mrs. Kirsted brought
their children over and parked them on our lawn, so that
we could sit on the porch together and sew and watch
them. I had made a fresh marshmallow cake and decided
to cut it and serve some lemonade and make it a real
social occasion. I called over to Dulcie to come, too, but
she didn't seem to be at home.

Rosie and Mrs. Kirsted were complaining about their

husbands going away every Saturday afternoon to play golf. They weren't bitter at all about it, just pleasantly grumbling and, though I really didn't mind much, I joined in. There is nothing that makes you feel so comfortable as when other women complain of their husbands to realize that you've got one to complain of, too. I do feel awfully sorry for unmarried girls.

"Howard didn't eat any dinner at all to-day," Rosie said plaintively. "He never does Saturday noons any more—Sister, don't put that in your mouth!—just bolts a few mouthfuls and dashes for the golf course. And then he comes home at six so hungry I simply can't get enough supper to satisfy him."

"That's just the way Frank is, too," said Mrs. Kirsted. "I've decided I'll have to have dinner at night on Saturdays though I loathe it—Frankie, bring that to mother, let me see what you've picked up!—I hate not to be able to get through the hot work and clean up in the afternoon."

"Will is perfectly awful about golf," I went on. "Of course I knew he would be, though; he never uses any sense about anything he takes up. He no sooner gets into the house than he's grabbed one of his clubs and gone out to the ravine in back to practice. And as I told him, while I don't mind his practicing 'putting,' whatever that is, all over our living-room rugs, when he asked me to sit still and let him try dropping balls in my lap with a mashie, I had to draw the line somewhere."

We all laughed comfortably.

"I used to be perfectly crazy about golf myself before I was married," said Mrs. Kirsted, "so I can understand it. It makes me kind of homesick to see Frank getting out his clubs. If it weren't for Frankie, I'd like to take it up again."

We all sighed comfortably and said how different your life was after you had a husband and a baby or so. At five I served the lemonade and cake and we got to talking about Betty Bartell and at quarter of six the girls were just going.

Suddenly, as though an electric switch had been touched, we all looked down the street at the same time. Roger Lane's flivver was coming with our three husbands and Dulcie in it.

At first, we thought of course Dulcie had just driven out after them, but as they all climbed out and came swarming up on our porch with their clubs, we found our mistake. Dulcie had been playing with them!

She sat on the railing in a green wash silk sports dress, swinging a pair of very good-looking golf shoes, and told us she had learned to play on her vacation. The boys were all teasing and jollying her about her game. I glanced over at Rosie and, though we scarcely exchanged a second's look, I could tell that in the same vague, uneasy way I was feeling, she didn't exactly like the idea. I glanced at Mrs. Frank Kirsted and she was looking like a person who doesn't really think there's a fire and yet seems to smell smoke.

If Dulcie were plain and low-heeled and athletic-looking nobody would have minded, of course. But with her yellow hair and pretty eyes, there's no denying that Dulcie is simply made to be the serpent in somebody's garden. Something came back to me out of the past. In the time since we've all been married, I'd almost forgotten the Dulcie that used to keep all the girls in town upset, the Dulcie who couldn't look at a new beau of another girl without wondering if it would be possible to get him away from her. Not that I thought she wanted to try to get any of our husbands now, goodness knows, but— well, I couldn't quite decide what it was that made me feel uneasy but I couldn't help wishing Dulcie had a pair of twins too and had to stay at home like any other married woman.

The next Saturday I had supper ready promptly at quarter past six as usual, and those men never got home till seven o'clock! Will was very apologetic.

"We wanted to finish up the eighteen holes," he explained, "and Dulcie said you wouldn't mind, supper being mostly a cold meal, anyway."

"I made popovers," I said rather chillily, "and I'm afraid they aren't fit to eat now."

Will was very sorry and ate the popovers which were cold and soggy, declaring they were good, of course. He went right on explaining being late and, as is always the case when Will starts smoothing things over, the more he smooths them, the rougher they get.

"I hated to start home ahead of the bunch," he said, "because we get in our best chance to play after five o'clock. All of us just learning, it makes us kind of nervous when the course is crowded and the Harvester crowd thins down late in the afternoon. You see, most of them keep maids and they have to get home right on tick for dinner so the girls won't get sore and leave."

I said nothing for several moments and the more I

thought of that remark of Will's, the less I liked it. A husband has to be too considerate of his maid to keep her dinner waiting two minutes, but he can leave his mere wife hung up for three-quarters of an hour while her popovers get as soggy as sponges.

"It seems to me," I said in a hurt tone, "that when I have to stay at home all the afternoon taking care of your children and getting your supper, the least you could do would be to get here in time to eat it."

Will was quite crushed by the justice of that remark but his way of fixing everything up was far less satisfactory than before. The next Saturday afternoon he called me up from the golf club.

"Listen, honey," he said, as though he were handing me money, "don't you bother with supper for me to-night. We're just going to get started now and it'll be late. Dulcie says she'll get us all something cold when we get home."

Most unhappily I put the babies to bed that night, got my own supper and ate it alone. At eight o'clock the flivver arrived. Will dashed in, dropped his clubs, shouted:

"Dulcie says for you to come on over, Dotty," and dashed over to the Lanes.

I didn't go over, however. Things had come to a pretty pass when if I wanted to see my husband I'd got to meet him at Dulcie Lane's. They ate out on the porch, I could hear them opening ginger ale and laughing and talking about the game. Will came home too enthusiastic to notice my coolness.

"Why don't you come on out and learn, Dotty?" he

demanded. "A lot of the Harvester bunch's wives play."

"Who would you suggest I'd leave the babies with?" I asked coolly.

"Couldn't mother—or your mother—" he began.

"The Ossili meet Saturday afternoons," I reminded him. "They'd scarcely care to stay home from that to let me play golf."

"Well, can't you hire Ella?"

"Ella has a beau who works in the bank. He has Saturday afternoons off. She'd scarcely care to come then, either."

Whenever I feel irritated at Will, I use the word "scarcely" a great deal.

"Well, you always seem to be able to get away to go to a bridge party," he said in a rather aggrieved tone. "I should think if you really wanted to—"

"I don't go to bridge parties Saturdays," I said. "Of course, I can get Ella occasionally on other days. You see, Will," I added, gently reproachful, "my life is rather different now that we have children. I can scarcely be as free as Dulcie."

"Say," said Will suddenly, "it's a funny thing about Dulcie. She doesn't get anywheres near as long a shot as the rest of us but she hits straight and we go off wild to one side a lot. When we come to count up strokes, she'll often beat us on the hole."

"Did she wear that green dress again?" I asked, curiosity overcoming resentment for the time being.

"No," said Will. "She's got a lolla pa looza. Stripes running round and round her like a convict. It sounds funny but it looks pretty slick on her."

"She showed me the pattern," I said. "I'd thought I might make me one."

"Well," said Will doubtfully, "I don't know that you'd like it for yourself."

If there is anything that makes me wild it's for a husband to admire something on another girl and then think it's too loud for his wife. Not till two days later did it occur to me that perhaps Will thought I was getting too fat to wear stripes running crosswise. This was hardly likely, though, I admitted. I was much slimmer than Rosie Merton and it wasn't fair of Will to go comparing me with a girl like Dulcie who has no children and nothing to do but doll herself up and serve meals in the middle of the night.

Oh, the strain was certainly on again. All the peace that had come while Dulcie was away, was flown. The next Saturday they didn't get home till half past eight. And I couldn't say a word, Will was raving so over what a good sport Dulcie was to be willing to get a late supper for them. Every weekday evening he'd dash out to the ravine to practice right after supper.

"Leave the dishes till it gets dark," he'd say, "and I'll help you."

And when I wouldn't, he'd go just the same and never come in till nine o'clock. I recalled Mrs. Collier saying that if she hadn't taken a firm stand, she'd have never seen her husband except when it was too dark for him to see a golf ball. I'll bet even Mrs. Collier would have had some trouble taking a firm stand with Dulcie right next door, like a serpent in a green silk sports dress.

And several days later, I found that I wasn't the only

one who found Dulcie a serpent. Rosemary and Mrs. Kirsted and I happened to be alone at a table at Corinne's porch bridge and during refreshments, we fell to talking of our husbands' golf. Strangely, all the pleasant, comfortable, complaining way we had had the last time we'd discussed it was gone. We all felt queer and uneasy. Not that the other girls admitted it, not that Dulcie was more than barely mentioned, but I never need any map to trace out how other girls are feeling. Both of those others were just as uneasy as I was. Mrs. Frank Kirsted because she hadn't known Dulcie before she was married and didn't know just what she might do, Rosie because she had known Dulcie and didn't know just what she might do.

"I went out to the club with Frank last Saturday," Mrs. Kirsted said, "and took Frankie, because Frank simply insisted. But I'll never go again. There were four Harvester wives playing bridge and a couple of old gentlemen on the porch. Of course, I had to watch Frankie every second. He played with the old gentlemen awhile, but after a bit they left and he got restless. I took him around to the south porch and the old men were there, but they only stayed a few minutes. You just have to keep changing constantly to keep Frankie quiet in a strange place, so pretty soon I took him up on the balcony. The old men were sitting there talking and as I came in, I heard one of them groan and say, 'Here comes that damn kid *again!*' "

Rosie and I said sympathetically how cold people without children always got. There was a little, rather suggestive pause. Then:

"Did you see Dulcie out there?" Rosie asked in a tone that any other woman could recognize as merely pretending to be careless.

"Yes," said Mrs. Frank Kirsted. "I watched her drive off the first couple of tees. That is what makes me so simply furious. Frank has been raving about her playing till I thought she must be a peach of a player."

"Isn't she?" I asked, afraid to believe anything so consoling.

"No," said Mrs. Kirsted. "I should say not. The boys don't play with the Harvester crowd so there's no other woman for them to compare her with. She's good-looking so they think she's wonderful if she manages to hit the ball at all."

I remembered the patronizing way Dulcie had told me that very morning that the day of the rocking-chair woman was over.

"It makes me so furious," said Mrs. Kirsted tensely, "because I know that if I just didn't have to stick home with Frankie I could go out and beat the life out of her."

Rosemary and I looked up the way you do at a scrap of blue sky when it's raining.

"Do you honestly think you could?" we asked. Hearing Rosie's heartfelt tone, I wondered what Dulcie had said to Rosie or worse still what Rosie's husband had said about Dulcie.

"I know I could," said Mrs. Kirsted. "With one hand tied behind my back. But you can't get Ella Crowninshield on a Saturday and I can't play golf with Frankie tagging along."

"Leave Frankie with me Saturday," I said. "And go out and beat Dulcie."

"And don't worry about supper," said Rosemary, "or hurry home. You and Frank come to our house for supper."

"Why, that's imposing on you girls too much," Mrs. Kirsted objected.

"Imposing nothing!" said Rosemary and I in the same tone exactly. "There's nothing in the world we'd like so well! You take your clubs and go out next Saturday afternoon and *beat Dulcie!*"

It was honestly kind of funny. Mrs. Kirsted brought Frankie over early Saturday afternoon and left him with me. And I saw that she had on Corinne's new silk sweater and knew that she was going to Rosie's for supper. It was kind of like a knight of old riding out with his lady's ribbon on his helmet. We were only too glad to lend her clothes and mind her child and cook her supper. Mrs. Frank Kirsted was our champion. She was going out to challenge Dulcie. And with her went the prayers of every girl in town who had to stay home to take care of babies. We might have to stick at home that afternoon in the flesh, but in the spirit every one of us was striding along the links beside Mrs. Frank Kirsted, helping her beat Dulcie.

And she did.

Will came home at nine o'clock amazed. Frank's wife, he said, was a whiz.

"How was Dulcie?" I asked.

"Oh, all right," he said in a careless tone, "but not in Mrs. Kirsted's class, of course."

I simply hugged that careless tone in my heart for two days. Monday afternoon all four of us were on Corinne's porch fairly idolizing Mrs. Kirsted.

"Mercy," she disclaimed our praises, "it was nothing to beat Dulcie. As a matter of fact, I licked the crowd of them. Our husbands, I beg to state, are noble lads but rotten golfers."

"Well, they're just learning," we all said defensively.

Mrs. Kirsted suddenly leaned forward, looking like the picture of Joan of Arc hearing the voices.

"Listen, girls," she said, "of course they're learning. And if you don't want to let a chance slip by that you'll regret the rest of your lives, you'll find some way to learn at the same time. Right now they want you to and would be glad to dub around with you. But if you wait a couple of years till they get good, they'll never be willing to play with you at all. Look at the Harvester crowd! Of course, no women play on the links Sundays but Saturday afternoons there are loads of wives playing with their husbands. And let me tell you, they're the ones who started playing at the same time. A good woman player can give a good man player a fair battle every time. Look at Dot, here. Tell me she couldn't learn to swing a golf club like a clap of thunder!"

"I used to play tennis pretty well," I admitted.

"*Used to,*" Mrs. Kirsted snorted. "That's the trouble. We're every one of us slipping into the 'used-to' class. We can't afford to do it. We've got to keep up with our husbands. We've got to or—"

She paused, and though no one said a word, I knew what each girl was thinking. Each one of them was seeing the same picture I was. It was as though Dulcie, pretty, gay, slim, laughing, had strolled slowly across the porch.

"How can we?" I asked faintly. "The boys can't play any time but Saturday afternoon and we can't get any one to take care of our babies then." I thought of Dulcie again. "There *must* be some way," I said desperately.

"There's *got to be!*" said Rosie.

"There's simply got to be!" said Corinne.

We sat for some little time, our chins on our hands, thinking, thinking as hard as I have ever thought in my life. It seemed hopeless. It was all I could do to make myself leave my babies with Ella, who, never having been a mother, couldn't feel responsibility as I do. Even if I could find somebody in town I could hire—and the town had been too well canvassed to leave much hope of that— but even if I could, I doubted that I could feel right about leaving them.

I would glance up and see the others looking hopeless, too. And yet I knew that every one of them had seen Dulcie's ghost walk across the porch. They would look up a moment, then bury their chins in their hands again and go back to thinking. And out of our desperation the idea was born. It happened to come to Rosie Merton.

"Why," she demanded, "don't we take turns? There are four of us and seven babies. Why couldn't each of us give up one Saturday afternoon out of four and take care of all seven?"

It was The Idea! We all knew it the instant we heard it. Why in the world had nobody thought of it before? It would be a terrible afternoon for the one left at home, as I knew, having watched spoiled little Frankie Kirsted last Saturday. But those who went away would go feeling perfectly easy, knowing that there was a mother on the job who would recognize the "trouble cry" when she heard it.

And after all, what was having one perfectly terrible Saturday afternoon out of four? It was certainly better than having all four kind of terrible.

"And we'll have a picnic supper on one of our porches all together afterward," we elaborated the plan. "Out on the porch so we can all put the babies to bed at home and hear them if they should cry. Just cold stuff we can get ready in the morning. The one who's been taking care of the children will just sit still and be waited on by the rest. Paper cups and plates so there'll be no dishes to wash."

It was a gorgeous idea, born, as I guess most gorgeous ideas are, out of desperate necessity. The funny part is that it has worked, as lots of gorgeous ideas don't.

Of course, it wasn't as simple as it seemed when we thought just getting away with the boys on Saturday afternoons was all there would be to it. I had no idea golf would be so hard to learn. All fall I've been working my head off at it. I haven't been to a bridge party in months. Every afternoon I can possibly hire Ella I'm out on the links with the old clubs. And every night Will and I are out back in the ravine, practicing approach shots till dark. Then sometimes we bring our mashies into the living room and practice popping balls into the big chair.

I went at it in this frantic fashion, of course, as a sense

of duty, spurred on and on by Dulcie. And then one day, after I'd been at it for weeks, a surprising realization came to me. I was actually crazy about golf. It is really Fun.

Three Saturdays out of every four are simply gorgeous. We didn't get home one week till quarter past nine. I certainly felt sorry to see poor Mr. Collier leaving at the end of the fifteenth hole and hurrying home so as not to keep supper waiting fifteen minutes. Mrs. Collier may be proud of having "trained" him, but I'd rather have Will look on in surprised admiration as he did the first time I drove a hundred and fifty yards than to have him as well trained as a sideshow flea.

And the way I've taken off weight! I made up the sports dress pattern with the stripes running around and the first time Will saw me in it was worth all the work. He said:

"If you want to hand somebody an awful laugh, just put on that dress and then tell 'em you've got two children. You look about fourteen."

But in spite of our success, the joke is on all four of us girls who saw Dulcie's ghost walk across Corinne's veranda. For, now that we've all learned golf just on account of Dulcie, Dulcie isn't playing golf any more. She told me first of all that she expected to be in the orange juice and spinach class herself next winter. I'm really pleased, but not at all for the reason I had once thought I'd be. It will mean no rest for me. It certainly seems like looking for trouble, but I've decided to hunt me up another childless chum right away. Every woman with babies ought to have at least one. It keeps her from getting fat and settled down before her time.

There's no telling when something else like golf will be coming along new, and if I just ran around with other mothers I might never even hear of it. I guess it wasn't such a bad idea, that slipping the serpent in along with Adam and Eve.

III

TOGETHER

"THERE are times," said Dulcie disgustedly, "when I wish there was something besides men that you could marry." She had brought back my sherbet glasses that she'd borrowed for her dinner party the night before and we were chatting in a pleasant, neighborly way in my kitchen. "Men just don't seem to have any sense of responsibility. I was so mad at Roger last night that I could have choked him. There I'd worked an hour setting the table for the party. I was busy in the kitchen when Roger came home and beyond calling Hello, I didn't pay any attention to him. I just happened to go into the dining room and I got there just in time. There he stood beside my beautiful table, looking over the evening paper and eating up every bit of the celery. In two more minutes he'd have started on the olives and the salted nuts, and give him ten minutes alone and the table would have been stripped as bare as a farm after the seven-year locusts have passed through!"

"Will is just the same," I said feelingly. "Nobody would ever believe that it was his party and his friends and his house just the same as mine. I simply can't get him to take any responsibility for anything. If I ask him what to have for dinner when we're going to have company, he'll say 'Mulligatawny stew.'"

"Does he help you any in deciding important things, either?" Dulcie asked.

"Does he!" I raised my eyes to the ceiling to show Dulcie that he decidedly did not. "When we got that new rug for the living room, I had every bit of the worrying to do, myself. It was as though he didn't care whether we had a good-looking living room or not. I tried to explain the different things to be considered, to him; how if we got a blue rug we couldn't use the curtains we had, but how if we didn't get blue the wing chair Mother Horton is going to let us have wouldn't fit so well, and so on; all the pros and cons you positively have to consider before you buy an expensive thing like a rug. There's no use pretending you can decide on anything big like that without talking a lot about it, but after the first two or three evenings, Will didn't seem to want me even to mention it. He seemed to think you could make a snap judgment and then just forget it. He'd either be flippant and say, 'I'll tell you what! Get a plaid rug, that'll go with anything,' or else he'd act kind of half exasperated and say, 'Oh, get whatever you like, Dotty, and let's forget it!' "

"That's Roger all over!" Dulcie said feelingly. " 'Oh, just any old thing,' or 'I wouldn't fuss so over it,' are his two favorite answers. It would serve men just right if we took them up on some of those answers. Funny-looking houses we'd have if we did, and funny meals and a funny life all around. They'd hate it just as much as we would, but they don't realize that it's just our fussing that keeps things halfway decent. And I suppose they know we will fuss, no matter what they say. They don't have to have any sense of responsibility; they know we've got enough for two."

I knew this was true, of course, but I didn't realize how very true it was until the week-end Will and I entertained the Kruses.

This was purely a business matter. I had never seen either Mr. or Mrs. Kruse before and neither had Will. Will always takes me into his confidence about all the business at The Horton Real Estate Company, but this time it was specially important for him to.

Father and Mother Horton had gone south for January and February, the first time they'd been away from Montrose in years and years. And while they were gone, Will found that the Kruse Leather and Bark Novelty Manufacturing Company was thinking of moving their factory from a Chicago suburb to somewhere in our district, either here or Verblen. Will was all excited over the prospect. It looked like a chance to rent the canning factory building at last. If Will could put it over, it would tickle his father almost to death as well as give him a fat commission for himself.

Will went right down to Chicago to see Mr. Kruse and talk Montrose up to him. He came back more excited than before.

"Kruse is a fine fellow," Will said, all enthusiasm, "and he said our place sounded pretty good. He's got his eye on the ramshackle old shoe factory building in Verblen, too, though. He could get that cheaper, of course, but it's a frame building and it's run down till there are about two boards left nailed together. They've written him, though, and to read their description—well, you'd never dream it was the old shoe factory they were talking about."

It always gives me the most delicious feeling of being extremely mature and important to have Will talk to me about business. Naturally, I was all interest. I was perfectly unprepared, though, for what came next.

"He wants to look our place over," Will went on calmly, "so he's coming up to stay over week-end after next to do it."

"It's a shame he can't make it without staying over night," I said, with the pleasant little feeling that it always gives me to be so understanding about business. "The hotel isn't anything to recommend Montrose particularly. It's a shame the new one isn't done."

"That's right," said Will, as though relieved. "I'm certainly glad you can see how it is. I knew it would queer the deal altogether for him to stop at the hotel. So I asked them to stay here."

"Here in this house!" I gasped.

"There isn't anywhere else," said Will apologetically, "with the folks away. You can get Ella Crowninshield to come and help you, can't you? So that there won't be too much work for you?"

"Oh, it isn't the work," I said faintly. And then, "They?" I echoed. "Will—will his wife come with him?"

"Sure," said Will.

Any woman can understand why it made me feel a little faint. When you do practically all your own work and have a pair of twin babies, the idea of week-end guests of any kind is rather appalling. And when they're

people you've never laid eyes on before and people rich
enough to own a factory at that—well, it's not like some
of your old crowd that it doesn't make any difference
whether you have everything just right or not. It was
a stupendous undertaking, of course, but I could see that
it was really necessary. The old hotel is awful—any
woman who stayed there overnight would go back to
Chicago feeling that Montrose was the most hick town in
the world and ready to do anything in her power to per-
suade her husband to move anywhere else.

"Do you think we can manage it all right, Dotty?"
Will asked anxiously. "I hate to put any extra work on
you, with all you've got to do, but—well, you can see
yourself how it is. Dad would never forgive me if I
didn't do all I could to get the Novelty to come here—
we've got a lot of property out around the old cannery
and it would all boom some. Then, on just this one deal
alone, there's the little old commish to think of. It
wouldn't hurt our budget's feelings any to crowd in a
little extra cash. I'll help you all I can. Do you suppose
we can swing it?"

"Oh, yes, I guess so," I said lightly and, as a matter of
fact, rather pleased.

Not that I was pleased at the ordeal ahead of me,
goodness knows, but there were other reasons. Mainly,
it was Will's putting it up to me the way he did. There
is quite a kick in feeling that you can help out your husband in a business way. Then, too, I felt flattered at his
explaining it all to me so carefully. There are plenty of
husbands who don't explain their business to their wives.
Why, just take Frank Kirsted for instance. If I'd been

in Mrs. Kirsted's place I'd have wanted to leave him, the way he acted when old Mrs. Long got a divorce from her husband.

It was the only divorce in Montrose for years and years. The Longs had been married thirty-five years and while everybody knew they fought like a cat and dog, we all thought they were happy. Then suddenly the news got out that she had filed suit against him a month ago for divorce. The whole town simply reeled on its foundations. We girls heard it first at Charity Club, and went home simply bug-eyed to tell our husbands. They were all as dumbfounded as we had been. All but Frank Kirsted. He is a lawyer, of course, and when Mrs. Kirsted went home all a-twitter and told him in bated breath, he said carelessly, oh, yes, Mrs. Long had talked to him about it before she filed the suit, and he had advised her to go to Mr. Grant.

"Before she filed the suit!" Mrs. Kirsted told me she echoed in a gasp. "You've known about it for a *month* and never told me! You've deliberately kept still and let me hear it from Rosie Merton when I might have had all the fun of springing it first!"

"That's exactly why I didn't tell you," Frank said. "Because you couldn't have kept from springing it first on somebody. Mrs. Long consulted me in confidence and anything you tell your doctor or your lawyer or your priest is sacred."

"You needn't think I would have told a living soul," Mrs. Kirsted said with cold dignity, "or that anybody I did tell would ever have dreamed of repeating it. It simply shows you don't trust me."

"You bet your life I don't," Frank had admitted cheerfully. "You're too good-looking to have good sense."

And along that line, he actually jollied Mrs. Kirsted
out of being hurt about it. It is strange how a woman
will swallow any insult in the world if it's hung on her
being good-looking.

Will thinks I am good-looking, too, and I couldn't help
being pleased to see that he also trusts me. It gave me a
comfortable feeling of superiority. Then, too, I rather
liked the idea of entertaining my husband's business
friends. Lots of the older married girls have quite a bit
of this to do and complain bitterly about it. And when
they had complained to me before, it had always placed
me at rather a disadvantage, not being in a position to
complain any, myself. Oh, take it altogether, for all entertaining the Kruses was such an undertaking, I en-
tered into it with interest and even a certain amount of
enthusiasm.

"They'll probably get in on the five-seven Saturday,"
I said. "We'll have dinner at night and I'll ask Dulcie
and Roger and the Kirsteds. They make the best impression of any of our friends on strangers. Then that'll
make just two tables for Bridge afterward."

"Bridge nothing," said Will. "Let's make it Mah
Jong or Five Hundred."

"Mah Jong is going out," I said, "and as for asking
people from Chicago to play Five Hundred, you might as
well suggest Lotto. Nobody in the world but you and
Frank Kirsted even remember that there is such a game as
Five Hundred."

"What's the difference if Mah Jong is going out,"

Will objected. "We've still got our set and if Kruse likes to play—"

"Now listen, Will," I interrupted gently, "Mr. Kruse isn't the only one who's got to be pleased. You'll make a terrible mistake if you forget that. The Kruses will live in whichever town they put the factory in, and you can be sure Mrs. Kruse will have something to say about which town it's to be."

"Well, you don't suppose the sight of a Mah Jong set will turn Mrs. Kruse against the town of Montrose, do you?"

"It might easily, Will," I said gently. "If she's very snappy and keeps right up to date on things herself. What we've got to do is to show her that the social life here is something that even a woman used to life in Chicago would never need to be ashamed of. If she once got the idea that there was anything provincial about Montrose—"

"But ye gods, Dotty, the way I play Bridge isn't going to raise the social tone of Montrose any! If Kruse knows anything about Bridge, he'll just think the other business men of Montrose must be half-wits, too, or I couldn't earn a living here. You know how I play Bridge."

Well, there was considerable truth in that. Actually, I've watched Will playing Bridge and thought he must have one of those dual personalities you read about. It simply doesn't seem possible that the same person can be smart enough to understand real estate law as he does or take a flivver all to pieces and put it together again and yet be thick enough to let a one no-trump doubled, stand.

"I'll tell you what," he said. "Let Frank and Rosie

and Dulcie and me play some game for simple minds at one table, and you and Roger play Bridge with the Kruses at the other."

That really was an idea. Roger plays a terribly keen game and I'm not so bad, if I do say it myself. In fact, I was so relieved at having this first problem so well settled that I didn't realize how significant Will's part of it was. I thought of it later, though.

"Then Sunday morning you can take them to church," I went on. "And I'll stay home and get dinner. I'll have Ella come early in the morning and take care of the babies. Thank goodness, the new church is done if the hotel isn't. I wish to goodness I could be there, too, but I can't possibly. You want to be sure to introduce them to the right people as you're going out. People like the Burrises and the Scogginses. Then in the afternoon I'll ask Miss Prescott and Professor Haynes and his wife to drop in for tea. They're fearfully cultured—a woman like Miss Prescott who goes abroad any time the notion strikes her would make a good impression on anybody. Then I suppose they'll take the eight-ten back to Chicago."

I drew a sigh of satisfaction as I outlined that program. You're always reading about the help a worldly-wise woman can be to her husband in a business way, and I'd like to see any wordly-wise woman get up a better program than that on first thought.

"You haven't left any time to go out to see the cannery," Will objected, however. "And that's what they're coming for, you know."

"That's so," I admitted. "I suppose we'll have to get

that in somewhere." I considered the advantages of the different parts of my plan. "Well, I guess we'd better leave out church for once and go out there Sunday morning. You can drive past the church and call attention to the building on your way. Then I'll ask the Burrises to come to tea, too. I'm sure they'd come and they'll add just the right heavy-respectable note."

"But isn't this going to be too much for you, Dolly?" Will asked anxiously. "I don't want to put too much work on you."

"I don't mind a bit," I assured him. "I've an interest in your getting that commission, too."

I really didn't mind. If anybody ever started off a hard job with her heart in her work, I started that one. Fortunately, the week-end was ten days off so that I had plenty of time. I invited the different people first of all so that I would know what I had to work with, and fortunately, they could all come. I engaged Ella to come all day Saturday and Sunday to help me. The very first evening I sat down and made out complete menus for all the meals we'd have. Will was greatly impressed at my having so much system and executive ability. I get it from Father, goodness knows! When Mother's going to have company she has no system at all. She's like a kernel of corn on a hot stove lid. We always had a big crowd for dinner Christmas, and the day after she could scarcely raise her head from the pillow.

Of course, I wanted Will's advice in making out the menus.

"Now, what do you think would be nice for dinner Saturday evening?" I asked him.

"Mulligatawny stew," said Will.

I could scarcely believe my ears. That he should be flippant at a time like this! Seeing that he had hurt my feelings, he sobered up right away and tried to help me.

"How about a chicken?" he said.

"I'd thought we'd have a chicken Sunday."

Just that little difficulty squelched Will completely. He likes almost anything to eat but, even when he tries, he can never think of anything but chicken. With the props pulled out from under his one idea, he was simply helpless.

"I'd thought about veal birds—you know, the kind fixed with toothpicks—for Saturday night," I said at last. "Do you think those would be nice?"

"Fine!" said Will enthusiastically.

"I thought we'd have grapefruit with a cherry in the center to start with," I went on, "then split-pea soup with croutons and cheese straws. Then the birds and riced potatoes and gravy and—well, either canned peas or scalloped squash or both, and peach pickles. Then salad with Roquefort cheese dressing, and ice cream and cake and coffee. How do you think that would be?"

"Fine!" said Will approvingly.

"Then for Sunday we can have chicken," I went on, "and all the trimmings, and mousse for dessert and—which do you think would be best for salad, boiled dressing or oil dressing?"

"Fine," said Will.

"Fine what?" I asked sharply. "Aren't you paying any attention to what I'm saying?"

He pulled himself together and said he guessed French dressing, but even then I could see that his heart wasn't in this thing as mine was. Why, I threw my whole soul into it. All the week before, no matter what else I was doing, I was planning that week-end. I made menus and changed them, decided to have popovers for breakfast, changed to pancakes, then back to popovers. I spent all one morning deciding just how I'd manage Sunday afternoon tea. Naturally, with anything on my mind so much, I mentioned some of the problems now and then to Will. He was not the slightest help though. Sometimes, especially after I had struggled with the same problem for some time, considering the advantages of first one way then another, it would seem to me he was scarcely listening to what I was saying.

I don't know when I first began to be a little hurt by this. I think, though, it was along toward Thursday when the real work began. Will was specially busy at the office, so I had most of it to do. He helped me all he could —he's always sweet about helping with work—but that kind of help wasn't what I wanted. What I wanted was for Will to take a little interest. He didn't seem to care even to talk about it, saying almost irritably, "Ye gods, Dot, how should I know?" when I asked him if he thought coffee kept Mrs. Kruse awake, or whether she would drink it after the Bridge game. He seemed to have no appreciation of the vast amount of intelligent thought that it takes to make a week-end a success. He actually seemed to think you could go on just the same as usual, thinking of nothing, and then when the time came, perfectly prepared meals, a perfectly clean house, a perfectly

dressed wife, and all the rest would simply happen by
magic.

We were going to give the Kruses our room. Since
the babies came, we haven't any guest room. Will would
sleep on the couch in the sewing room and I on the davenport in the living room. I didn't care much about sleeping on the ground floor, but I was afraid to trust Will.
Sometimes I think he has no sense of responsibility at
all. I couldn't depend upon his leaping up at the first
sound of the alarm clock and dashing upstairs with all
the bedding and being wary about not meeting the Kruses
in the hall. It's a terrible thing to feel you can't trust
your own husband, but there's no dodging the fact that
there'd be a chance of his shutting off the alarm, thinking he'd lie just a minute longer, and then be found sleeping abandonedly right in the middle of the living room
when the Kruses came down for breakfast.

I worked like a dog all day Wednesday, Thursday and
Friday, using the new vacuum Father gave us for Christmas on the rugs and the draperies, waxing the living-
room floor, doing up the curtains in our bedroom, polish-
ing the silver, washing the windows, washing the best
dishes, washing and ironing the monogram napkins—
doing all the million necessary things that, combined with
my regular work and taking care of the babies, were
enough to lay anybody low. Of course I got terribly
tired and the tireder I got, the more I found myself re-
senting Will's attitude.

He did the best he could to help me, doing the dishes
Friday night so that I could finish up my new beige velvet
dress that I wanted to wear Saturday, even shellacking

the kitchen floor when he found I was going to do it myself, if he didn't. But he didn't see any sense in it. That was what hurt my feelings, tired as I was. He didn't appreciate all my work. He was even flippant about it.

"It's a shame we didn't know about this week-end last spring," he said, "and maybe you could have got the town to pave the street in front of the house." Or, "You mean to tell me you haven't cleaned the attic and the cellar? How can we have a couple overnight without the attic and cellar cleaned?" Or, "Don't you want me to buy a piano? As likely as not, Mrs. Kruse plays."

Will never seems to have learned that there are times for being funny and other times when it's just as well not to try to be.

Saturday itself, though, was the most hectic of all. The Kruses were to come on the five-seven and Will promised to shut up the office and get home by three to help me with last-minute things. Ella would be no good; she's got a one-track mind; when she's taking care of the babies she can't be counted on for another living thing. I was busy all the morning with making cake, getting the vegetables ready, making the stuffing for the birds—I wanted as little as possible to do after the Kruses came. At the last minute, I decided to clear out the closet in our bedroom; it would make it seem more like a guest-room, so I ran back and forth upstairs, putting our clothes in the attic for the time being.

I left a few things for Will to do, thinking I would manicure my nails and dress and maybe rest ten minutes or so while he was doing them. I was so tired that I could have gone to sleep standing up except for the terrible strain of responsibility I was under. And Will never came into the house until half past four. He was terribly apologetic.

"At the last minute I had to go clear out to the Crossings to get the cannery keys," he explained. "Old Dutton swore he'd leave them at our office and then didn't. Anybody'd think I was trying to rent his property against his wishes, all the coöperation I get."

I could see he was annoyed about it, but not half as annoyed as I was. At a time like this to be thinking about keys! I'd had to keep going ever since three, doing the things I'd counted on his doing. Now, I wouldn't even have time to manicure my nails. And I was so tired that when I'd talk it sounded as though somebody else was working my voice. I told Will I didn't think it was very nice of him, setting the table briskly all the time.

"Would you put two butterballs on for Mr. Kruse?" I asked in the midst of my talking, kind of thinking out loud.

"Put the butter on in the jar for all I care," Will said suddenly. "I've heard nothing but this miserable weekend for ten days. I wish to Heaven I'd never asked them at all. I certainly wouldn't have if I'd known you'd have to clean house and get an entire wardrobe for the occasion. You're so worn out and cross you don't know whether you're afoot or a-horseback."

"Well, of all things!" I said, feeling the tears come to my eyes—they do so easily when you're tired and responsible—"Any one would think I'd been working myself to skin and bone for days for my own selfish pleas-

ure! The Kruses aren't any friends of mine, you know.
I've been doing it to help you and this is the thanks I
get!"

"I know it," said Will quickly. "I didn't mean to be
cross, honey. I just hate to see you wearing yourself
out. I didn't mean to be cross—I'm just kind of jumpy,
myself. It's a pretty big deal to put over with Dad
away—don't be mad at me."

"All right," I said. I forbore making the obvious
remark that I didn't see what Will had to make him
jumpy. I had the whole thing on my hands. But you
can't be mean if a person apologizes and besides there
was no time to waste quarreling with the train coming in
about twenty-seven minutes.

Never as long as I live shall I forget that hectic week-
end. The Kruses arrived on the five-seven according to
schedule. He was a great, big, fat, jolly man. He
brought me a burnt-leather table cover which would have
seemed very nice to any one who likes burnt-leather table
covers. And she was a nervous, thin, talky little woman.
Talk-talk-talk-talk every second of the way up home in
the flivver. It took her about two minutes to change her
dress for dinner; then she was back following me around,
talking to me more.

She followed me out into the kitchen where Ella, the
babies in bed and asleep at last, was fixing the salad.
Ella's nothing of a cook. I had the dinner to cook myself, of course, and there were a million things to think
of.

"Oh, what a darling little kitchen! I love your checked
curtains!" Mrs. Kruse gushed. "And how cute to have

the inside of your dish cupboard painted red! Now, I
know there are loads of things to do—just give me an
apron and let me help."

"No, there isn't a thing you can do, really," I assured
her. "Ella and I can manage splendidly. You just go
in and keep the men company."

"Indeed I'll do no such thing," she said sprightlily.
"Just because I keep two maids at home, I suppose you
think I don't know how to do a thing. But I'll show
you. Why, every Thursday I let both the girls off at
once and get dinner myself, and I get perfectly wonderful
dinners, too. Just ask Mr. Kruse if I don't. Now let's
see, for instance, last Thursday I had—"

And on and on she chattered, while I tried to listen
politely with one ear and think about my own dinner with
the other. It was awful. Every few minutes she'd stop
long enough to say, "Now just give me an apron and tell
me what I can do to help." What I'd have adored to
say was, "Just stop talking and get out of the kitchen
so that I can hear myself think," but naturally, I didn't.
Instead I went on, doing my best to concentrate on what
I was doing and yet make her think I was paying attention to what she was saying.

I hadn't got anything done when I heard the doorbell
and Dulcie and Roger in the hall. But I thanked goodness anyway. Mrs. Kruse had to go in and talk to them
and I could fly at things in peace.

The dinner went beautifully. Of course I didn't know
what I was eating I was so nervous watching to see that
everything was being all right. More than once during
the dinner, I thanked Heaven for good friends. I simply

couldn't keep from being a little preoccupied, wondering
if Ella would remember to put the dressing on the salad
and such things, but Dulcie and Mrs. Kirsted were wonderful. They appreciated what I was up against and did
their best to help me out. Dulcie flirted with Mr. Kruse
just enough to please him and not enough to displease his
wife, and Mrs. Kirsted listened politely to Mrs. Kruse,
which was all that Mrs. Kruse needed.

We played Bridge afterward, Roger and I and the
Kruses. Godness knows, Will needn't have worried, he'd
have been right at home playing with the Kruses. Mrs.
Kruse never stopped talking while she or anybody else
was playing a hand, just intersecting her remarks with
"Oh, dear, hearts aren't trump, are they? I meant to
put on a trump," or "Oh, dear, partner, was that *your*
king?" And I began to think Mr. Kruse was even worse.
He played all right, but he was so fat and hot and com-
mon. Why, he sat there and took every bit of varnish
off my best Windsor chair!

I was up before dawn the next morning. Of course
I'm always up at six with the babies' bottles, but on
Sundays I always go back to bed again. Not this Sunday, though. I had the living room to clean up before
breakfast. It looked the way a room always does after
eight people have been playing Bridge and having cake
and coffee in it. Then I had to get breakfast. I made
popovers and, of course, the only way you can tell that
popover dough has been beaten long enough is to beat
till your arm falls off. Ordinarily I never think of minding this, but this morning I minded everything. You're

likely to when you don't get enough sleep. And then, too, I was feeling more and more aggrieved at Will.

Here, this was his party, really, and he took no responsibility for it. He might almost have been part of the company, the way he took everything for granted. He did get out into the kitchen a few minutes before breakfast time to ask if there was anything he could do, but that isn't taking responsibility. He had never once thought about how we'd left the living room when we went to bed. He wasn't thinking of anything. Except maybe that I was making too much fuss about everything.

We had a fine breakfast, if I do say it myself. Mrs. Kruse dried the breakfast dishes and talked to me while the men looked over the Chicago papers. When they were ready to start out to see the cannery, I got Will aside.

"For Heaven's sake, Will," I begged, "take her along with you. Ella isn't used to bathing the babies and she doesn't know how to strain the vegetables—I'll have to keep showing her and I've got dinner to get and sandwiches to make for the tea. I simply can't have Mrs. Kruse around talking to me every second. I'll never get things done and I'll go stark staring mad trying."

Will looked horrified at the suggestion.

"I can't take her with us!" he said. "She'll talk every mile of the way. I'm awfully sorry, Dotty, but you'll just have to put up with her this time."

I said nothing. Selfishness like that simply stunned me. There was Will, just off for a pleasant ride in the flivver; I was at home with a billion things to do and all the responsibility of the entire enterprise shunted off onto me, and he wouldn't even help me by taking Mrs. Kruse off my hands.

"Well, will you please get home by quarter past one?" I asked resignedly. "And drag her off me for the last fifteen minutes? We've got to have dinner at prompt half past one—that's absolutely necessary in order to get it over and cleared up before the tea people come—and I simply can't make the gravy and meringue fluff and tend to all the last-minute things if she's in the kitchen."

"All right," Will agreed. But there was an absent-minded note in his voice that made me nervous.

"Now don't forget," I cautioned him. "Quarter past one. Not half past, just in time for dinner. *Quarter past.*"

"All right. Sure," Will repeated.

But I had a queer premonition that he wouldn't be there. He went away with an air of having his mind anywhere in the world but where it ought to be. I had a feeling that once he and Mr. Kruse got off in that flivver, he'd never once think of gravy or the fancy meringue dessert that had to be tended to at the last minute. As I worked around that morning and pretended to listen to Mrs. Kruse, I thought about what Dulcie had said. Let two men get off together and they're just like two no-count boys. Years of married life don't seem to give them one bit of the sense of responsibility that a girl is born with.

But, in spite of my premonition, I really never thought Will could play me the mean, mean trick that he did.

At quarter past one, there was no sign of the flivver.

Well, I sighed resignedly and went on with the meringue as best I could between Mrs. Kruse's syllables. I hadn't really expected he'd get back though it did seem as though he might have, under the circumstances. By superhuman effort, however, I managed alone, in spite of the handicap of Mrs. Kruse. At half past one to the minute, I had as delicious a dinner as I've ever laid eyes on, done to a perfect turn, ready to sit right down to.

I was actually about to pour out the soup when I suddenly remembered that the men hadn't come yet. I went into the living room and scanned the street anxiously. Not a sign of the flivver.

Nervously, Mrs. Kruse and I sat down in the living room to wait. I had potato balls, which were as light and fluffy as egg whites now, but which would be soggy and horrid in ten minutes. There are dinners you can keep ten minutes and dinners that you can't. I had prepared a perfect wonder of the kind you can't.

Ten minutes! At two o'clock they hadn't come. I was really worried by then and telephoned out to Rita May White, who lives on the road to the cannery, to see if she had seen the flivver go by. She never misses a thing that goes by and she had seen it go out and come back. Then I was worried in earnest. If they had started back a half an hour ago, as Rita May said, they should have been home before now. Maybe something had happened. Something must have. Will is a good driver, but even good drivers do have accidents. I completely forgot my dinner in my sudden anxiety.

Mrs. Kruse wasn't worried at all apparently, just talked on and on and on. I stood in the window where I could watch the road, getting more cold with fear all the time. Quarter past two—twenty minutes past—something had happened, there was no doubt of it. Time drags so fearfully when you're worried. Half past two.

Suddenly, around the corner from Beekman street, appeared the familiar flivver sedan. And there were both the men in it, safe and sound. For a moment, I was simply limp with relief. And then I thought of the dinner. It's a strange thing but the more frantically you worry for fear something has happened to somebody, the madder you are when you find that nothing has. Those men blew in as coolly as though being an hour late for dinner wasn't anything.

"Had a fine ride," Mr. Kruse told me, rubbing his hands cheerfully. "We've had one fine ride. Out by the cannery and then took in all the surrounding country. Over to Verblen. Mighty pretty country you've got around here, even in the winter. Well, I suppose you girls have had plenty of time to get dinner. We're starved, aren't we, Horton?"

"You bet your life!" said Will, with an air of bluff cordiality. But he looked guiltily at me. At the first chance he got me off alone.

"Sorry to be late, Dotty," he said, "but it couldn't be helped. I took him over to Verblen." Will gave me a meaningful look. "Never thought of it, either, till we started back home. Thought first I'd try to steer him off, but he had it on his mind. Then I got the hunch to take the bull right by the horns and drive him over there myself. I think it was a good stunt."

And he actually had the nerve to look at me as though I'd think it was a good stunt, too!

"As long as you had a pleasant ride and saw all the adjoining country," I said sarcastically, "I don't suppose you'll mind that the dinner is ruined."

Will didn't even seem to know that I was being sarcastic.

"Oh, no," he said with an air of large-handed good nature, "don't worry your head about the dinner any."

I said nothing. There was nothing to say. As I hurried around the kitchen doing the best I could with the wreck, I faced the fact that as long as I lived, I should have to carry all the responsibility for the family. Will was, apparently, not capable of taking his share of it.

Someway or other we got through the rest of the day. Someway or other, the tea went off, the Kruses caught their train back to Chicago, assuring us they had had a fine time.

We came back to the house and Will pitched in and helped me get things straightened up. He talked to me all the time about the ride they'd taken and unimportant things like that. I didn't even tell him what I thought about his being an hour late for dinner. I would some time, but right then I was too exhausted even to fight. After all, it was all over. The Kruses were gone, they had said they had a good time and maybe they had. Anyhow, I'd done my best. Anyhow, it was all over.

As I slid out of my velvet dress at last and fell into bed, I did think again, though, about what Dulcie had said about wishing there was something besides men that you could marry. I remembered how in one glance the night before, she and Mrs. Kirsted had taken in the whole

situation and how conscientiously they had pitched right
in to help me. Catch one of them going for a ride and
forgetting all about dinner! If your husband could be
like another woman, was my last thought before I
dropped off to sleep, between the two of you, you'd
manage anything pretty well.

Monday morning both of the twins were sick, actually running a temperature. Each one, I learned Tuesday, was cutting an eye tooth and any woman who has
ever heard one baby cut an eye tooth can fill in from imagination what it would be to have two doing it in the same
house. It was the first catastrophe that had ever struck
the two of mine simultaneously. Night and day are all
alike to an eye tooth, and the strain of it knocked the
Kruses and the week-end and everything else completely
out of my mind.

Wednesday afternoon, however, when I was wheeling
the baby carriage—Will calls it our twin-six—home from
marketing, I got to thinking about the way Will had
acted that week-end, and the more I thought about it, the
madder I got. There I had had every bit of the thinking
and managing as well as the work to do and Will hadn't
even realized the importance of the occasion enough to
get home in time for dinner. It is all very well to say tolerantly, "Oh, men never do grow up; they're always just
boys," but it's no fun to feel that all your life you'll have
to do all the thinking and carrying all the responsibility for
the family. And Will is so dear in most ways, too. He
helps me loads with the work, and the babies, and is
really sweet in most ways. Somehow that made it all
the more exasperating. If he were horrid and selfish I

could just set it down as a hopeless proposition, but when a person is so nice you can't help loving him, and it is hard to have to realize that he hasn't got good sense.

As I was passing the bank, Mr. Burris came out and walked along with me toward his house.

"Well, I hear your week-end party was a success," he observed.

"No, I can't say it was a howling success," I said honestly. "I barely pulled it through. That's as much as I'd say for it."

Mr. Burris looked puzzled.

"Why, I was just talking to William and he seemed greatly pleased. Or maybe he hasn't telephoned you this afternoon?"

"I haven't been home. I've had the babies out all afternoon," I said, thinking there wasn't much Will could telephone me about that awful week-end that I didn't already know. Mr. Burris fairly beamed.

"Ah, then I can be the first to announce the good news," he said. "William has just heard that the Kruse Company will lease the cannery building."

For a moment I stared at him blankly. I had been thinking about the week-end and this sudden change of subject was so abrupt.

"A very keen young man, that husband of yours is, Dorothy," Mr. Burris went on approvingly. "He keeps his eye right on the ball. It was a neat piece of work for him to land Kruse when the Baker people have been trying to get that Verblen shoe factory building off their hands for two years. It's quite a feather in William's cap."

I suddenly thought about the commission, about what Will's selling the cannery would mean to us. In the excitement of entertaining the Kruses the cannery had slipped out of my mind altogether.

"The Baker people," Mr. Burris went on, "weren't expecting Mr. Kruse to get up this way till next Sunday and they were going to camouflage their old ruin as well as they could—they'd even considered painting it over." Mr. Burris chuckled. "A very neat idea of William's to drive Mr. Kruse over there last Sunday and let him see it as it really is—without any fresh paint covering up rotten boards."

Mr. Burris gave another nice, elderly, approving chuckle.

"Mr. Kruse thinks very well of William, indeed. He told me so Sunday afternoon when we were drinking our tea at your house. Said William certainly had had all the information he needed right at his tongue's end. William had looked up the insurance rates—the cannery being brick of course made them a lot lower than the Verblen place—showed him the railway switch the cannery had had put in, pointed out that Verblen isn't on the main current line; if he should want to use electric power he'd have a lot of expensive poling and wiring to do. William had gone into it, Mr. Kruse said, as though he were going to manufacture bark and leather novelties himself. A very shrewd young husband you have, Dorothy."

We had reached Mr. Burris' house and he left me with his nice, deep, old-fashioned bow.

I walked on home with the strangest feeling of seeing for the first time in my life the sort of thing Will has to think about. Why, with all that on his mind, no wonder he was jumpy about the Kruses' coming. Somehow, always seeing him just at home, I forgot that he has anything in the world to do but just what I see him doing: have a good time with me and our friends and families and help me out some with the work and the babies. And yet, really—

Suddenly I thought of last Sunday morning, the one really important part of the week-end as far as all that the week-end really was for at all. On that ride in the flivver Will had had to put over the whole deal, show Mr. Kruse about the electricity and the insurance rates and all the rest of those things I'd never even known existed, when, as a sudden clinching thought—and it had really been little short of an inspiration—he had taken Mr. Kruse over to Verblen and killed the shoe factory's chance of getting the factory away from us by foul means. That ride was the crucial time of the entire enterprise, what it had all been leading up to. And I had actually wanted Will to take along that silly, talky Mrs. Kruse! Why! she would have chattered every mile of the way; Will wouldn't have had a Chinaman's chance of getting in a serious word with her husband.

Here Will had gone off with a deal of this kind to put over—and done it, too! And I had been mad at him because it took him a little longer than he had figured on! "He keeps his eye right on the ball." I suddenly remembered what Mr. Burris had said, and realized how true it was. I'll bet not once during that week-end had Will forgotten for a single moment what he had really had the Kruses come to Montrose for. And not once—

not for one single fleeting moment had I remembered it.
I would have worried myself sick over whether to play
Bridge or Mah Jong or whether to have pineapple mousse
or chocolate loaf, and then if it had all depended on me,
actually let the Kruses go back to Chicago without even
showing them the cannery building, without so much as
mentioning the factory at all.

I pushed the baby carriage in at our front door, thinking exactly the same thought I had been thinking when
I had pushed it out, but in a mighty different way. Thank
goodness, I was thinking, one of the family had some
sense!

Will was there; he had come home early to tell me
the news.

"And listen, Dot," he said excitedly, "I shouldn't wonder if you were the one who put it over."

"Me?" I gasped.

"Yep. In a postscript, in his letter, Kruse says, 'Give
our regards to Mrs. Horton. She certainly gave us one
grand time. My wife's talking about it yet. She
wouldn't even let me think about going anywhere but
Montrose; says she's never seen another town where
there were such nice young people, or where they seem
to have such good times.' There, you see!"

Will beamed proudly on me and I suppose maybe, if
I hadn't had that talk with Mr. Burris I'd have actually
kidded myself into thinking I'd done the whole thing.

"A man's wife has got a lot of influence with him on
a change like this," Will went on appreciatively.

That was perfectly true, of course. I didn't want to
do my part out of any of the credit it really deserved.

Mrs. Kruse had doubtless had something to say. But she hadn't had it all. No man who's smart enough to run a factory is going to decide to put it wherever his wife happens to like to play Mah Jong.

"Will," I said suddenly, moved to rash honesty by his being so dear and generous, "don't give me too much credit. I did the best I could, but I certainly didn't keep my eye on the ball. I was so busy thinking about just the right flowers for the table and everything like that that I—I never once remembered what we were having the party for. Never once did the faintest thought of the cannery even enter my head!"

"Oh, well, women aren't expected to have much real sense of responsibility," Will said tolerantly.

I suddenly began to giggle. I had thought of Roger eating the celery, and I couldn't help it. Will laughed, too, just because he was feeling so happy and triumphant; put his arm around me.

"Maybe it was the right flowers for the table that turned the trick," he said. "We'll never know. Anyhow, between us we've put it over."

Between us! Giggling happily there with Will's triumphant arm around me, I had a funny feeling that was kind of like a vision. Between us! A vision of Will and me, so different from each other that we can't help rowing about it every once in a while, yet loving each other and fitting together like two pieces of a scroll puzzle into the scheme of things. Women are all right in their way and men are all right in theirs, but I guess it's a good thing for both that when they come to get married there has to be one of each.

IV

FROM the time our crowd changed the Lodge Night Club into the Charity Club our husbands made fun of it. Miss Prescott, the only rich, unmarried woman in Montrose, got us to change it. Eight of us whose husbands go to lodge Thursday evenings had been meeting then to play Bridge. We always had grand refreshments and it was really quite like a party. I had little Ella Crowninshield every Thursday night to do the supper dishes and stay with the twins so that I could go.

Miss Prescott said she thought that, as the young matrons of Montrose, we ought to be doing some charity or welfare work. All the girls were perfectly willing, so the Lodge Night Club became the Charity Club. It continued to meet Thursday evenings and to have refreshments. The only difference was that instead of playing Bridge we sewed. We made sheets and pillowcases and nightgowns and so on for the charity ward of the new State Hospital that's being built just outside town.

We all liked the change. It does give you a comfortable self-satisfied feeling to realize that you are doing something for the poor and at the same time, we had just as much fun as when we'd played Bridge. I'm not sure that we didn't have more fun, as a matter of fact, because sewing gave us a chance to talk. Any one who isn't a fool can cut and baste and talk at the same time and we all got so we could even run the sewing machine at top speed and never miss a syllable. The boys would always call for us after lodge meeting and when Will would come in, he'd usually say:

"Well, how's the Ladies' Thursday Night Gossip and Scandal Association?"

We always jumped on him, of course, but, while he was just joking, there were times when it occurred even to me that those club meetings were getting the least little bit gossipy. You have to talk about something, though, and nobody can tell me that they honestly enjoy discussing politics or books or music as much as talking about somebody they know and don't exactly like.

Of course, we might have stuck to the general subjects of conversation. Such as the servant problem. None of us keep any regular servants, but we have the problem, just the same. And it is really more interesting to discuss than as though we each kept one instead of all of us having the same ones. For we can all speak feelingly of how much America Hawkins, the colored woman who washes for practically all of us, eats.

"I'm just sure"—Mrs. Frank Kirsted would stop running the sewing machine so that we could hear her lowered voice—"I'm just sure she *takes food home with her*. No human being could eat all that disappears. And why else"—triumphantly—"why else does she always bring a satchel?"

We all sighed.

"And little Ella Crowinshield is getting worse by the day," Rosemary Merton took it up plaintively. "She's honest enough and she hasn't much appetite, but her mind isn't on what she's doing more than half the time."

"I should say it isn't," I agreed feelingly. "Why, last Thursday night before Will had got the front door open, I could hear both the twins crying. They were making noise enough to be heard down to Water Street, and yet right there in the kitchen sat Ella with a beau, insisting that she hadn't heard a sound. And she had forgotten to give them their ten o'clock bottles!"

Mrs. Frank Kirsted stopped the machine.

"I thought maybe she'd be better after she broke off with that bank fellow she'd been going with, but, my word, it wasn't a week before she had another."

"It'll be a wonder," said Dulcie, "if she keeps straight. Her sister Lulu, you know!"

"Of course, two of the other sisters married, though, and are respectable enough," said Rosemary. "I've given them a lot of Junior's outgrown things for their babies."

Mrs. Kirsted slowed down the machine.

"I've given Ella a lot of my clothes, too, but she doesn't appreciate it. Do you suppose she'd come and stay with Frankie on a Saturday afternoon to help me out? Not much! The bank is closed Saturday afternoons."

"Well, thank goodness, she's broken off with him," said Rosie, "so we don't have to plan all our social life with banking hours in mind. Her new beau works in a garage over in Verblen and, thank goodness, a garage gives a man something to do."

We all sighed. Yes, we had the servant problem to discuss, like any other women.

But there's no denying that there isn't a subject in the

world—even servants—that is quite as interesting as gossip. In a town like Montrose there are always general subjects that everybody discusses, like how on earth the Bartells can live the way they do on Chandler Bartell's salary, and why in the world Veda Knopf and Fred don't get married—they've been going with each other since before the war.

We started on subjects of that kind, but they didn't last more than an evening or so; they've been so worked over there's no life left in them. Then one night Roger had a toothache and Dulcie didn't come to the meeting.

We sewed along for awhile, talking about America and Ella Crowinshield and Betty Bartell and Veda Knopf, all the old stock subjects. Then about nine o'clock there was a little pause. Rosie slowed down the sewing machine.

"Dot, do you know what Dulcie paid for that green sports dress she bought in Chicago?"

"Twenty-three seventy-five," I answered promptly. There was no secret about that.

Rosie stopped the machine altogether and leaned over it.

"I knew that was what she told me!" she said triumphantly. "But yesterday Howard walked home with Roger and Roger got to talking about how clever Dulcie was, always picking up bargains. 'Look at that green dress she got in Chicago,' he said. 'Only fourteen-fifty!'"

There was a little silence among all seven of us.

"Why, I always thought Dulcie told us the truth!" I exclaimed.

"So did I," said Rosie. "I simply can't understand it."

There was another silence. Mrs. Frank Kirsted cleared her throat hesitatingly.

"You don't suppose she—deceives Roger, do you?" she asked.

"Oh, no!" we all said. But we were all wondering. It certainly did look queer.

Well, that was the beginning. They all began to discuss Dulcie. I held back as long as I could, but it is queer how a subject like that affects you. I held back and held back and all the time I could feel myself weakening. It was as I imagine getting drunk must be. All of a sudden, you just let go. At last my strength of resistance gave way altogether and I told them how Dulcie had had two golden-light rinses and sworn me to secrecy, said Roger would have a fit if he knew.

After that we all let go. In the excitement Corinne put a cuff on the neck of the night shirt she was sewing on and Rosie kept the machine going for ten minutes without noticing that the thread had run out.

We got out on the street after the evening was over and I had the queerest feeling. Kind of excited, exhilarated. There is something about talking confidentially like that that gives you an awful kick. I felt strangely near to those other six girls and terribly fond of them all.

But the next morning, I got a kind of reaction. Dulcie brought me over a half a jelly roll she'd made and helped me enamel the kitchen table. I thought about the things we'd said last night and it made me feel guilty. I knew that Dulcie doesn't really deceive Roger any more, that is, than all of us deceive our husbands. And she told me all about those golden-light rinses in strict confidence. I felt miserably guilty over having told.

I felt a little better about it the next week, though, when Rosemary Merton had to go home early and we all got to discussing her. For Dulcie told how Rosie's own sister lives in a kitchenette apartment in Chicago and washes her dishes *in the bathtub*. Rosie had certainly told that to Dulcie in the strictest confidence and would have died to know it had got out.

I didn't feel quite so exhilarated or fond of the other girls after that meeting. It seemed to me that Dulcie was a shade cool to me the next day and I wondered if Rosie could possibly have told her that I'd told about the golden-light rinses. Rosie is the kind who gets attacks of conscience and there is no telling what a person in an attack like that will do. If she felt impelled to confess her part in the gossip to Dulcie, she'd be just as likely to feel impelled to confess my part, too. I felt nervous and ill at ease with Dulcie, and I didn't like Rosie Merton as well as I had. I kept watching her with a cold, suspicious eye.

And before the month was over there wasn't a girl in the club that, for one reason or another, I didn't feel edgy at. I'd resent what Corinne had said about Rosie and then feel miserable and guilty over what I'd said about Corinne. There wasn't any one I felt just easy and friendly with any more. I was always wondering what they'd said about me or feeling myself as much in somebody's power as though I were being blackmailed.

Being at those meetings was like being under the influence of liquor. I'd hear myself saying things that the next day I couldn't see how I could ever have said.

It was really the Charity Club that gave me the grippe. If I'd stayed at home that Thursday night that I came down with such a hard cold and taken a hot lemonade and everything the way Doctor Horne told me to, it would never have gone into grippe. But I didn't dare stay home from the Charity Club. In a moment of weakness I'd told Dulcie about the first quarrel I'd ever had with Mother Horton and I knew well enough that if I didn't want it to be all over town by the next day, I'd better be first at the club and the last to leave that night. I was, too, but the next day I was down in bed with the grippe.

Oh, take it altogether, the club was a terrible worry to me. It was pleasant to have Miss Prescott so pleased when I'd take her a pile of nightgowns and pillowcases for the hospital and when Doctor Wellins mentioned right in the pulpit the splendid welfare work the young married women were doing. Sooner or later, though, we would certainly have broken up in a terrible row if it hadn't been for the scandal about Peggy Scoggins.

That tied us together again. We stopped talking about each other and all talked about Peggy Scoggins. Peggy Scoggins is Judge Scoggins' youngest daughter and lives in the beautiful stone house out by the park. She is only seventeen and terribly pretty. She has always had a flock of boys running after her, but her mother and the Judge are terribly strict. She couldn't even go to the Dancing Club parties unless she went with her married sister.

And she's the only girl I ever heard of who couldn't go skating without a chaperon.

The Scoggins are the richest people in town so that anything about them is always interesting, and of course a scandal about a girl like Peggy was enough to make any club stop talking about anything else.

It started with Corinne and Scott seeing her at White's Tavern in Verblen.

White's Tavern is a kind of roadhouse and they sell bootleg liquor and have a very bad name. They also serve perfectly marvelous food and lots of the nice older married people go there on account of White's seafood. There's no other place around that serves seafood at all. The first thing every young married couple in Montrose does after they're married is to go to White's alone. It makes you realize as nothing else could that you're grown up and married.

And Corinne saw Peggy Scoggins there alone with a man!

It was enough to cause any Charity Club to rock on its foundation. Peggy, just seventeen, who couldn't go skating alone! Of course Peggy must have slipped out to go, of course her parents didn't know a thing about it. Peggy had carefully kept her back turned all the time, Corinne said, and Corinne couldn't see the man's face, it was behind a candle.

Well, we discussed that the whole evening. Discussed who the man could possibly be, how on earth Peggy had ever dared. We couldn't help being just the least trifle pleased about it because Mrs. Scoggins has been quite superior about the way she brought up her girls;

rather criticized our mothers for letting us go around alone so much. This was what she got, we told each other with a shade of mean satisfaction.

I watched Peggy in church the next Sunday, looking so prim and proper between her mother and the Judge. It just didn't seem possible. And yet that week, Dulcie saw her at White's again. Even Will was shocked at that.

"White's is no place for any nice girl," he said. "They get those tough motor parties from Chicago."

We almost forgot to sew at all at the meeting after the second time. Dulcie hadn't been able to see the man with Peggy, either, and we were simply seething with curiosity. They were leaving just as Roger and Dulcie got there.

"I stopped just inside the vestibule," Dulcie said, "and watched them go out. She had on that red coat with the gold buttons that Clemence Scoggins brought her back from Paris winter before last. And the man helped her into the sportiest looking car you ever saw, a pale blue sport roadster."

"It can't be anybody in Montrose, then," we said all at once. In a town the size of Montrose, you get to know all the cars by sight.

The next day Dulcie and Corinne were in Verblen and they saw the pale blue sport roadster standing outside the Vance building. Corinne recognized it. The car belonged to one of the Vances, who own the Vance building. And every one of the Vances is married.

This was a real scandal. The most exciting that had ever come into my life. We discussed whether we ought

to tell Mrs. Scoggins. Nobody wanted to be the one
to do it. Mrs. Scoggins might be glad enough to know,
but she is terribly haughty and would certainly be awfully nasty to whoever told her. The week that she ad-
dressed the Parents' and Teachers' Club on "How We
Can Help the Adolescent Girl" we almost died.

We talked of nothing else. Just as the thing was almost dying down for lack of fresh fuel, Rosie happened to be up at two o'clock in the morning with the
baby and looked out the front window and saw the
blue roadster coming down Water Street. It stopped
at the corner of Jackson, two blocks away from the
Scoggins' house. They were foolish enough to stop under
a street light and Rosie could see Peggy's red coat.

That brought the subject back to fever heat again,
and it was still simmering hot the night of Corelle Pat-
terson's dance in Verblen. Will had to go to Lodge first,
so I went to the Charity Club, but left early. Mother
Horton came over after prayer meeting to stay all night
so I let Ella Crowinshield go home early.

It was one o'clock when we left the party and it must
have been half past when we got to the bridge. We were
both sleepy and driving the flivver along in silence. There
isn't much travel on the Bridge Road late at night, but
when we turned the corner just before the bridge, we
saw a tail light. We thought at first the car was moving,
but as we got closer we saw that it was parked.

"You'd think it'd be too cold for neckers," said Will.
And just to be mean he turned the new searchlight he'd
just got for the flivver, full on the other car. I gasped.
It was a long, low, sporty-looking pale blue roadster.

As we came along the side, I saw a man's shoulder and Peggy Scoggins' bright red coat.

It gave me a shock that almost took my breath away. That is the way it is—you can hear things and hear them and yet the first time you actually see them yourself, it gives you as much of a turn as though you'd never heard a word.

Will's searchlight swept past the man's shoulder, over his dark hat, and full on the girl's face. My heart turned a double flop.

The girl in Peggy Scoggins' red coat was little Ella Crowninshield!

Will looked at me and I looked at Will as he drove on, blank, simply aghast. Ella, who had washed our dishes that very night and stayed with our babies till Mother Horton got out of prayer meeting. Ella that I'd known ever since she was a funny red-nosed baby, toddling along beside the toy delivery wagon when her brother Billy used to deliver her mother's fancy washing!

It all came over me in a flash. There had never been a word of truth in all these stories about Peggy Scoggins. Corinne had seen her from the back at White's, Dulcie across the driveway getting into a car. Nobody had seen her face and hadn't thought they needed to. That red coat was so unmistakable. Of course, that night that Rosemary had seen her getting out of the roadster at the corner, two blocks from the Scoggins' house, it had been at the very corner where Ella lives.

Of course, Mrs. Scoggins had given Ella Peggy's coat. It had been Ella all the time. And I had intended going back home and spreading it all over town that Peggy had been in a parked car on the Bridge Road at one o'clock in the morning.

I felt scared limp, as though a gun you'd been playing with had suddenly gone off and almost killed somebody. Not scared over what we had almost done to Peggy Scoggins. That was bad enough, but after all, you can't really hurt a Scoggins in Montrose. Even if it had all been true about Peggy and had got out, it would just have made a terrible stir for a while, Peggy would have been packed off somewhere to school and the whole thing hushed up. By the time she got back nobody would dare really snub her—Judge Scoggins is president of the bank and the richest man in town—and after a while, Peggy would marry somebody who'd be only too glad to be Judge Scoggins' son-in-law and the whole story would be forgotten. No, a little gossip wouldn't really hurt Peggy Scoggins much.

But Ella Crowninshield!

Nobody'd be afraid of offending her family. Her father had been dead since just before she was born and her mother was just a fancy washwoman. There was no bank back of Ella Crowninshield. There'd be no money for Ella to go away with until things had been hushed up and forgotten. And things would never be forgotten, either. Look at Lulu Crowninshield! It was in the blood, people would tell you. The two sisters who had married and turned out all right wouldn't count a second against Lulu. Everybody in Montrose and Verblen would hear all about it. No decent man would ever think of marrying Ella. She would have to live on right here in Montrose and she would be utterly and completely damned.

I felt simply limp and scared to death. Didn't Ella have any sense? Didn't she know what people would say when she started running with a married man? Didn't she know that even if he'd been single, she could ruin her reputation for life just by going to White's with him or staying out all hours in a sporty-looking car? Didn't she have any sense at all?

I was simply furious at Ella. The danger she was walking right into, herself! Of course, I'd keep still, but somebody would see her some time who wouldn't. I had got to stop her in time, that was all. I'd give her a terrible talking to the very next day. I'd tell her!

She stopped in the next morning to return the babies' best dresses that I always have her mother do up. I was out in the kitchen making cookies and all primed and ready for Ella. I'd tell her!

I don't know what kept me from jumping on her the second she opened the door. Goodness knows, I was all ready to. Something stopped me, though, and made me think it would be just as well to start a little easy, work up to jumping on her by degrees. So I just passed her a hot cookie on my pancake turner and said:

"Sit down a minute. There are raisins in the panful that's in the oven now. What's all the news?"

We talked a few minutes about nothing at all. Then I said carelessly:

"What'd you do last night?"

I expected she'd turn red and act guilty, which would

give me my chance.   But instead she lighted up like a
room when you turn on the floor lamp in the twilight.

"Went riding with Joe," she said.

"Joe who?"

"Joe Miller.   He works over in the Verblen garage,
you know.   He's got a night job there now, but they're
going to give him a swell place in the repair department
when old Evers leaves in the spring.   He's just wonderful
with machinery.   He fixed up Mr. Vance's French car
when the mechanic they'd got clear up from Chicago
couldn't locate the trouble.   Mr. Vance thinks he's grand."

"Is that light-blue roadster Mr. Vance's car?" I asked.

"M-hm," Ella just beamed.   "We was out in it last
night.   Mr. Vance lets Joe drive it sometimes on his
night off."

"Last night?" I said innocently.   "Why, you were
here with the babies last night."

"Oh, afterward," said Ella.   And then, as though
she were afraid I was criticizing her, "He didn't come
here at all.   I met him down at Gray's corner.   I knew
you didn't like it the other night I had him here."

"But it must have been awfully late," I said.   "You
were here till nearly ten."

Ella giggled.

"We never got home till ten minutes of three," she confessed.   "Mr. Vance starts south to-day in the car and
it was our last chance."

By the kid way she giggled about it and the way she
acted so tickled, I knew that it was really all right.   Which
made it all the worse in a way.   For her to get herself
talked about the way she would, all for nothing!

"But, Ella," I said, "you can't stay out till three o'clock in the morning in a gossipy little place like Montrose without getting talked about."

Ella shrugged her shoulders.

"It's the only time I can see him," she said. "Thursday's the only night he gets off and I have to be here every Thursday night. You don't get home from the Charity Club till eleven o'clock."

Well, there was something in what she said. She'd lost a lot of jobs by not wanting to work when she had her bank beau. Jobs like Ella's you have to take when they're offered.

"Then you ought to have him at home," I said.

Ella's face hardened.

"Ma sleeps in the parlor and she goes to bed at nine. And I'm never goin' to have a fellow at home again, anyway. I had a swell fellow—worked in the bank— used to come Sundays. It'd be just the same if I had Joe there as it was with him. My sister's kids stuck right in the parlor all the time and she came in once and sat the whole time he was there, telling him about the time she was operated on, and Ma'd come in at nine and yawn and look at the clock and the place always smells steamy anyhow. Then one day Lulu came up from Chicago and she and Ma had an awful row in the kitchen and he could hear every word of it. That was the last straw! He never came another time."

Just as suddenly as her face had hardened, it got all soft again.

"I don't care, though. Joe's worth ten of him if he did work in a bank. But you can bet I'm not going to have

Joe at home. Ma's still got Lulu on her mind and like as not the second time Joe came she'd stalk up and ask him if he meant to marry me. You know how that'd scare any fellow to death. I—I just *gotta* have everything go right. You know how it is."

In that instant the long lecture I had all ready and waiting for Ella died on me. I simply couldn't say the first word of it. It was the way she said, "You know how it is" confidentially, as woman to woman, that stopped me. For I did know how it was. I didn't want to know. I would rather have remembered that I was six years older than Ella and married and come from a good family and couldn't understand how she could do such foolish things. I didn't want to understand, but I simply couldn't help myself.

"I—I just *gotta* have everything go right!" Oh, couldn't I remember when I'd felt that way about Will! When I first began to be crazy about him and wasn't sure whether he was crazy about me or not. I could just remember the goosefleshy excitement when the very ringing of the telephone would make me positively sick with uncertainty. When I'd be all trembly with hurry and yet afraid to take down the receiver, feeling that if it shouldn't be Will I should die.

I must have done a stack of silly things, too. Mother and Father hadn't seemed to care, though. I could remember how they used to sit inside on hot stuffy nights so that Kathie and Elmer could have the front porch and Will and I the back. How Mother would be as worried as I was for fear a new dress wouldn't be done in time for a party. And the night Will and I had gone to

Verblen for a sundae after the Dancing Club and missed
the last car and had to walk home and got back so late
and Aunt Ellen, who was visiting us, was so shocked
and said, "But why did you have to go clear to Verblen
for ice cream in the first place?" How Father had just
said, "Oh, come, come, El, I can remember the time
when you thought the farther from home you bought a
slice of watermelon, the better it tasted."

And all the other girls, too. Dulcie would be horrified
to know that Ella had spooned in a parked car out on
Bridge Road, and yet she and Roger used to put out
the streetlight and sit out on Dulcie's steps summer nights
after parties till Mr. Dunwoody would call out of the
window and tell Dulcie to bring in the morning paper
when she came.

It was all silly. And yet it wasn't just silly. It was
pretty important, too. Just silly little things like that
might make all the difference in the world to Ella. The
difference between baking cookies in her own sunny
kitchen some time with somebody who'd look as good to
her as Will does to me coming home at noon to eat them,
a baby of her own to take care of and worry over and
love till just thinking of it brought a lump into her throat
—the difference between that and spending her life in
other people's kitchens, washing other people's dishes,
taking care of other people's babies. Or maybe even—
I remembered Lulu Crowinshield, the last time she was
in town with her fur coat and her gold mesh bag and
decent women crossing the street so they wouldn't have
to speak to her.

Why, Ella was in the scariest position in the world!

Her whole life might swing either way. And there wasn't a soul to give her the right push. No mother to help make things go smoothly, no safe, comfortable father to call out the upstairs window when she stayed out too late. Nobody but a whole town waiting to call her wicked if she was silly. And Ella was just as sure to be silly as I was when I was first crazy about Will or Dulcie was when she was first in love with Roger Lane.

I looked over at Ella and she smiled at me, an excited, kid smile. Suddenly I thought of Will coming around the corner at suppertime, of my babies blowing bubbles and grabbing hold of my hair, of everything that was dear and safe and happy; then of Ella, likelier than not to let it all slip through her fingers. Something had *got* to be done about it. Things couldn't be *let* go as terribly wrong as that.

And I knew that it was up to me.

"Listen, Ella," I said briskly, pulling a pan of cookies out of the oven, "don't go meeting Joe around on corners and riding all hours of the night with him. And don't ever go to White's. You'll get yourself talked about and you know what that's likely to do to any beau. You're all wrong about my not wanting him here. I don't care at all. Have him come here every Thursday night. You can have the supper dishes washed and your dress changed before he can get over here from Verblen. Take him into the living room and play the Songola or do anything you want to. Will's always at Lodge that night, so we never use the room."

"Hon-honestly! You—you really wouldn't care? If we didn't stay in the kitchen?"

Ella's face made my throat get all tight and achey. She was so surprised and excited and half scared, as though I were handing her the grandest thing in the world and she was afraid to believe it for fear I might change my mind and snatch it back. The poor kid! To feel like that over something the rest of us had taken as for granted as the air we breathed! Looking as though the heavens had opened! And for just a decent place to see her sweetheart!

So nobody had ever offered her anything like that before! Had nobody else ever seen how important it was? Oh, there was no use dodging. It was up to me.

"Have you worn that red coat much?" I asked anxiously. "The one Mrs. Scoggins gave you?"

Ella shook her head.

"Just out with Joe. It's a swell coat, but I don't know —I kind of hate to wear it around Montrose here. I guess maybe it's too swell for me. I'd feel as though everybody was looking at me and thinking, 'Oh, look, there goes Peggy Scoggins' coat!' "

For a second I felt almost wobbly with relief. It was like the moment Dick Barthelmess dragged the girl back from the brink of the falls. There wasn't a thing in the world that need ever connect Ella with the scandal. Nobody had really seen Joe, the car had gone south, and the coat— Why, Ella was safe! Safe—she didn't even know the falls had been there!

"Of course, I will wear it," she said. "It's a grand spring coat."

"Of course," I said, making my voice sound careless. It was like watching a scary, exciting movie. Only I was caught right into playing in it, too. I couldn't help myself. I knew I was doing something wild and crazy, but I couldn't stop myself. I couldn't make anything seem important but dragging Ella back, well away from those falls.

"By the way," I said, and nothing in the world seemed necessary except to make my voice casual enough so that Ella wouldn't suspect anything, "by the way, I've got a coat that I can't wear and I'm going to send out to my cousin in Kansas. If you'd rather have it, I'd just as soon trade and send my cousin Peggy Scoggins' red one. Mine is really almost as nice a coat if it didn't come from Paris. Tan with fluffy fox collar and cuffs."

"The one you showed me Sunday!" Ella gasped. "Why, that's brand new!"

I guess Ella had never had anything new in her life to wear.

"Oh, I haven't had it long," I said, brandishing my pancake turner casually. "But Will doesn't like it."

That was a terrible lie, of course. But it worked! It worked! Ella never suspected a thing. She went home, looking kind of dazed, with my coat in the box it had come in. I was to stop for the red one in the flivver that night. Ella wanted to bring it over, but I was taking no chances of anybody in Montrose ever seeing that bright red coat again.

I stood watching Ella walk down the street. Slowly, the enormity of what I had done came creeping over me. I had given away my new spring coat! A brand new coat that I'd never even worn. It was a beautiful coat, the first really nice thing I'd bought since the babies came.

Will was crazy about it. I hadn't meant to send it to any cousin in Kansas. I haven't even got a cousin in Kansas. But I didn't have any other coat except a black one three years old that was nothing I could have offered Ella in place of that beautiful Paris coat. Of course, I couldn't go around Montrose in Peggy Scoggins' coat, either, so I should simply have to wear the old black one.

What on earth would Will say! We run our budget together. I couldn't blame him if he were perfectly furious. He'd be justified enough. It was a perfectly crazy thing to do. I knew it, and yet even realizing the enormity of what I'd done, I knew I'd be fool enough to do it right straight over again if Ella were sitting in the kitchen now.

I told Will fearfully the instant he got in the house for dinner. I tried to make him see how necessary it had been, but I was afraid I couldn't.

"I know I shouldn't have done it," I said, "but, honestly, Will, there just didn't seem to be any other way. I can wear my old black coat and—well, there just wasn't any other way. Do you mind an awful lot?"

Will is the dearest man in the world. He just looked at me a minute.

"Doll," he said solemnly, "you'll never be able to get that black coat on over your wings."

I felt the load of the ages fall off my shoulders. Everything was all right, after all.

And it's working out gorgeously. Of course, I'm sorry that I've had to give up the Charity Club, but I simply don't dare leave the babies in the house with nobody but a girl entertaining a beau. I know how any

girl with a beau is. The house might catch fire and burn
down and Ella'd never even smell smoke.

I have to be careful, always making Ella think I intend
to go to the club but that something has come up at the
last minute. She's proud and wouldn't come if she didn't
think she was staying with the babies. I sit upstairs in
my new little sewing room where I can't hear them talking in the living room. Sometimes when Will gets home
from Lodge, Ella and I make hot chocolate and we all
four play Five Hundred for an hour or so. Will thinks
Joe is a fine young fellow.

I suppose the Charity Club has gossiped about me
till I'm as stale a subject as Betty Bartell or Veda Knopf
and Fred. But I don't care so long as they're too busy
to talk any more about the places they saw Peggy Scoggins' coat. I did feel awfully guilty when Miss Prescott
said she was so sorry to hear I'd dropped out of the club,
that it seemed as though even a busy young matron
should find time to do a little welfare work. But I con-
soled myself with the knowledge that, though I can't explain to the rest of them, I haven't really dropped charity
work for good. I shall get right back into it as soon as
I get Ella Crowninshield safely married and off my
hands.

V

LET DOT DO IT

ELLA CROWNINSHIELD certainly started something in our crowd when she got married. Nobody had ever thought of thin, stringy-haired little Ella as being so important, but when she was suddenly pulled out from under us, so to speak, everybody realized how much had rested on her narrow shoulders. Was America Hawkins pokier than usual? Get Ella to finish up the ironing. Was somebody sick? Get Ella to help out in the kitchen. Did you want to give a party? Get Ella to wait on the table. Did you want to go to one? Get Ella to stay with the babies. For twenty-five cents an hour, Ella would tackle *anything*.

Being able to call on Ella at a moment's notice like that for such a variety of things, had built up a sort of false security, and when she suddenly got married and her husband wouldn't let her work out by the hour any more, our young married crowd was thrown into a perfect state of flapping and floundering. Mrs. Frank Kirsted had to postpone entertaining the Charity Club till she could gather strength to do it without Ella, and when Dulcie came home from the hospital with little Dulcie, Roger said actually he'd have to stay home from the bank if it hadn't been for my helping them out. Dulcie's mother was down with the flu and while Dulcie had a trained nurse to take care of her, it always takes at least one more to take care of a trained nurse.

It was while I was fixing a tray of our dinner to take over for Dulcie and the nurse that it suddenly dawned on me that I was flapping and floundering the least of any one in our crowd. I ran them over in my mind, Rosie Merton, Corinne, Dulcie, Mrs. Kirsted—surely I had just as much work to do as any of them. Of course, Rosie did have three babies to my twins, but she buys every stitch of her own clothes ready made so that evened things up. And yet her house always looked like a cross between housecleaning and a day nursery while ours, if I do say it myself, was pretty slick most of the time.

I sprinkled a little chopped parsley over the creamed potatoes and laid a crisp new radish on the bread-and-butter plate. If I really was getting along better than the other girls—and I knew it wasn't just conceit, I really was—it was because of my "time budget" that they had all laughed at so at the start. So many minutes to prepare the grapefruit, the babies' clothes in the boiler before we sat down to breakfast, the dishes done by five minutes past eight—everything had to go just by schedule. Will sometimes made fun of my budget, telling how one morning when I was specially hungry I ate an extra piece of toast and didn't get caught up all day. But it was an admiring sort of fun that he made of it because he knew that it worked.

I laid a daffodil across the napkin and carried the tray across the lawn to Dulcie's, continuing my pleasant thought. It was thanks to my budget that I had the afternoon ahead of me free. Having no system at all, Rosie never knew where she was at. No wonder she was usually kind of harried looking. When she was strain-

ing carrots for the baby she'd be figuring how she ought
to have led out trumps sooner at the party the day before
and then when she was actually at a party, she'd be wondering whether to have chops or kidney stew for dinner
the next day. Every Sunday evening I made out my
menu for the week to come and, barring accidents, such
as the butcher not getting any fish, or there being more
roast beef left over than I'd figured on, I didn't have to
give meal planning a thought during the week.

Mother Horton had said I could park the twins on her
this afternoon so it was with nothing on my mind but
my new pink horsehair hat, that I strolled down and
dropped in on the High School Alumnæ Club. The
members were pleased and surprised to see me because
most of the girls drop out as soon as they get married
and those who stick past that give up the ghost completely when the first baby comes along. I explained
how with my time budget I was able still to find time
for such things, and the girls all agreed that it was wonderful.

"Dot is the very person to be chairman of the Bazaar,"
Girlie Whittaker exclaimed. "Isn't it the limit we
haven't thought of it before! If any place needs a capable
person!"

"Oh, I'm afraid I wouldn't have time to undertake
that," I exclaimed.

"There won't be much work for you," Girlie assured
me. "You just have to appoint committees and sort of
get things started—the committees do all the work. The
chairman is just a figurehead."

"But she's the most important person in the whole

shebang," Ellen Llewellyn said hastily. "You simply have to have a capable head or the whole thing will be a flop."

"You're the one person who could put it over," Rita Birney assured me. "It takes somebody who's both tactful and knows how to organize. There isn't another member who could do it."

I ran over the members in my mind and I realized that they weren't just jollying me. I couldn't think of anybody else, either.

"Wel-l-l," I began doubtfully, but they snapped me up so quick that before I hardly knew I'd accepted, 1 found myself appointing Marge Kitteridge to take care of the advertising.

I walked home from the meeting in a pleasant glow. Rosie and Corinne wouldn't even find time to go to the Alumnæ meetings and yet I, with as much home work as either of them, had been appointed chairman of the Bazaar. It is a marvelous satisfaction to suddenly find that you're capable. I undressed the twins briskly, knowing that, thanks to my own planning, the lettuce for supper was all washed and in a bag on the ice, the cheese potatoes ready to slide into the oven, the table all set out on the porch. I drew a deep comfortable breath of peace, the busy, active sort of peace that is the nicest sort of all.

It's well I drew that breath while the drawing was good. Looking back, it seems to me that it was the last peaceful breath I drew for weeks.

If there ever was a pleasant fiction that sits combing its golden hair like the Lorelei and luring you on to your own destruction, it's the idea that all a chairman has to

do is to appoint committees, that then the committees do
the work. Before a week was over, I discovered that idea
for the false fair thing it is. I found that I could parcel
out the work among the committees as much as I liked,
but then I had to do the thinking for all of them. It
simply appalled me, the important things they forget all
about.

Marge, for instance, had charge of the advertising, yet
she never once thought of going to Mr. Vose and getting
him to run an editorial about the bazaar. Jeanne Garden
was supposed to have charge of the soliciting and it never
occurred to her to write all of the girls who had married
and left Montrose, and ask them for contributions. The
girls were simply amazed at the way I thought of things
and I was simply amazed at the way they didn't.

"I suppose it's having seen your husband handle
things," said little Betty Leach respectfully.

I don't think that was true but I didn't deny it. It
is rather flattering, the attitude of girls who haven't husbands to those who have.

The attitude of the married girls is entirely different.
When I stopped in at Dulcie's and asked her to take a
table for the bazaar, she looked at me in the most superior
way.

"Mercy, I haven't time for bazaars," she said, "with a
brand new baby and a husband to look after." She
paused for a moment. "I don't think it's fair to Will for
you to neglect your family in order to run a bazaar."

I shouldn't have paid any attention to that, of course,
knowing by experience that a girl with her first-month

baby is always so heady with responsibility that she thinks she invented the domestic life. It must have had some effect on me, though. Without it, when Will said wistfully that evening:

"I wish I could get somebody to work up that mind-reading stunt with me."

I'd have said sympathetically, "I wish you could," and let it go at that. But Dulcie's hint had taken root and it occurred to me that if I was the only one who could run the bazaar, I was also the only wife Will had. So I looked up with interest.

"Could I help you with it?" I asked brightly.

Will was suddenly all enthusiasm.

"You bet your life you could," he said enthusiastically. "Say, it's the greatest stunt I've seen in a long time. I've got the directions all here and it's a lulu. You're blindfolded, see? And I go around and get things from people and ask you what it is."

"How am I going to know what it is?" I asked, "if I'm blindfolded."

"That's the stunt," said Will. "Here it is. It's a code. It all depends on the way I ask the question. Now for instance, I say, 'What have I here?' All questions beginning with What mean metal. So you know what I've got is metal and go on to the next word. If I said, 'What *is* this?,' the "is" would mean it was a key. But saying What *have* means that it's a coin. If I said, 'What have *we* here?' it would mean a half-dollar, but What have *I?* means a penny." He looked at me all bright eagerness. "Do you see how it works?"

"Why, yes," I said. "It sounds quite simple. I suppose there are scads of ways we can think up to ask a question that would sound all right to the audience."

"That's the eye!" said Will enthusiastically. "I knew you'd catch on right away. That's all there is to it—just learn the code."

"All there is to it—just learn the code!"

The next afternoon after I'd fed the babies and got them to sleep, I got out the code and looked it over. I nearly dropped dead. Just learn the code—why, it was practically a whole book to learn. You might be given anything from a blank check to a potato. There was page after page of stuff to memorize. Will, however, when he arrived home for supper was quite optimistic.

"Oh, sure you can learn it," he reassured me. "You've got a good bean. It'll take some time, of course, you never get anywhere in parlor magic without putting a lot of time into it. Look at the time I practiced on taking off my thumb."

Will has a perfectly gruesome trick of taking one thumb in the fingers of the other hand and apparently pulling it off—you actually see the thumb in his other hand and the stump it's supposed to have come off. He has it worked down to the fine point where it just makes my blood run cold every time he does it even though I know how it's done. He was practicing it one night when we and the Lanes went to the hotel for dinner. Just as the waiter arrived with the soup, Will managed a pretty good one. The waiter stopped short, his jaw dropped open and he let one plate of soup skid right off the tray. "My God!" he gasped. "L-look what you done to your hand!" I guess he thought Will wasn't paying much attention to what he was doing and hadn't noticed that he'd pulled his thumb clear off.

"Sure you can learn it," Will insisted.

"Wel-ll," I said.

It was certainly some combination I had wished on myself, tending to the bazaar with one hand and learning parlor magic with the other. And in the meantime doing all my own work. And my own work suddenly increased a millionfold by Jill wanting to walk. (Since we call little John "Jack" everybody calls Katherine "Jill.") She could do it if you held her by both hands and she wanted to do it all the time. No more putting her in her pen and peacefully forgetting her. And she never got tired. I'd have to bend to reach her little hands and my back would be ready to break after doing the tour of the downstairs three or four times. But not Jill. She'd kill off a half a dozen grown-ups and still be on the job.

I was telephoning about the bazaar one afternoon and Jill was yelling her head off when Mother Horton came in. I explained that Jill just wanted me to walk with her. Mother Horton thought it was perfectly awful that I should be telephoning about a bazaar when my child needed me and after she went out, I did get to feeling kind of guilty about it. Jill would look up at me so dear and funny with her one curl standing right up on top of her head and I knew that after all it was more important for a little human being to learn to walk than anything else. So I'd walk her around one room after another, studying over Will's code and worrying about the bazaar.

Every night that we weren't going anywhere, Will

would want to practice the mind-reading stunt. I'd usually have to call up a lot of people about the bazaar first
and by the time I'd get to try to read his mind I'd be so
dead sleepy I couldn't remember whether I'd put out
Buster, to say nothing of knowing a code. Will would
get so impatient with me that I'd vow I'd study on it
harder the next day.

Then one day when I was up at mother's, she told me
I ought to invite Dr. Elincourt and his wife to dinner.
He is the new minister at our church and mother said he
felt hurt that the young people weren't taking him into
their hearts more. As I said to mother, I'd just as soon
take him into my heart but I didn't see how I could find
time to ask him to dinner. It did seem to me that some
of the other girls might ask him, somebody who didn't
have to be chairman of a bazaar daytime, and mind-reader
nights, but nobody did. I waited ten days or so and
then could see that it was up to me. That was the terrible
part of being capable I suddenly saw. Everything is up
to you.

Mrs. Elincourt seemed very appreciative and said
they'd love to come. Mr. Elincourt has lots of committees and so on evenings and the only evening we could
agree on was two nights before the bazaar. So we agreed
on that night and I invited Howard and Rosie Merton
too. If you've got to get a dinner fancy enough for a
minister you might as well give somebody else the benefit of it, too.

It is queer how that one dinner seemed to be the last
straw. I feel quite sure I should have gotten by with
all the other things if it hadn't been for that. I was

even getting along fairly well with the mind-reading code, the bazaar was shaping up all right and though I didn't walk Jill as much as she wanted me to, I felt I was doing enough. But from the minute the Elincourts accepted my invitation, everything began to go wrong.

Mostly about the bazaar. Everybody began blaming me for everything. The school principal didn't like Mr. Vose's editorial, the out-of-town girls didn't send things as fast as they should—everything went wrong and I had to straighten out everything. From the time I got up in the morning till I went to bed at night, the telephone was ringing. Would I ask Mrs. Long to send in flowers, the flower committee hadn't thought of her. Why hadn't anybody had the Lodge announce the bazaar? The Masonic Hall would charge us an extra five dollars if we held over into the evening and used light. Where was the bunting they'd had for the last banquet? Why had I ever put Girlie Whittaker on the candy committee? Didn't I know she makes everybody she speaks to so mad that they won't do anything for her? And so on.

I would never turn away from the telephone that Jill wouldn't begin Yeh! Yeh! and hold up her hands for me to walk her and when I'd go on with my work and just let her cry, I'd feel mean and guilty and wonder if I was one of those modern mothers who tends to everything outside their own home and lets their own children starve for need of a little mother love. Then one noon Will came home to dinner all pepped up over a dinner that the Lodge was going to give to the Rotary Club and their wives.

"They're trying to get up a program of stunts," Will

said, "and I told them you and I would do our mind-reading stunt."

"Oh, Will," I simply wailed, "I can't possibly learn that code well enough in time. Why, the dinner's only a week after the bazaar."

"Sure you can," Will insisted. "You've got it pretty well all ready and I'll help you."

"But to do it at a public affair!" I protested. "You never said you expected anything like that."

Will looked kind of hurt and reproachful.

"Well, if you want to run bazaars and do everything like that for total strangers and then can't find time to do anything I want you to—"

I sighed resignedly.

"Oh, all right, I'll do the best I can," I said. "But you needn't blame me if you ask me what a fountain pen is and I say a fresh egg."

The prospect of that dinner put a new phase on learning the code. It made it a terribly serious thing instead of just a useful pastime. Will got so serious about it that he seemed to think I ought to not pay any attention to anything but studying it. And all the time the bazaar got closer and more worrying.

Everybody kept telling me that I was a marvel, so capable; but in spite of it I began to doubt this myself I simply never got through. There was always somebody to call up about something. Or if there was nothing else, by daytime there was always Jill to walk, and by evening that miserable code to study. I would actually have nightmares, something I'd hardly ever had in my life and would wake up thinking that Jill was blindfolded and Will was holding up a handkerchief and asking her, "And now what have I here?", and I would try to tell her that any question beginning with And was made out of cloth and that the Girls' Friendly had never returned the bunting and that we'd have to trim the booths with crêpe paper.

It was awful. I got so tired that just seeing Jill stick up her hands all the time for me to walk her made me feel cross. Sometimes it seemed to me I didn't love her as much as I ought to or I wouldn't feel that way.

It was terrible. I began to look at people like Dulcie and Mrs. Frank Kirsted, who weren't capable, and just envy them. Nobody expected anything of them. Capable people seemed to have to bear all the burdens of the world.

I knew that I was bearing all the burden of that bazaar. When it came right to it, everybody left everything for me to see to. There were girls enough who would say, "Oh, I'll do anything, just tell me what to do," but then I'd have to do all the thinking and if I'd tell them to do anything they didn't want to, they'd be too busy. I began to feel kind of hurt and mad about the bazaar. Having put my hand to the plow, I was going to make a success of it, but it seemed queer to me that I should be the only one to take any real interest in it. So I'd keep after them, nagging the slow ones, checking up on the careless and everything. And I kept having to stay up later at night every night and getting tireder and tireder and crosser and crosser every day. I couldn't even look forward to the time when the bazaar would be over because there was still that miserable mind-reading ahead.

Then there was the dinner for Dr. Elincourt. It had
been easy when I could get Ella to come, she knew
right where I kept everything and was a real help. I
did engage America to come and wait on the table and
do the dishes afterward, but there was no comfort in it.
She is so fat, she looks funny in the dining room anyway and then I had to teach her everything about waiting on the table. And while she was willing, she was
dumb. I just knew that in spite of all I could teach her,
when the critical moment came she would stack the
plates.

I planned a very nice dinner, pork chops split and
stuffed—everybody speaks well of those—pear and
cream cheese salad, maple mousse and all the trimmings.
A minister certainly has it soft, he gets the peach pickles
and wild grape jelly wherever he goes.

Never as long as I live shall I forget the day of that
dinner. The night before I began to sneeze with a cold
and by that morning I felt perfectly miserable, head-
achey and a little deaf and so dopey that all I asked of
life was to lie down and shut my eyes. I had as much
chance of being elected mayor of New York as of lying
down and shutting my eyes.

By afternoon I had my regular work done and dinner
pretty well under way. I wished the twins on mother
for the afternoon and figured I was going to get along
pretty well. Then Marge called up to say that the printer
said he couldn't get the tickets done in time for the
bazaar and the flivver being on the fritz I had to walk
down to see him. Walking home, it seemed to me that
Marge might have done that herself, instead of leaving

everything for me.   Then Girlie called up to say the
candy boxes had come from the factory and they hadn't
sent a single half-pound box.   It took me an hour to get
that straightened out.   It occurred to me that Girlie might
have tended to that.   In fact, by the time America got
there at five, I was beginning to see what a martyr I was
being made.

There is a certain satisfaction, of course, in being a
martyr, in knowing that everybody thinks you're so much
more capable than anybody else, but it's hard to keep going on just gratitude.

I had set the table and showed America how to fix the
pear and cream cheese salad, and I'd just dragged myself
down from changing my dress when the telephone rang.
Before I had time to say Hello I heard voices and knew
they'd rung me by mistake.   I should have hung up right
away, but suddenly I heard my name.

"Oh, might as well let Dot Horton do it," a girl's voice
was saying, "She thinks nobody else can do anything
right.   She's getting so bossy—"

I hung up quickly and stood staring at the telephone
so mad I could hardly see it.   So that was what the girls
were saying!   That I was bossy.   A fine bazaar they'd
have had if I hadn't been bossy.   And I'd been just managing to keep going by thinking how grateful they were.
It's an awful thing to suddenly have gratitude pulled out
from under you.   In my anger it occurred to me tempt-
ingly that there were people who would just drop right
out and let the bazaar fail.   It's easy to be moral and say
that you don't want gratitude, that you're working for
the cause, but—

"Now what would this be I have?"

I hadn't heard Will come in and his voice made me jump. He was always springing those everlasting mind-reading questions at me, but this was certainly at the wrong time.

"I don't know what you have and I don't give a darn," I said.

Of course, Will didn't know that I was just miserable with a cold and had just had a taste of human ingratitude or he would never have said, as he did, crossly:

"Well, if I'd known you weren't going to take any interest in the stunt, I'd have got somebody else to help me, you can bet your bottom dollar on that."

He turned and walked away. Suddenly the mad feeling all went away, I just felt blue and hurt, and I could feel a great ball coming in my throat and the telephone blurred. It may make you mad to work your head off for a lot of girls who don't appreciate it, but when you've tried as hard as I had to do your duty to your husband and then he turns on you—

Just then the doorbell rang and I had to brush away the tears and go and let in the Elincourts. Howard and Rosie came right afterward and at half-past six we all sat down at the dinner table.

It is a nervous strain at best, entertaining a new minister for the first time. My cold was so bad that I couldn't tell whether things tasted right or not. I kept a nervous watch on America, but aside from looking comical, which of course she couldn't be kept from doing, she didn't seem to do anything very wrong. The food looked all right and I could only hope it tasted all right, too.

In one way, I soon saw, my carefully planned dinner was almost a total loss. Dr. Elincourt was the kind of man who doesn't know what he's eating. He started talking to us about the missionary in China and from the far-away air he had toward his cream of tomato soup, he might have been in China with the missionary for all he knew what he was eating. The stuffed chops were a triumph but he'd moved on to India by the time they came and I might just as well have given him chipped beef—you could feed that man sawdust and he'd never know the difference. It was annoying after planning so much on a dinner for him.

By the end of that course my cold was getting worse so fast that the room seemed about ninety and I forgot to see whether America stacked the plates or not. I did come to, though, when she brought in the salad. I'd told her just how to make it but I hadn't stood right over her while she was doing it. To my horror, I saw that she hadn't taken the tin foil off the cheese, just sliced right down through it. Dr. Elincourt's piece was a corner and almost completely covered with tin.

I was so mortified I didn't know what to do. I couldn't decide whether to apologize or not. Mother had always told me that nothing was worse manners than to apologize for anything on your table but then mother had never served tin foil. I felt that really required some explanation. I looked nervously at Mrs. Elincourt, she was scraping the cream cheese out with her fork delicately and pretending, like the lady she is, that there wasn't anything funny about serving it that way.

I opened my lips to apologize but Dr. Elincourt was
holding the floor and I couldn't get in a word.

"The fruit in Custer County," he was saying, "has
never justified the land that's been put into orchards—"

I glanced at him and suddenly my blood ran cold.
There before my very eyes that man was *eating the tin
foil.*

"Oh, Dr. Elincourt!" I gasped in shocked protest.

But he just smiled a genial smile as though to include
me in the conversation and, looking at his salad with eyes
that couldn't see anything nearer than Custer County,
finished the last corner. If there'd been a doily on the
plate, no doubt he'd have eaten that too.

I looked at Mrs. Elincourt in horrified reproach.
Everybody left everything for me to do. It did seem as
though in this case she might have taken a little responsibility and stopped her own husband, herself. Would it
kill him? It seemed to me I had heard of metal poisoning.
Had I been a murderer at my own table. At best, it
seemed to me it would undermine his constitution. It
surely couldn't be good for anybody to eat tin foil. If
it made him sick, would it come upon him right away or
would it be a slow weakening? It seemed to me he was
already beginning to look a little pale.

Or maybe it was just the lights. My head was throb-
bing so that the candlelight seemed to blur bright and
then go almost dark. People's voices seemed queer and
miles away. The room felt as though it must be ninety
and yet the next minute I couldn't seem to keep from
shivering Suddenly Jill woke up upstairs and began crying in a plaintive, conversational tone. She wanted me

to come and walk her. I thought of walking upstairs to put her down in bed and the ache in my legs swept all over me—it suddenly seemed as though I could never walk upstairs again.

Walk upstairs—I didn't feel as though I could drag myself into the living room. In a few minutes I should have to do that. We were having our after-dinner coffee. I drank my little cupful down in two swallows—maybe it would give me strength. But it just made me feel sicker than ever. I squeezed my hands together under the table; they were like ice. The water goblet in front of Dr. Elincourt suddenly seemed to move and float—

Suddenly there came the clang of the fire engine. Everybody rose and rushed to the window. It went banging right past our house on downtown. Howard and Dr. Elincourt hurried out to the porch, Will dashed to the telephone. A moment later he turned back.

"It's the Busy Bee," he said, "and the Masonic Building."

"The Masonic Building—" I gasped. And with the goblets and the candles on the table reeling and dancing before me, I pulled myself up and started for the door. The porch steps seemed to tip and wobble but I got down them and started toward the gate.

"Going to the fire?" Will asked.

"I've got to," I said. "The Masonic Building can't burn—it's where the bazaar's to be—day after to-morrow—"

"Well, for the love of Pete," said Will, stopping to help Mrs. Elincourt down the steps, "what do you think you can do about it? Go down and put it out yourself?"

I was halfway to the street before Will's words finally filtered into my mind, reeling on in a kind of daze, hardly knowing where I was going, just feeling that, once more, it was up to me.   And suddenly his words soaked in along with the distant clang of the fire engine.   I stopped short—that fire engine was going to put out the fire, I didn't have to!   If the Masonic Hall burned down and they couldn't have the bazaar at all, I couldn't help it.   I couldn't do anything about it.   So I didn't have to.   I didn't have to go another step.

"Going to the fire?" Will asked me.

The street light flared suddenly in my face—I put one foot ahead of the other and it felt as it does when you come to an unexpected step down when you're walking in the dark.   Will turned and looked sharply at me.

"Dot!" he said, "you're sick!"

I just slid down into the dark step-off and didn't even try to answer.   I was at the very end of my rope.

When I woke up the next morning, the sun was streaming into my bedroom.   It must be terribly late!   Hadn't the alarm gone off?   What about the babies?   Breakfast! I started to spring up and then suddenly I saw Ella Crowninshield in the corner of the room.

She hurried over and pushed me back down.

"You just lie still," she said.   "You've got the la grippe."

"The—what?" I asked.

"The la grippe."

"Are you—sure?" I asked, afraid to believe it.

Ella nodded.   I lay still for a few minutes while the heavenly, unbelievable relief of it swept over me.

After a bit—

"Did the Masonic Hall burn down?" I asked.

"To the ground," said Ella.

I shut my eyes and went back to sleep.

After a while Dr. Horne came and said I really did have the grippe. I was to stay right in bed. Ella explained that mother had taken Jack and Mother Horton would keep Jill. Ella was going to stay and keep house for Will and take care of me. Joe would let her do that, she said, though she wasn't working out any more, because Will and I had been so nice to them. Will had arranged everything.

Never shall I forget those next three heavenly days. People who think sickness is bad have never had anything worse. The peace of hearing the telephone ring and knowing that I didn't have to answer it! What was a chill or sore throat compared with the bliss of being able to go to sleep whenever you wanted. I realized that I ought to feel regretful about the bazaar having to be given up but I couldn't seem to make myself care even enough to speak about it. The Rotarian dinner too— the peace of knowing that it was flatly impossible to rise from a bed of grippe and read minds.

By the fourth day I was feeling much better. I was propped up in bed, when Will came home to dinner. He came in and sat down on the edge of the bed and visited with me.

"Well, I hear the bazaar was a great success," he said.

"A success!" I gasped. "The bazaar! Why, they didn't have it, did they?"

"Oh, sure," said Will.

"But—but—" I stammered, "they didn't have any place to have it."

"Oh, they rustled around and got the Universalist church," Will said.

I lay for several minutes, dashed into utter silence.

"I wonder how they ever got the stuff moved over," I said finally. "And who got the tickets and what they used for decoration, the bunting must have been burned—"

Will didn't know any of the particulars. All he knew was the one staggering truth. Those girls had had the bazaar without me. They had not only pulled it off, they had made a success of it. It had never occurred to me but, that if I had given up, even if the hall hadn't burned, they would just have lain down and died. Instead of which they had had the bazaar and it had been a success. There's no denying that it was a shock.

That afternoon both the mothers came in to see me. Mother brought some chicken broth and Mother Horton some jelly and Jill. They wouldn't let Jill come into the room for fear of her catching the grippe, but I could see her through the hall door and she did look so sweet and funny with her little yellow curl on top. I couldn't see how I could ever possibly have felt cross at her even for a second. Suddenly I gasped, "What's she doing?"

"Walking," said Mother Horton carelessly.

"All alone!"

And she was. She'd go along a few steps all right, then she'd cross her feet or something when she didn't mean to, like a person just learning to skate, and sit down hard, but she'd be right up and at it again, staggering along without anybody to help her at all. I could hardly believe it.

"Oh, yes," Mother Horton said carelessly. "I just left her alone and she learned to go by herself. Mercy, I've been too busy to walk that child by the hour."

After she'd gone I told Mother about the terrible episode of the tin foil. She said she'd seen Dr. Elincourt yesterday and he looked to be in perfect health.

"I'm sorry I urged you to have them for dinner when you were so busy and half sick," she said. "Some of the other girls ought to have done it."

After they went out I lay there in my nice quiet room and thought. Mother Horton had taken Jill back home with her. I could faintly hear Ella in the kitchen getting supper. The sun shone in the room and everything in the world seemed peaceful. And I thought.

And I made up my mind to something.

Maybe I was capable but I wasn't going to spend my life on the ragged edge of nervous prostration doing every single thing that every single person thought I ought to, letting everybody from Dulcie to the Alumnæ Club decide my duty for me. From now on I was going to make up my own mind on what was my duty and then I was going to do it and not be kidded into doing any different. If the High School Alumnæ Club couldn't run without a married woman with two children it would have to collapse. And it was half a reassuring, half a humbling feeling to realize that it probably wouldn't collapse, that it would probably run just as well without me as with me.

I wasn't even going to do everything the two mothers

thought I ought to. I'd be polite to them but I was going to let Jack learn to walk hanging on to the edge of his pen.

By the time Will came home for supper I was in the happiest, most peaceful frame of mind I'd known in months and months. There is a wonderfully safe, comfortable feeling in knowing that you can make up your own mind about things.

"What are you going to do for your Lodge dinner stunt?" I asked him, safe in the knowledge that no mind-reading could be expected of a person just arisen from a bed of grippe.

Will's face lit all up with enthusiasm.

"Say, Mert's got a dandy new stunt that we're going to work out together."

"We?" I repeated doubtfully, "you don't mean you and I?"

Will hesitated and acted awfully fussed.

"Well, I—I sort of thought that maybe Mert and I might do it together," he said uneasily. "You won't be feeling up to anything by that time, you know. You were certainly fine at that mind-reading stunt but of course—"

I just laughed and reached up and pulled Will's rough cheek down to mine. He's so funny when he's trying not to hurt your feelings.

"You needn't try to fool me," I said. "You think I was rotten—"

"Oh, no, I don't, honey, dear." He denied in such a horrified guilty tone that it gave him away completely. "I—I just can't get over your plugging away at that when you were so rushed and half sick and—oh, honey, you are a little peach."

I rubbed my cheek against the back of his hand.

"But not so good as a mind-reader," I insisted.

"Yes, you are," he insisted, too. "You were really fine. And if you'd had lots of time to put on it, you'd have been a perfect pippin. You—"

But he was altogether too earnest. I was a good mind-reader in this, anyway. With every word of his praising, I realized more clearly that I couldn't have been any-wheres near as good with the code as I thought I was. But I didn't care. I just kept on rubbing my cheek against his hand and smiling contentedly. It was darling of him to keep on insisting how good I was. It proved that he likes me as a wife if not as a parlor magician. And, someway, knowing I wasn't very good at it any-way, gave me the same sort of comfortable let-out feeling I had had when I heard the fire engine clanging in the distance, taking the Masonic fire off my hands. There were a few things in Montrose it wasn't ever going to be up to me to run.

VI

WILL DEALS WITH THE TROUBLE-MAKER

EVERYBODY was sorry for Will and me when Jervie and Irma moved out of the bungalow next door to us and Miss Waters moved in. Miss Waters was the Montrose trouble-maker. Father said that every town he'd ever heard of had at least one. Will said it was too bad Miss Waters was born into a small place like Montrose, a woman with her talents. Just give her one or two capable assistants to direct and she could supply plenty of trouble for Chicago.

The queer part of it was that Miss Waters didn't seem to be really mean. It was just that she couldn't mind her own business. And it is amazing how just as soon as anybody else takes to managing your business it doesn't make any difference whether they're mean or not, they make trouble just the same. If Miss Waters had been rich with lots of time on her hands, people would have said that was the trouble, that she didn't have any business of her own to mind. But nobody could say that of Miss Waters. She is a dressmaker and she keeps house for herself and makes all the clothes for her sister's children in Verblen for nothing. She is always busy. It seemed to me till she moved next door that I'd never seen her except with her mouthful of pins.

When she took Jervie and Irma's house, of course, I was all forearmed. I knew how snoopy she was and I wouldn't make the mistake of giving her any chance.

"Thank goodness," I said to Dulcie, "our living room and our room are on your side of our house and I'm going to keep the other shades down tight and never speak a word above a whisper on Miss Waters's side."

Dulcie laughed. Before she was married, she herself used to live next door to Miss Waters.

> " 'You don't know Nellie like I do,'
> Said the bird on Nellie's hat,

she sang. "A hot lot of good it will do you to pull down your shades. Thurston hasn't anything on Miss Waters, she can see through seven thicknesses of heavy woolen cloth just as well as he can. And as for lowering your voice! Well, I never would have believed in mental telepathy if I hadn't known Miss Waters. She doesn't need to *hear* anything. Actually, when I made up my mind to marry Roger, I'm dead sure she knew it before Roger did."

In spite of Dulcie's being so discouraging, we made all the preparations we could, like a city getting ready for a siege. We had our telephone put on a private wire because her house would be on our party line. It had never made any difference when Jervie and Irma lived there. Every once in a while Irma and Dulcie and Rosemary Merton and I would all get on together and decide what to take to a picnic or something but being on a party line with Miss Waters would be something else again, Mawruss.

She moved in on a Tuesday and the rest of the week I was inclined to think she had been slandered. I couldn't

see that she was so bad. I invited her in to supper the
day she moved,—even if a person is a trouble-maker,
you've got to be halfway neighborly and moving is a terrible mess. Even Will, who kept cautioning me not to
get on clubby terms with her, went over home with her
after supper and helped her put up her curtains. She
was crazy about my cold baked ham—she'd never tasted
it baked with two tablespoonfuls of chili sauce before—
and complimented Will on having such a long reach with
the curtains and said he looked like Father Horton but
was better looking. Take it altogether, Will and I agreed
that evening that she might have been made a victim of
that give-a-dog-a-bad-name idea. We couldn't see that
she was so bad.

I remembered how, when I was a little bit of a girl
and she used to come to our house a week every fall and
spring, I used to like her. She'd sometimes bring me a
hard peppermint and I liked the way her needle made a
sharp singing noise against her thimble. When she began
making my dresses, I didn't like her any more because I
hated standing still to be fitted. Then father put in a
ready-made department in the store and mother and
Kathie and I got our clothes there except those we made
ourselves, so I hadn't seen Miss Waters for ages. I
hadn't even heard of her. Most of the girls and the
young married women get their clothes ready-made so
they didn't see her.

It was funny, though, how much Miss Waters knew
about all those girls who didn't see her from one year's
end to another except maybe in church, and who never
thought of her at all. It was more than funny, it was

downright uncanny. A few of their mothers still went
to her for their clothes and I suppose they'd drop a word
here and there about what their daughters were doing.
I don't suppose any of them figured they were dropping
more than a word or so and yet when they'd all got
through, Miss Waters knew more about what their
daughters were doing than they did.

"Oh, I just put two and two together," she'd say when
anybody asked her how she knew about something she
couldn't possibly have heard about.

She must have sat there, sewing on Mother Horton's
blue silk poplin or Dulcie's mother's flat crepe, and putting two and two together by the hour. Once in a great
while, of course, she'd make three or five out of it but
mighty seldom. She usually got four all right. That was
what made people so furious. You don't mind having
something that isn't so told about you half as much,
when you come right down to it, as having something
that is true but that you wanted to keep dark. When it's
true, you simply haven't any come-back.

It wasn't just our young married crowd or the Center
Street Church crowd or any other one crowd that Miss
Waters kept tabs on. It was all the crowds from the
swift new Harvester bunch to Mother's and Mother
Horton's Ossili Club. There's no use denying that it
made her a fascinating person to talk to. In spite of
all Will's cautioning and in spite of all I'd heard about
her, myself, I'd find myself listening to her in spite of
my better judgment. It was twice as interesting as reading the society column of the Montrose Monitor. Miss
Waters' talk had, as father put it, so much more scope.

I'd see her sewing out on her side porch of a nice afternoon and I'd resist as long as I could, then I'd give in
and take the peas I was shelling over and sit on her steps
and talk to her. I never went like that once that I didn't
come back with something to pay me for my trouble.
I'd keep Will entertained all through supper with the
racy bits I'd picked up. "Veda Knopf has broken off
her engagement to Fred," I'd tell him. "It seems that
she'd made him stop sending her candy or taking her
into the city to shows or doing anything else like that so
that he could save every penny toward getting furniture.
And then she found that he'd met a girl in Chicago and
was sending her flowers twice a week and spending the
money Veda was helping him save, like a drunken sailor."

Will whistled through his teeth.

"Where'd you hear that?" he asked.

"Miss Waters told me," I admitted.

"Good Lord," said Will. "I should think Miss Waters
would have been the last person Veda would have told
anything like that to."

"Oh, Veda didn't tell Miss Waters," I corrected him
hastily, "Miss Waters told Veda. About the Chicago
girl."

"How the dickens did Miss Waters know about it?"
Will demanded. "Surely Fred didn't tell it."

I shrugged my shoulders.

"I tried to find out," I said, "but she just looked mys-
terious and said a little bird told her."

"Gosh," said Will, "she must keep a flock of homing
pigeons." And after a minute or two, "I'd be careful
about talking to her too much," he cautioned me again.

"People might get the idea she gets her information through you."

This was good sense all right but Will, himself was the one who got caught first. About Mrs. Long's well.

"Mrs. Long isn't going to have the well dug," I told Will chattily one evening. "Miss Waters told her that they're going to run the city water out past the Crossing in six months and that she'd better hold her horses."

"Well, Miss Waters is wrong for once in her life," said Will. "I was at the special committee meeting in father's place last week and they decided not to run the water out to the Crossing at all, the estimates were too high. That's the danger of a woman like Miss Waters. Now Mrs. Long will worry along for a year or so without her well and then have to have it put in just the same. I wish Miss Waters would mind her own business."

Will went out of his way that evening when he was mowing our lawn to stroll over to Miss Waters' side and tell her that she was mistaken about the water.

"Oh, I think you'll find I'm right," she said firmly; "they'll have the city water out there inside of a year as sure as you're born. Don't worry your head about Mrs. Long's well, Willie."

"I happened to be at the committee meeting which decided that the water was *not* to go out there," Will said with extremely crushing dignity. He's fit to be tied when anybody calls him "Willie" and I could see what a satisfaction it was to him to be in a position to put Miss Waters in her place for once.

And then three weeks later, a special meeting of the committee was called and it was decided to recommend the council to accept Byer's estimate and run the city water out as far as the Crossing, after all. Will wasn't at that meeting. Father Horton had got over his cold.

"Miss Waters couldn't *possibly* have known about it when she told Mrs. Long," he said at supper, so baffled he was mad clear through. "The very men who voted to do it were against it until they heard that Verblen had designs on that tract out by the Crossing and might offer to run their water out there and include it in Verblen."

But if Will was mad that night he was about fifty times as mad the next, for his father gave him an awful calling down and said he'd never send him to another committee meeting in his place. It seems Mrs. Long had told everybody out that way and they had quietly got hold of a lot of property.

"Dad's figured out that I must have blabbed something about the water to Miss Waters," said Will, so mad at the injustice of it that he could hardly talk. "I asked him how I could have told her anything as the only meeting I went to decided *against* it. But you know how Dad is when he gets an idea in his head. He's seen you and me talking to Miss Waters and he's made up his mind I must have dropped something. 'Oh, I don't say you did it on purpose,' he said, 'but you're the only person who's been at any of those committee meetings who isn't old enough to know how to keep his mouth shut. I thought of course you knew the committee's work is private till they report to the council. I don't say you did it on purpose but you must have dropped something. Where else could

Miss Waters have got it?' He kept saying, 'I don't say you did it on purpose,' as though that was all that I was objecting to. I'd rather be called a crook than a chump."

"Oh, well," I said soothingly, "there's no use getting mad about it. You know how your father is when he gets an idea into his head and there's no point in letting yourself get all stirred up about it."

"It makes me so blame mad," Will insisted. "When I'd finally got him to pay any attention to what I was saying, he said, 'Well, probably Dot dropped it, then. She's always talking to Miss Waters.' "

"Well of all things!" I gasped. "I never in my life heard anything to equal that. How in the world could I have told her. I didn't know it myself. And I *never* repeat anything about business that you tell me. The idea of your father laying it onto me! I never heard anything so downright unfair in my life! I'll—"

"I thought you said there was no point in letting yourself get all stirred up about it," Will said.

"But this is different! It's so unfair it's simply ridiculous. How could I have told Miss Waters anything I didn't know myself?"

"How could I, either? That's what I've been saying right along. That's what happens when you get mixed up with anybody like Miss Waters. I told you all along you were making a mistake having so much to do with her."

"That *I* was making a mistake," I echoed angrily. "I wasn't the one that told her to tell Mrs. Long to go ahead with the well. I wasn't the one—"

"You were the one she told about the well in the first place," Will pointed out. "If you'd let her alone from the start it never would have come up at all."

"That's just like a man," I said. "When anything goes wrong, he's just tickled to death if he can trace it back far enough to find a woman to lay it on. I'd like to know who it was that went over in the first place and hung her curtains for her. I notice you were just as interested as I was in hearing about Veda Knopf."

Talk about stirring up trouble! Before we got through we were both mad at Father Horton and mad at each other. We talked so loud it woke up the twins and when they began to howl I felt mad at them, too. It seemed to me there wasn't anybody I wasn't mad at. And all because of Miss Waters.

Will and I made peace though, of course. When we got cooled down we could both see that it was really kind of funny and I told Will maybe I wouldn't put arsenic in his father's coffee after all. But it had been an awful row all for nothing. We both decided that the less we saw of Miss Waters the better for all.

I stuck to this pretty well, too, but it was really quite a strain. It is hard in a neighborly place like Montrose to keep from seeing anything of your next door neighbor especially in the summer when everybody's out in the yard most of the time anyway. And there's no denying that it was an awful temptation to talk to her. When Veda Knopf and Fred made it up and Veda came out with her diamond ring again, neither of them gave a word of explanation, just tried to pretend that nothing had happened. Naturally everybody discussed it and I'll say it took character to live as I did right next door to where I could get the low-down on it and never find out.

Once in a while, I wouldn't be able to keep away from Miss Waters. I'd be in the kitchen and she'd call out of her window and start talking to me. And the things I'd pick up in those brief chats! When Mr. Welkins decided to give up his church because the congregation was so reactionary, I knew it before any of the congregation did. On a Wednesday, Miss Waters told me that Roger was going to get a raise at the bank. By sheer force of character I kept from saying anything about it to Dulcie and on Sunday Dulcie told me. Roger hadn't known it himself, she said, until Saturday.

When the president of the Harvester's wife gave a dance at the new country club, Miss Waters told me that the Bartells wouldn't be asked. She didn't know either the president's wife or Betty Bartell to so much as speak to, but she was right. Nobody in town could figure why the Bartells were left out of the dance, but they were. When Dulcie gave a luncheon for Marianna Cox, she kept the menu a dead secret to have it a surprise, even Ella Crowninshield, who came to help serve, didn't know what she was going to serve till she got there. I had to leave early, all the rest of the girls were still there when I went into our house. But when I stopped a minute at our kitchen window, Miss Waters called over from her porch to ask if I had had a good time at the luncheon and were the clover-leaf patties good?

It was worse than snoopy, it was downright spooky. She told the president of Roger's bank that she'd never trust that cashier if she had anything to do with the bank.

The president just laughed, he was so sure everything was all right. But I suppose it made him a little bit uneasy because he began checking up and having the cashier watched and sure enough, he was laying plans to get out with ten thousand dollars.

That was the only time, though, as far as I know when anything that Miss Waters told did anybody any good.

When Don Underhill married that pretty little blond girl from Chicago, Miss Waters had gone out of her way to drop a word here and there about how she'd used to be in cheap vaudeville. This was true enough and after people got acquainted with Mrs. Underhill, she'd told them herself, but she wasn't a bit like it would make you think she was and having it get out like that ahead of her made it awfully hard for her to get acquainted and she'd put in a lonesome year that she didn't need to.

And it certainly didn't do any good for Miss Waters to ferret out that Roberta Wills couldn't get into Holly Hall School in New York because her father had been a butcher, or to tell young Mrs. Bottomley how her husband had tried to get Portia Shubert right up to the day Portia was married and had said more than once that he'd never look at another woman while there was a chance of marrying Portia, or her finding out—goodness only knows how—and telling all over town that John Dewey lived in constant terror of losing his job. When that got around to Vance and Edwards where John worked, it naturally made them think he couldn't amount to as much as they'd really thought he did.

And so on. There were dozens and dozens of things— Will was right in saying Miss Waters had talents too great for Montrose when it came to trouble making. By almost superhuman caution Will and I managed to get 'along next door to her without stepping into anything, at least so far as we knew. Of course, she made an excuse to run in or call up and pump me after every party I ever went to—Who was there? what did they have to eat? why hadn't Marge Kitteridge been asked? did Mrs. Curtis wear that blue crêpe again? And it made Will perfectly disgusted when she criticized poor Miss Carroll's funeral. Miss Carroll had been society editor on the Monitor for twenty years, she used to be Will's Sunday School teacher and he'd always liked her. So it made him especially mad for Miss Waters to go prying into the funeral arrangements and making nasty comments.

"Can't she even let a person *die* in peace?" he demanded of me.

However, nothing might ever have broken if it hadn't been for the beautiful afternoon when I went out in our yard to pick currants. They were ripe and I wanted to make jelly the next day so, though the bushes grow right on the lot line toward Miss Waters and she was sewing on the porch, I kept on picking. She chatted with me a few minutes about this and that and then she said:

"What's all this about Will buying diamonds?"

"Buying *diamonds!*" I echoed, so amazed that I didn't stop to realize that of all things I shouldn't let Miss Waters know that I didn't know anything about it.

She smiled, that delighted little smile she always wears when she gets hold of some bit of racy news.

"Oh, bless my soul!" she said, "I do hope I haven't said anything I shouldn't."

"Of course not," I said carelessly. At least, I hope I said it carelessly.

I went on picking currants so dumbfounded that I'm afraid there wasn't a chance that it didn't show on my face. My husband buying diamonds! Any married woman knows what a turn that would give you. If anybody but Miss Waters had said it, I'd have known it was some crazy mistake and never thought of it again. But Miss Waters was so everlastingly accurate. If she said Will was buying diamonds, I felt pretty sure Will was buying diamonds.

If it had been anywhere near my birthday or wedding anniversary or Christmas or any earthly reason like that it wouldn't have knocked me so cold. But there wasn't a ghost of a reason now! And not giving me so much as a hint. And diamonds of all things on earth! I was so puzzled and amazed that it was all I could do to get supper that night. And the second Will had got inside the kitchen door, I shut it behind him—I'd already closed the window on her side of the house—and asked him what in the name of heaven he'd been buying diamonds for.

He acted fussed and tried to deny it.

"I haven't bought any diamonds," he said. "What the dickens are you talking about?"

I could tell there must be something in it, because he was so fussed and that gave me a suddenly queer feeling.

"You may just as well tell me," I said. "Miss Waters has already."

Will's mouth fairly fell ajar at that.

"How the mischief did she get hold of that?" he demanded.

"Then you have been?" I demanded in turn.

"Well, there's the best surprise I ever planned gone bluey," said Will disgustedly.

"A surprise on who?"

"Why on you, of course. Charley White called me up the other day and told me that he'd got hold of an old-fashioned diamond ring cheap and that if I wanted to have the stone cut over and let him set it in an up-to-date setting, he'd see that I got a bargain. I'd told him quite awhile ago to keep his eye out for something like that. I made up my mind a long time ago that just as soon as I could swing it, I was going to get you a decent engagement ring. I've always been ashamed of that pin point I gave you. I figured that I ought to be able to manage it by our anniversary this fall so I went in and looked at Charley's stone. I didn't get it, though. It was bigger than I could swing."

"Oh," I said. "Well, she must have seen you looking at it, or else Charley told her, then. I'm terribly sorry I said anything and spoiled your surprise. But it gave me such a turn I couldn't help it. I knew she was probably right and yet I couldn't think what under the blue sky you'd be buying diamonds for," I giggled. "You're not expecting an engagement ring when you're the mother of twins, you know."

"A person ought to be shot at sunrise for telling things like that," he said. "Suppose you hadn't trusted me, or were just the least bit doubtful. Look at the trouble it would have stirred up. I'll bet more than one happy marriage has been started going wrong just by some old harpy like her."

I went on fixing the salad and let the thing slip out of my mind, but Will must have kept on brooding on Miss Waters. All through supper he hardly said anything except to speak about Mrs. Long's well and Miss Carroll's funeral. And all at once the second he'd finished his chocolate pudding, he got up as though he'd suddenly made up his mind to something and started toward the door, with a queer purposeful look on his face.

"Where are you going?" I asked apprehensively.

"I'm going next door," said Will, "to tell that confounded old busybody to mind her own affairs."

"Will!" I gasped, horrified. "You can't do that! Why, she's old enough to be your mother."

"I don't care if she's old enough to be my grandmother and calls me Willie. I'm going to tell her where to head in."

I just stared helplessly, as he went out, slamming the screen behind him and stamping across the lawn toward Miss Waters'. There are times when I can stop Will with the merest glance and there are other times when I just have to keep out of his road. This was one of those other times.

I heard Miss Waters' back door slam and knew he'd gone in. I tried to pick up the supper dishes but I couldn't get my mind on anything. I kept watching Miss Waters' windows uneasily. I couldn't hear a sound. Her kitchen was on the other side and she had probably been in it.

I washed the supper dishes and put them away but Will

didn't come back. I kept glancing over at Miss Waters'
house uneasily. What in the world could be keeping him
so long? I took the Monitor into the dining room and
sat down by the window, but I couldn't get my mind on
it. I kept watching Miss Waters' back door. Half-past
seven, eight, and he didn't come. Half-past eight and
still no sign. I stopped trying to read and watched that
tiny bungalow uneasily, almost as though I were expecting to see words come blowing out of the chimney as they
do in the comics. But it looked as peaceful as a church
from the outside, nothing came out of the chimney and
neither did Will come out of the door.

What on earth—what on *earth* could be going on inside! It suddenly occurred to me—Will had been so
awfully mad—could he have done Miss Waters violence?
That was a wild crazy idea, of course, but what on earth
was taking him so long?

At nine o'clock, I decided to go over and see. Much
as I disliked to get mixed up in whatever was going on,
I couldn't stand it any longer. But just as I was on the
point of going out our side door, I saw Will come out
Miss Waters' front door. To my amazement, however,
he didn't come home but turned in the other direction
and struck off toward town, walking fast. Merciful
heavens! Was he going after a doctor?

I waited on pins and needles, one minute thinking I
ought to go over there, the next running to our front
window to look for Will. It was a half hour before he
came back and when he did he went back into Miss
Waters' house for a minute before he came home. When
he finally came into our house at last, I was almost beside

myself. To my surprise, instead of having the scared, guilty look of a man with blood on his hands, he looked the way he does when he comes back from a lodge committee meeting and has put over a good lot of business.

"Did—," I began, but Will interrupted me.

"Well," he said, "I got her a job all right."

"You—what?" I gasped.

"I got her a job," he repeated. "Why, Dot, do you know that woman's been hardly getting enough to eat?"

"Miss Waters?" I gasped again.

"Miss Waters," he repeated firmly. "Do you know what she gets for making a dress? And how long it takes her to make one?"

A person would have thought he was accusing me of under-paying her.

"Well, she isn't a very good dressmaker," I told him. "She can make the fussy clothes that some of the older women like but she couldn't make anything slim and plain to look like anything at all. All the girls and young married women buy their things ready-made anyway and they're the only ones who'll pay much for a dress."

"A woman could hardly live decently just herself on what she makes," he went on, "and she sends *ten dollars* a week to her sister in Verblen—the one that was left with all those kids—besides making them all their clothes. And do you know what she gets herself for dinner when she wants a good square meal? A can of baked beans!"

"Why, for mercy sake!" I exclaimed, horrified, "I never thought but what she was getting along all right." And after a moment, "How did you ever find out?"

"That's the part that scares you to death," said Will,

"it's been going on for years and she wouldn't let any-body know for anything. If I hadn't happened to come crashing in on her at just a critical moment to-night, nobody might ever have known. But she's just heard that Mrs. Vance was moving away from Montrose—she's been her best customer—and just before I got there, she'd got a dress back from Mrs. Long to do all over. And she'd heard that that old Scrooge is going to raise her rent October first. It had all come at once just before I got there and she was so scared that she *had* to tell somebody. She was kind of half crying when I went in; she wouldn't have answered the door but I just rapped and then opened it, myself. She was right in the kitchen and she couldn't get away. I guess she was about at the end of her rope anyway, and she just got desperate and told me."

"Isn't that terrible?" I said. Someway you never think of anybody you know being really poor, so poor that they hardly get enough to eat. "We'll have to do something about it," I said. But as I said it, I realized how awfully hard it would be to do anything. Miss Waters is not the kind of person you can give charity to—if I even started asking her to dinner two or three times a week all of a sudden she'd know why I was doing it and probably wouldn't come. It would be terribly hard.

Then suddenly I remembered that Will said he'd got her a job. He swelled out proudly when I asked him and said Yes, he had.

"What kind of a job could she do? A woman of her age?" I asked, completely puzzled.

"Miss Carroll's," said Will.

"On the Monitor?"

"Betcher life," said Will. "It's funny I didn't think of it right off. Old Smith asked me just this morning if I knew anybody who'd be good to get to do the society column. He's divided up all the rest of Miss Carroll's work among the men and he'd decided just to keep the society stuff separate. Of course he won't pay a lot but it'll be enough to put Miss Waters on Easy Street on top of what she makes now. It won't take long to write it out and"—Will grinned—"well, just gathering the news won't be any trouble to her."

It seemed almost too good to be true.

"And Mr. Smith'll hire her, will he?"

"I beat it right down to his house, tonight. And the second I mentioned her name he said, 'Cat's Foot! Why didn't I think of her myself? She's perfect. She knows all the different crowds—she's got the background, knows who's related to who, who works for which. Why, man, she's got a *talent* for it!'" Will grinned again, "He was just afraid she wouldn't have time, I told him I thought I could fix it up with her, as an accommodation to him."

Well, we sat and talked about it till bedtime and when I finally reminded Will that he'd gone over to tell Miss Waters to mind her own business, he smiled sheepishly and said he guessed he'd found her the kind of business she'd like to mind.

And he certainly had. It's just funny how beautifully it's worked. Mr. Smith is tickled to death with her— everybody says the society column is the most interesting part of the Monitor,—she gets in all sorts of interesting stuff that Miss Carroll never used to hear about. And happy! You never saw any one so changed as Miss Waters! She doesn't have to go gum-shoeing after news any more—all kinds of people invite her to their parties just to be sure they'll get in the paper. And she's actually got herself a new dress, the first she's had in years. She's like a different person.

But the funniest thing of all is the way she's changed her tactics. The other day when I went to Jessie's luncheon for the college girl who's visiting Marge, Jessie asked me if I'd mind stopping and giving Miss Waters the list of guests and the decorations. So I did. Miss Waters was finishing up a dress for Mother Horton and I sat down and visited with her a few minutes. She was cooking something for her supper that smelled awfully good, she wasn't just opening a can of beans that night.

I gave her Jessie's lists and she thanked me, said she was awfully rushed—in that happy way that a popular girl talks about being rushed. She asked me about the menu and I told her everything we had, how the cakes were in the shape of banners and everything in the college colors. And then, having been thrown a little off my guard, I forgot myself and said:

"It was kind of funny—Ella Crowninshield was there waiting on the table and Marge's friend looked at her so funny. And it seems"—I lowered my voice a little the way you do when you're telling something a little racy—"it seems that at the party Betty Bartell gave for her yesterday, Betty had Ella, too, and had tried to palm her off as her own regular maid. I could see Marge's friend recognizing Ella and looking kind of puzzled. And the joke is"—I had to stop to giggle—"she'll be more puzzled than she is now before she leaves. Everybody's entertaining for her and she'll see Ella's familiar face almost everywhere she goes. Isn't that just like Betty Bartell to try to get away with silly swank like that?"

Then suddenly I realized that I shouldn't have told anything like that to Miss Waters. But I needn't have worried. She was pulling out bastings, while she looked over the paper Jessie had sent her and she had scarcely heard what I was saying.

"Um-hum," she answered me in a downright absent tone of voice. "Of course I can't use anything like that in the Monitor though," and before I could say that of course I hadn't expected her to, she looked at me over her glasses and said in a gently reproving tone, "Of course, in my position, I have to be awfully careful not to say anything that might make trouble."

VII

I NEVER was superstitious, believing in signs and things like that and I haven't changed my mind now, in spite of all that happened while Aunt Hattie was staying with us. Though I admit there are plenty of things that looked queer, from the very minute the horseshoe over our door fell down just as Aunt Hattie was coming in for the first time.

It was Will who suggested that I get Aunt Hattie to come for July and August and help me out with the babies. Aunt Hattie is our family's one poor relation and she lives sometimes with one part of the family and sometimes with another and helps them out. I really did need help, too. Mother had gone up to Minneapolis to visit Kathie and Father and Mother Horton had gone East with some of the Kiwanis Club so that, now with Ella Crowninshield married, I hadn't had a living soul to leave the twins with for a minute. Two sixteen-months-old babies together are without any comparison the cutest, sweetest things in the world, but after two months all alone with them there are moments when any mother wishes that they woudn't start being sweet at five o'clock in the morning or would hurry up and cut enough teeth so that you wouldn't have to strain carrots and prunes and scrape beef by the hour.

Dulcie, living right next door with little Dulcie just eight weeks old, had made my work more difficult, too. I never could have stood it as long as I had without Aunt Hattie if I hadn't been able to get down to Rosemary Merton's once in a while and get Dulcie out of my system. Rosie, having three babies fifteen months apart, could be counted on to be even more irritated at Dulcie than I was.

"I ran into her in the Busy Bee market this morning," Rosie would say, "and I could just see her taking in my old tan dress. We walked home together and she got to telling me how well she was able to manage. She had on another new printed cotton with the inverted pleat in front and everything; said she did all her sewing while little Dulcie was asleep. Merciful powers! I should think that she could. An eight-weeks-old baby sleeps all the time! 'Why, I even still have time to manicure my nails every day,' she said. 'I do it while little Dulcie is having her ten o'clock bottle. I really believe it's all in planning your work.'"

Rosie and I just looked at each other.

"I suppose she thinks she can plan her work so that she'll always get by with nothing to do but shove a bottle in little Dulcie's mouth," I said. "I'd like to see her manicure her nails while she's feeding applesauce to twins."

"I hope she has another," said Rosie venomously.

"Oh, I don't really mind her only having one baby," I said tolerantly, "and not having anything to do to speak of if she only wouldn't be so smug about it, thinking it's all in the way she manages. She told me yesterday that she had little Dulcie trained so that she sleeps right

through the night. Trained! Why, you can have a brass
band playing in the room all night and any healthy two-
months-old baby will sleep right through it."

"Trained!" snorted Rosie. "Just wait till little Dulcie
starts cutting her molars, and then let her tell me about
'training.' "

However, it wasn't just having Dulcie next door for
contrast, I really had had an awfully busy time and Aunt
Hattie's coming for July and August was as a breeze on
the front porch. I had a nice supper the night she was to
come and got the babies all in bed by the time Will was
ready to start down to meet her. He had scarcely driven
around the corner and I was putting a basket of sweetpeas in the center of the supper table out on the side porch
when I heard somebody at the front door. To my amazement, there stood Aunt Hattie.

"Why, how on earth did you get here so soon?" I
gasped, as I opened the screen and kissed her. "Will's
just gone to meet your train."

"The train was ten minutes early," Aunt Hattie explained.

"But why didn't you wait for Will in the station?" I
asked, lifting her suitcase. It weighed a ton and the poor
soul had carried it all the way up in the heat. It seemed
so inhospitable. "Didn't you get my letter? I told you
Will'd have the flivver down to meet you."

"Oh, that's all right," said Aunt Hattie. "I don't
mind. And I know these flivvers. Sometimes they get
there, sometimes they don't. My niece in Peoria has one
that they call 'The Perhaps' because perhaps it'll start
and perhaps it won't."

"We never have a bit of trouble with ours," I said proudly. "But come in anyway. I'm awfully glad to see you."

It was as I pushed the screen door open wider to get Aunt Hattie's suitcase through, that the horseshoe fell. The horseshoe was one that Will had found in the road just outside our house and gilded and stuck up over the front door, just for fun. A piece of honeysuckle vine had trailed along the porch ceiling and caught on the screen. When I gave the door a sharp, hard push, the horseshoe came tumbling down, landing at my feet on the porch floor with a dull thud.

"My stars!" said Aunt Hattie. "Is that a horseshoe? Mercy me, what an awful sign!"

I laughed and picked it up and laid it on the bench for Will to stick up again.

"We just have that up for a joke," I said. "You aren't superstitious, are you?"

"Oh, no," said Aunt Hattie, "though it would have been just my luck to have had that thing hit me on the head. It's just as I always say about ghosts. I don't believe in them but, still and all, I don't want to see one."

"Well, you won't see any around here, I promise you that," I assured her comfortably. And just then Will got back from the station.

"Well, how are all Uncle Henry's people?" he asked Aunt Hattie genially, as we sat down to supper.

"They're all well," said Aunt Hattie. "Except his mother, of course. She died of Bright's disease this spring. Poor thing, she suffered horribly."

"I remember her; she was an awfully nice old lady," said Will sympathetically.

There was a little pause while I helped Aunt Hattie to the creamed dried beef.

"Did you ever know your Uncle Henry's brother-in-law, Austin Sears?" she asked. We never had met him. "He just failed in business," said Aunt Hattie. "He had the nicest little hardware store in Harrisfield; everybody thought it would run on beautifully as long as he lived. Well, well, you never can tell."

"That's the truth," Will agreed. "Business takes some awfully queer turns sometimes."

"How's the real estate business?" Aunt Hattie inquired politely.

"Oh, about as usual. It's dull right now, of course. We always get a slump in the middle of the summer."

"That's what Austin Sears thought it was, at first," said Aunt Hattie. "Just a slump. Well, well, you never can tell."

"You were down in Peoria last winter with Aunt Philippa, weren't you?" I asked. "How is all her family?" I didn't give a rap how Aunt Philippa's family was, but when you're making conversation the first meal like that, you do certainly have to drag in a lot of relatives.

"They're well," said Aunt Hattie. "Or at least they were when I left them. It was a shame about their losing their lovely home. It burned right to the ground when they went away over a week-end. Not a thing left standing but the chimney."

"Insured?" Will asked practically.

"Not for anything like its value, of course," said Aunt Hattie. "They got a little something out of it, I guess."

When we were undressing that night, Will observed:

"All your Aunt Hattie's folks seem to have been playing in tough luck."

"I should say so," I agreed.

And then, speaking of luck, I told him about our horseshoe falling down.

"Well, I suppose we've got a few knocks coming to us one of these days," Will observed philosophically. "According to Ye Old Law of Averages. We've had a pretty good break ever since we started out together. Every family's got to expect some tough luck once in a while. Not that I figure we're due to get ours just because our horseshoe fell down," he added hastily.

Well, whatever bad luck we might have coming to us, I was certainly in luck now, I thought that next morning as I came downstairs and heard Aunt Hattie singing "Lead, Kindly Light" in the kitchen and found that she'd already started the coffee and got the babies' cereal on. It was like a vacation for me, just having Aunt Hattie in the house. Since Mother'd been away I hadn't had anybody to help me at all except America Hawkins, and she was so dumb that I had to tell her just how to do everything and then stand right by and see that she did it that way so that by the time we were through I might about as well have done it myself. Aunt Hattie was as different as day from night. She just took right hold of things herself.

"Now you run along and see some of your girl friends," she said the first afternoon. "I'll see about supper. And don't worry an instant about Jack and Jill. I'll never take my eyes off them."

"Oh, you needn't watch them like that," I assured her gratefully. "Just put them out in their little yard and they'll be all right." Will had fenced in a good-sized place for them with chicken wire and I always left them there while I did my work in the mornings. "Just give them a glance once in a while, or if they start crying; that's all you need to do. The fence is high enough so that they can't get out and no dog or anything can get in. There's nothing that can possibly happen to them out there."

"Nothing that can possibly happen to them!" Aunt Hattie echoed, shocked. "Why, there are dozens of things that could, Dotty. I found little Jack with a stone in his mouth just this morning that was big enough to choke him if he'd swallowed it. Or suppose somebody lost control of their car at the turn of the road there—it would come crashing right into your yard and through that flimsy wire fence like nothing at all. Or suppose when Jack gets to playing rough as he did his morning he should push Jill up against one of the stakes at the corner. And hit her head!"

The idea of Jill's hitting that dear, funny little tow head of hers against a sharp stake made me sick to my stomach, and it scared me to realize that I hadn't really broken Jack of putting everything in his mouth, after all.

"But don't ever think of the babies this afternoon," Aunt Hattie ordered me cheerfully. "I'll be right here and I'll never take my eyes off them once."

So I went down to Mrs. Frank Kirsted's. Dulcie was there, having parked little Dulcie with her mother for the afternoon, and we called to Rosie next door and she brought her three over on the Kirsted lawn, and we sat down to have a game of bridge on the porch. But in spite of knowing that Aunt Hattie was right on the job, I couldn't seem to keep my mind on the game for thinking of all the things that might be happening to the babies. I spoke of it at last.

"Oh, that's just because they're your first," Rosie assured me comfortably. "If you'd had three, one after another, choking on zweibach and getting croup and falling downstairs and pinching their fingers in doors, you'd know by now that a baby'll live through pretty near anything. Junior, see what that is Sister's putting in her mouth this minute. Spit it out, Sister. I double one no trump."

Which was all right for Rosie, having all her three right in sight. But Dulcie let Rosie's double stand, a thing which no partner in her right mind ever does, and after a couple of hands more, she said she guessed she'd better be getting back, she didn't want little Dulcie to get in the way of being rocked and her grandmother couldn't seem to keep from rocking her. Very glad of the excuse, I said I'd better be going along with Dulcie.

Of course, I found everything all right; Aunt Hattie crocheting and talking baby-talk to the twins. She was awfully disappointed I hadn't stayed away and had a nice

long afternoon of it; she said she just loved staying with
the babies.

And that was the beginning of the way that the vacation I expected to have while Aunt Hattie was there,
went bad. The Law of Averages Will had talked about
certainly began to get in its dirty work. The first thing
was Will's losing the Whittaker building sale.

Will had felt almost sure of the sale and was tickled
to death. With his father away, he was specially anxious
to have the business make a good showing. He told us
about it at dinner one day.

"They're within five hundred dollars of each other
now," he said, "and they'll never stop as close as that.
Mr. Howard wants the building all right and old Whittaker's got to sell. I guess it'll be a sale, all right."

"Oh, I do hope so," said Aunt Hattie, sugaring her
berries. "If you can just make a good sale like that,
it'll prove there was nothing at all in your horseshoe falling down. I suppose lots of sales do almost come off
and then don't though."

"Oh, sure," Will agreed. And that was just what
happened to this one. While Will was working on Mr.
Howard, Jackson Vierley, the new agent over in Verblen,
appeared with a client from Chicago and got Mr. Whittaker's full original price for him. Will was disappointed,
of course, but as he said, it was all in the day's work.
If you could sell every place you ever put any work in
on, everybody'd be in the real estate business.

I believe Aunt Hattie was actually more disappointed
than Will. She is the really unselfish kind who just
throws herself into your life.

"You don't suppose your father's let the business get into any old-fashioned ways, do you?" she asked anxiously. "Austin Sears decided afterward that that was what the trouble was with his store. He had a new competitor, a fellow just like this Jackson Vierley you speak about, with a bigger organization and more money to spend. Of course, though," she added hastily and sensibly, "just losing one sale doesn't mean your whole business is going to fail."

"Well, hardly," said Will.

Jackson Vierley beat him to a couple more little sales out in the country right after that. Having two men with cars on hand all the time, it was easier for Vierley than for Will when his father was away and he had just Miss Halloran in the office. Will had got in the way of telling me things like that at supper, so of course Aunt Hattie heard them, too, and she said both times cheerfully that of course the real estate business was entirely different from Austin Sears' hardware.

Things were certainly not going well for us that summer. All sorts of little things began going wrong. Like the garden. Will's had a garden every year since we've been married and we get all our vegetables out of it and I put up a lot.

"I do hope you'll be able to pull it through this year," Aunt Hattie said when we first took her out to see it. "All the weather forecasts say we're going to have a terribly dry July and August."

"Oh, I'll water it," said Will. "I've had an extra length put on the hose so she'll reach out there."

We did have a terribly dry spell. So dry that the

village water department requested people not to use their hoses at all but to conserve the water. It was just pitiful to see our garden. Just when we should have been beginning to get the real good out of it, everything turned yellow and each day we could pick less than the day before. The dry spell lasted all through July and August, and finally Will got discouraged and didn't even work in the garden any more. I had to buy nearly all the vegetables we ate.

We did get some crabapples, though, and one Wednesday I decided to make crabapple jelly.

"You don't suppose it's going to be a cloudy day, do you?" Aunt Hattie asked anxiously, looking at the sky. "Jelly won't jell if it's cloudy."

"Oh, I don't think it'll cloud up," I said. The sun was out bright and hot. It did cloud up for an hour or so, though, and Aunt Hattie thought I'd better leave the jelly till to-morrow. But it was almost cooked, and I went ahead just the same. And it didn't jell. The sun came out later and I'd never in my life had any trouble with crabapple jelly before, but this didn't get hard.

"I'll have to cook it over to-morrow," I said resignedly.

"That may help," said Aunt Hattie, "if only it doesn't make it leathery."

Of course, there's nothing worse than leathery jelly. I decided to give mine two or three days longer to see if it wouldn't set. It didn't though, and I got so busy with other things that I never did fix the crabapple jelly at all.

Then there was the remnant of silk I bought. Aunt Hattie didn't think I could get a dress out of so little, but as everybody knows, you can get a dress out of a man's handkerchief these days. I made a mistake in cutting the back, though, and of course, the goods being a remnant, I couldn't get any more like it.

I shouldn't have thought so much about the bad luck we were having if it hadn't got Will kind of worried. After all, they were mostly little things that happened. For one, the flivver began to go bad. Aunt Hattie said that of course we had to expect it. She'd known people who had lots of different kinds of automobiles and they all had more or less trouble with them. It seemed as though every time we went out something went wrong with ours. Of course, once it was just that we ran out of gas, but we were miles from a filling station and Will had to lug a three-gallon can through the heat.

We had quite a bit of engine trouble, too, and Will said he'd have to take an evening pretty soon and change the oil and clean the spark plugs and put in new somethings or other. Aunt Hattie asked him if he didn't think that after a car had been run a certain distance, it began to have to have so many repairs that it cost as much as a new car. Not that she knew, herself, she said, but she'd heard so many people say this. Will said that of course it cost more to keep an old car going than a new one, but that ours ought not to be old enough for that. The evenings were hot all the time, though, and he kept putting off working on it.

Then they raised the taxes on the land we were buying over toward Verblen and that worried Will. Aunt Hattie said she knew just how he felt. Her brother carried some land for years and it just ate itself up in taxes. And one morning when I first came downstairs, she no-

ticed that I looked kind of peaked and, though I hadn't
realized yet myself that I wasn't all right, by night I
was running a fever with an ulcerated tooth. Oh, nothing did seem to go right! It would take ages to tell all
the little things that went wrong, none of them amount-
ing to anything in itself but altogether sort of getting
your goat. Here with Aunt Hattie helping out and
perfectly delighted to stay with the babies any time, Will
and I had a wonderful chance for a little vacation, to get
out together evenings and things like that. And we
weren't making the most of it at all.

We tried to, but every time we tried something came
up to spoil it. It was blinding hot the day of the picnic
we gave for Mrs. Kirsted's sister who was visiting her,
and as Aunt Hattie said when she saw the glaring sun
first thing in the morning when she was making the
sandwiches, a day as hot as that just takes the fun all out
of a crowd. I'm sure nobody had a really good time.
Then late in August when it was too late to do the garden
any good, it began to rain and it rained almost every day.
Aunt Hattie felt so sorry for the babies, it makes them
cross to have to stay on the porch all the time. Once we
let them out anyway, but it worried Aunt Hattie all the
time about getting their feet wet—she'd heard of a baby
who got pneumonia that way—and sure enough Jill
caught a terrible cold. Honestly, I told Will, if I had
the faintest touch of superstition in me, I'd think the
horseshoe really had put the jinx on us.

"Oh, I don't believe in any of that nonsense," said
Will, "but it does get on your nerves the way nothing
will seem to go right."

He let young Whipple use our car and take a couple of prospects out to Fieldstone—Miss Halloran was sick and Will couldn't get out of the office that day—and found afterward that Whipple hadn't even tried to sell the farm; they all went fishing and never even went near the place for sale. When Will got out there two days later, Jackson Vierley had already sold the farm.

"A business that's gone on all right for years does sometimes take a turn and just go down to nothing," Will confided in me, kind of worried. "Of course, things are always dull in the middle of summer, but I've been looking over the books this afternoon and we're not doing as well this summer as we did last. Last year the insurance we picked up during the summer pretty much kept things even. It's not a very good sign, running lower than you did a year ago."

At dinner the next day he said he thought he'd go out and talk to Van Holderen again about putting more insurance on his big dairy farm.

"He'd thank me for it one of these days," said Will, "If I could get him to do it. And if he'd put on anything like what he ought to be carrying, it would bring our books up to last year all right, all right. It'd be just as good business for him as for us, too. Why, he doesn't carry enough insurance on that whole big place to replace one barn if it burned down."

"Van Holderen," said Aunt Hattie. "Well, I'm afraid it'll be like arguing with a stone. I've known two Van Holderens in my life and they were both as stubborn as mules. And stingy! Why, one of them borrowed a brewing of tea for his wife and then made her dry out

the tea leaves and return them instead of fresh ones."
Will sighed.

"Van Holderen's stingy, too," he admitted. "And
stubborn. I don't suppose it'll do any good, but I've
nothing on for this afternoon and I might as well give
it a try."

He came home for supper quite disappointed even
though, as he said, he really hadn't expected to do anything there. Still, you always feel if you'd only gone at
it a little different."

"I'd never blame myself," Aunt Hattie cheered him
up. "I'm sure you did the best any one could. That's
the Van Holderen of it. I'd never waste another drop
of gasoline or another second thinking about it."

"There doesn't seem to be any use of it," Will agreed.

But just the same it made him gloomier than before.
When we were going to bed, he was so quiet I thought he
must be mad at me. But when I asked him, he said he
was figuring on that Verblen land we were buying.

"It's about all we are saving, you know," he said, "and
if the business is going to be bad—it'll be some time before
that land will be worth much—"

"But when they put the trolley through," I reminded
him. "And even with the taxes it doesn't cost much to
carry it. You've always said—"

"Oh, I guess it's all right," Will said hastily. "I had a
chance to turn it over to-day, though, and it set me thinking. I wouldn't make anything on it, just pull out. Still,
with things going the way they are—we seem to have
kind of lost our stride."

It always depresses me when Will gets worried, so we

were both pretty blue for a couple of days. Then it was
getting toward time for Aunt Hattie to go. Mother Horton had decided to go on up to New Hampshire and visit
her cousin awhile as long as she was so near, and Elmer
broke his leg so Mother would have to stay another month
in Minneapolis to help Kathie. I'd be all alone with all
the work and nobody to leave the babies with again. Not
that I'd think of minding that, only it did seem too bad
that we hadn't been able to make the most of having had
Aunt Hattie. I tried to get her to say she'd stay through
September and she would have been glad to, but Uncle
Henry wrote just begging her to come back and she felt
she ought to.

Monday, when she was packing her trunk—she was
going early Tuesday morning—was the darkest, gloomiest day. I had to keep little Jill inside because her cold
was worse, and Aunt Hattie was worried about her. Of
course, she didn't know much about babies' diseases, but
there was that baby who had got pneumonia. It made
Jill cross to stay in the house and Jack was lonesome and
fussed out on the porch without her. Will had gone
away that morning terribly low in his mind, and take it
altogether, it was not a very cheerful day.

In the afternoon we had a terrible thunderstorm, the
lightning fairly blinded you. I thought maybe it would
clear up after that, but Aunt Hattie said she doubted it;
she was afraid we were in for a long rainy spell, to make
up for the hot, dry one. It did look a little brighter but
only for an hour or so, then it settled into a slow, steady
drizzle again. Rosemary, who had been going to bring
her sewing over in the afternoon, called up to say she

couldn't make it. Their electricity had all been put out of commission by the storm and she'd got to wait for the repair men. She wanted us all to come over there, but I didn't like to take Jill out. She told me that the storm had done a lot of damage; it had killed four of Van Holderen's cows; they'd all been huddled together, wet, under a tree, and the lightning had struck the tree. As I told Aunt Hattie, mean though it was, that news was the one bright spot in a gloomy day.

It was a terribly dull afternoon. Aunt Hattie finished her packing and I mended while Jill fussed and whined in the living room and Jack fussed and whined on the porch. While I was putting the babies to bed, the telephone rang and Aunt Hattie answered. It was Will, and she couldn't quite get what he said, but he'd had to go somewhere or other and wouldn't be home for supper. He said not to worry if he was late. So that took away the break that having a man come in does give to a blue day.

Aunt Hattie and I weren't very hungry so we just ate a bite on the corner of the kitchen table. When we went to put the light on to read by afterward, it wouldn't light. Our electricity was evidently on the blink, too. So we sat down in the dark. The rain dripped on the tin roof over the porch in the gloomiest way in the world, and I got to thinking of all the bad luck we'd had. Was that the way life went, just to let you get a good start and then suddenly make everything you tackled go wrong? Could a person fight against that when it went that way? You couldn't get up much pep to try, someway, when you knew ahead that it wasn't going to do any good. Suppose the

Horton Real Estate and Insurance should go down the way Austin Sears' hardware store had; suppose— The clock struck nine and I said suddenly I guessed I'd go to bed. Aunt Hattie said she might as well, too; she had a hard day ahead to-morrow.

I had some candles somewhere out in the garage, but Aunt Hattie said not to bother looking for them. I could never find them in the dark, she said, and we could undress all right without a light. I must have gone right to sleep because, though it was only half an hour later, it seemed to me it must have been the middle of the night when I heard Aunt Hattie at my door. She was crying.

"Oh, Dotty, come quick," she said, "come quick! Jill is dying!"

I was out of bed while I was still only half awake and running toward the babies' room. Jill had been all right when I went to bed, just a little sniffy with her cold. It seemed as though I was going ahead of myself, my feet couldn't keep up.

"What's the matter with her?" I gasped in a queer loud tone.

"Oh, I don't know—she's choking and gasping," Aunt Hattie said. "I'm afraid she's dying."

At the babies' door I could hear her, a terrible harsh choke.

"Oh, Jill darling!" I fumbled for the switch but no light came when I turned it, of course. It was terrible, in the dark with that terrifying choking sound. I picked Jill up and she just stiffened against me, pushed with her little hands and struggled for breath.

"See if you can find the candles in the garage," I said,

and I ran downstairs with Jill in my arms. I knew Dr. Horne's telephone number in the dark.

It was a year before anybody answered and when they did—

"The doctor's gone out to the Ridge. Mrs. Hollis's baby's coming," a voice said. "His wife's gone with him to help."

"Can't you find a candle, Aunt Hattie?" I begged frantically.

She came in with one just then and by its light I found Dr. Prescott's number and gave it to Central before I remembered that he was down sick with appendicitis, himself. My hand shook so I could hardly find Dr. Norris' number, and it didn't answer at all.

"I'm afraid the lines are out of order out that way," Central said.

"Can't I get Verblen?" I begged.

I couldn't. Not a doctor I could get and little Jill choking, struggling for breath in my arms. Dying— Aunt Hattie said. I couldn't even think that word. Bad luck—everything going wrong—nothing you could do to stop it.

"Oh, Jill, sweetheart!" I held her up, fanned her frantically with a folded paper—I had got to do something.

"Call up Rosie Merton," I gasped suddenly. "Montrose 77."

It seemed as though Aunt Hattie would never get her. —"Tell her Jill's—choking—pneumonia—"

"She'll be right over," Aunt Hattie said, the tears streaming down her face. "Oh, Dotty, poor little Jill!"

The candlelight flickering was weird and the room was

full of dark shadows—babies did die, in a minute like that—I could see Jill running around her play yard, holding up her arms for me to take her out, saying "Byee-byee" in her high sweet little voice—suppose I should never hear her say it again—the flickering candle shadows —Aunt Hattie crying—it was all like some terrible dark omen—something awful that you couldn't struggle against—fearful luck you couldn't keep from happening —terrifying, so horrible it didn't seem real—ghostlike—

"There she comes!" I heard hurrying footsteps on our front porch, a sound of clinking tin.

The door was standing open, waiting, and Rosie, her rubber coat over her bathrobe, a tin pail with a long spout in her hand, came in.

"Oh, Rosie," I cried, "Jill—" Jill coughed, a hard dry choking cough, a terrible rattle, she couldn't catch her breath—the flickering shadows—my baby choking in my very arms and nothing I could do— "Oh, Rosie, is she dying?"

"Ye Gods!" said Rosie. And in that spooky, flickering, terrifying night, Rosie's voice sounded suddenly safe and sure and familiar. "Ye Gods, Dot! What's the matter with you? The child's just got the croup."

"Cr-croup!" I gasped.

"Get her back upstairs in her bed," Rosie ordered me briskly. "Isn't it the limit not to have any light! Get a sheet"—to Aunt Hattie—"and we'll drape it over the bed. Where are the matches? I brought my croup kettle; I thought that was probably the trouble. Here, fill this half full of water, the benzoin's in it already.

Mix up some flour and mustard, six times as much flour
—we'll try a plaster, too."

Aunt Hattie stopped pressing her handkerchief to her
eyes and ran from one errand to another, making a little
moaning noise under her breath, saying she didn't believe
just steam or mustard could do any good.   But pretty
soon she stopped; Rosie was rushing her so fast she didn't
have any breath for moaning.   Rosie lit the alcohol lamp
under the croup kettle and the sweetish fumes of benzoin
rose in the room—she had me fixing the sheet so they
would all go into Jill's bed—Jack woke up in his crib
and started to scream; Rosie told Aunt Hattie to take him
into my room—

It was queer how in five minutes everything had
changed.   From terrifying, almost ghostly, everything
seemed sensible and practical and sure.   As competent
as Rosie's voice.   She sat down by Jill's crib.

"Might as well sit down," she told me.   "There's nothing else to do; just wait."

Jill kept on coughing, but pretty soon it began to sound
different, looser.   Rosie nodded.

"It's breaking," she said.   "She'll begin breathing easier
pretty soon."   She looked at me.   I guess I must have
looked kind of pea-green in the candlelight.   She laughed.
Not a mean laugh, just a comfortable, understanding
laugh.

"Croup scares you to death the first time you see it,"
she said.   "I'll never forget the night Junior had it.   We
had him out at the farm and we couldn't get a doctor.   I'd
studied our baby book, though, and I was pretty sure it
was croup.   We rigged up the kettle and got it going.

Part of the time I'd pray and part of the time I'd think how the baby book said, 'No child ever dies of uncomplicated croup,' sort of hanging onto heaven with one hand and Dr. Holt with the other." She laughed comfortably. "After the first time," she said, "you get the old croup kettle to going first and pray afterward."

Long after Jill was all right and Rosie had gone back home, I sat in our room watching for Will. The kettle was still simmering in a corner of the babies' room, but Jill was sleeping quietly and peacefully. Aunt Hattie had at last gone back to bed. I don't suppose the whole thing had taken over an hour and a half. I got to thinking about Aunt Hattie having been so sure Jill was dying. She had been afraid the croup kettle wouldn't do any good. Aunt Hattie never seemed to think anything would do any good.

I don't know what made me, but suddenly I thought about my crab-apple jelly. Maybe, if I had got right busy and cooked it over it wouldn't have been leathery at all. And the garden. Roger Lane, right next door, had hired the Peters boys to carry water down from Meadow Brook for a couple of weeks in the dry spell, and their garden was yielding fine again now.

Just then I heard Will's key. After I'd told him all about Jill, I asked him where he'd been.

"I've been out to Van Holderen's," he said.

"Oh, did you hear about his losing his cows?" I asked.

"You bet your life I did! That's why I went out. I said to myself, 'Those cows weren't insured. This is the psychological moment to point out the advantages of insurance.'"

"And was it?"

I could just feel Will grinning there in the dark.

"I've got him signed up," he said, "for enough to replace every stick and stone and every piece of live stock
on the place."

"Oh, Will," I gasped, "how gorgeous! That must be
an awful lot—his place is immense."

I could feel Will continuing to grin.

"I don't think Horton, Real Estate and Insurance, will
have had any special slump this month," he said.

I sighed peacefully.

"I didn't know where you were," I said. "Aunt Hattie
couldn't get it over the 'phone."

"You bet your life she couldn't," said Will, "because
I didn't tell her."

"Why not?" I asked.

"Because," said Will, "I'd just about figured out I'd
do better if she didn't tell me first that there wasn't much
use trying at all. You know there's such a thing as looking for bad luck so hard you can find it."

Will chuckled.

"I had to stop halfway out there in the pouring rain
and change two spark plugs," he said. "The old boat
stopped completely. My first thought was that it was a
bad sign, that the chances were there wouldn't be anything in the trip anyway, and it was raining harder all
the time and that maybe I might as well turn back. My
second thought was better though. I said to myself that
anybody who can't get around to do the things he knows
a car needs is going to have considerable bad luck with
his engine. And that I'd go right on to Van Holderen's."

Suddenly, though goodness knows it had nothing to do with engines, I thought of a way I could fix the dress I'd started to make out of that remnant; such a simple way I couldn't see why I hadn't thought of it before. And then about the picnic we'd given for Mrs. Frank Kirsted's sister. What if it had been a scorching hot day? I'd had wonderful times on hotter picnic days. Maybe ours wouldn't have been such a flop if we hadn't started out with the idea that it would be. And Will's losing the Whittaker sale—why, it didn't mean a thing. You've got to go right ahead in business and set things like that down to profit and loss.

"Do you know, Dot," Will said suddenly, "I believe a person like Aunt Hattie who's always afraid things aren't going to come out right is a dangerous person to have around."

"Isn't that funny? That's just what I was thinking. Kind of like when you're learning to skate. So long as you don't think anything about falling you swing right along, and then the second you begin to get scared, you wabble like everything. I suppose you must begin to do something differently, some little thing—"

"Just as I came darn near not going on to Van Holderen's this afternoon," Will said.

"Of course," I said hastily, "I'm not saying there's nothing in luck; things do seem to come in waves, but I'll bet if a person has bad luck right along, all the time, there's something—"

"I'll bet," Will interrupted, "you could usually look back afterward and see a place where you figured there wasn't any use bothering to clean your spark plugs."

Aunt Hattie's train was to leave early in the morning, but just the same she was up ahead of me, starting breakfast. Before I was dressed I could smell the coffee and hear her singing in the kitchen:

" 'The way is dark and I am far from ho-ome—' "

Poor Aunt Hattie! She was so kind, and so unselfish. And as far as that went, she always seemed happy enough. When she left she said she'd had the loveliest two months with us and she was perfectly delighted with the book and candy Will had brought her for her trip, and she did hope the babies' cereal that we'd left cooking on the stove wouldn't burn before we got back.

And it hadn't—we got there just in time. Will went upstairs a minute to see the babies, just long enough to tip Jack over in a somersault and say, "Hello there, old Wheeze-in-the-Dark" to Jill. Then he said he'd be off. He'd got to get busy and beat Jackson Vierley's time. As he was going out the front door, though, he saw the old gilt horseshoe still lying on the porch railing.

With a grin he stopped just long enough to tack it up again over the front door, points up, the way it holds the luck.

VIII

ELLA PLAYS HER OWN GAME

EVERYBODY has picked on me about Ella Crownin-shield. Even Will made fun of the present I gave her for her hope chest. She had plenty of presents that were sensible, though. When it got out that Ella was to marry a young man in the Verblen garage, everybody in town that she'd worked for, felt kindly toward her and wanted to do a little something to start her off right.

She was only nineteen, but she'd been going out doing odd jobs ever since she was fourteen and you get to know a lot of people doing that for five years. For twenty-five cents an hour she'd mind your babies or wait on table or darn stockings, or clean out the ice-box. And while she wasn't exactly an expert in any one line, she got by in all of them. The only job I ever heard of her really falling down on was the time of Dulcie's bridge party when Mrs. Frank Kirsted disappointed her at the last minute and, rather than have a whole table thrown off, Dulcie insisted on Ella's taking a hand. As I told Dulcie, though, she might have foreseen how that would work out. What good is fifteen minutes coaching in Bridge going to do anybody who'd never played anything but euchre and railroad casino.

However, Dulcie didn't hold this against Ella for long and gave her her old polychrome table lamp for her hope chest. Of course polychrome is simply out now but as Dulcie said, the lamp was perfectly good. Mother Horton gave Ella her living-room curtains. She was getting some new pongee ones and as she said, all Ella'd have to do would be to darn up the old ones and dye them and they'd look as good as new. Betty Bartell said if Chandler came across with the new breakfast set she's been hinting about for her birthday, she'd give Ella her blue and white set which, while they were a little chipped, had loads of good wear in them yet.

Oh, Ella had lots of sensible presents. Even the few people who didn't give her something they had in the house, bought something terribly sensible for her, good crash dishtowels or cotton stockings or nice warm knit underwear. I suppose the jade satin negligee I made for her did look kind of out of place. It had long traily silver lace sleeves and a bunch of silver rosebuds at the side.

"When in the dickens do you figure she's going to wear that?" Will demanded when I showed it to him. "Getting a six o'clock breakfast for Joe?"

"When do I wear the rose chiffon Kathie made for my trousseau," I countered triumphantly. "And how often does Dulcie get to wear her cream lace one? Or Rosie Merton her black and gold?"

Will looked bewildered.

"That's a hot argument for giving Ella one," he said. "The fact that nobody you know has been able to wear theirs after they got it."

"It's a very good argument," I answered firmly. "Ella's human and she's a bride, even if her mother does do fancy washing and she's always worked out herself. She's got as good a right as any other bride to have a fancy negligee that she can't wear."

Will is very democratic so that squelched him.

"Gosh!" he said. "To think we gave 'em the vote!"

However, as I told Will, I'd got the jade satin in a remnant for almost nothing and Father gave me the silver lace out of the store, thinking I wanted it for myself, so the whole negligee didn't cost hardly anything and Ella cried when I gave it to her; it was the only beautiful useless thing she'd ever had in her whole life. Will, however, is like all other men; he's got dumb spots. When I told him triumphantly about Ella crying and said how happy it made me, he just looked positively baffled.

Ella and Joe having done most of their courting in our living room, Will and I felt a regular matchmaker's interest in them. Just as soon as they were settled they invited us over for a Sunday supper. We parked the twins on Mother and went with great pleasure.

I could understand exactly how Ella felt. A bunch of taximen that Joe knew had clubbed together and given them a set of silver for a wedding present and Ella's table looked lovely. She knew just how to set it, of course, having set the table often enough for the fussiest people in Montrose. She had a glass bowl of lavender sweetpeas and baby's breath in the center, just as she'd often fixed it for my parties, and as nice a dinner as you'd ever want to eat: fruit cocktail and roast chicken and a salad with nasturtium leaves in it and Lover's Delight for dessert.

They'd rented a three-room flat over the garage and

that was just as nice as the dinner. Not as fancy, of course, but really awfully nice. The living room was quite good sized and Ella had her table set at one end of it. Then there was a small bedroom and a very nice kitchen and a back porch that Joe had screened in where they could sit evenings. It was all tiny and simple, but Ella had made it pretty and she was so happy and proud. She was getting acquainted with some girls in Verblen. The other man in the garage with Joe had a nice wife and the four of them went on picnics and the wife was introducing Ella to her friends.

Will and I drove home in the late afternoon in a perfect glow of satisfaction for them. It is a great pleasure to feel that you've helped make a match that's turning out well.

"Joe'll get along all right," Will said. "He's steady and hard-working and he told me to-day he was going to save his money and invest it and get ahead. He was asking me about those bungalows Pierce is putting up on Picard Street, whether I thought they were good investments. I told him they were well-built houses, but I didn't think any real estate except your own home was the best investment for a person who hadn't had any experience."

There is nothing that makes me feel so pleased with Will and so mature as to have people asking his business advice. And when Ella would ask my advice about household things, I just nearly burst with pride and satisfaction. I gave her lots of good tips, too. She didn't know a thing about planning meals for food value. She thought you did it according to color, one dark vegetable, one light. I showed her about buying canned goods by the dozen and how to tell a ripe canteloup and lots of other things. I also got her to take exercises every day to see if she couldn't get over stooping so, and I got her to bob her hair. It had been thin and stringy and Ella, having about as much figure as a drink of water, had always looked little and thin and stringy and poor. Keeping her hair short and curled made all the difference in the world in her looks.

Take it altogether, Will and I felt kind of responsible for Ella and Joe. Terribly proud of the way they were getting along. But of course, feeling that way, I had to stick up for Ella whenever people criticized her and, believe me, it wasn't long before the criticism began.

I had told Rosemary about our dinner there and the silver the taximen had given them for a present. She must have told Dulcie, because the next time I saw Dulcie she began:

"Of all things! For Ella Crowninshield to have salad forks! Did you ever hear anything so idiotic in your life?"

Of course I had to stick up for Ella, said they came in the set and that besides I didn't see why Ella shouldn't have salad forks if she wanted them and they were given to her, anyway, just as well as anybody else. But Dulcie was not at all convinced.

"Salad forks!" she sniffed. "I'll bet her mother eats with her knife!"

I said nothing to that. Thank goodness, it wasn't up to me to stick up for Mrs. Crowninshield, too.

Next it was Mrs. Frank Kirsted.

"Who do you suppose is going to buy our flivver as soon as our new big car comes?" she demanded. "Ella Crowninshield's husband."

Will helped me stick up for them on that. He said that the way Joe'd take care of that flivver it wouldn't cost them scarcely anything to run it, and he could probably keep it in the garage for nothing, and they'd get a lot of comfort out of it. Mrs. Kirsted, however, couldn't see it for dust.

"Well, I don't know what things are coming to," she said, "when I've got to wear that mangy old raccoon coat for another winter and Ella Crowninshield drives her own car."

Mrs. Kirsted had never spoken of "driving her own car" when the flivver had been hers—a flivver never looked like "a car" to her till she thought of Ella Crowninshield having one. Honestly, it just made me sick the way nobody seemed to think Ella was human. They wanted her to be kept warm and fed, but they all hated the idea of her having any fun.

Ella did, however, give even me a turn when she and Joe bought one of the Pierce bungalows. Not for an investment, but to live in. It was a six-room stucco bungalow, very nearly as nice as any of ours, with the bathroom plastered and marked off to look like tiles and lovely electric fixtures that looked like candles in the living room and a faucet that the hot and cold water came out of at once in the kitchen.

"And window-boxes, if you please!" said Mrs. Curtis in as disgusted a tone as though window-boxes were like getting drunk or something. Mrs. Curtis's husband is

president of the Harvester Company and she has a perfectly huge house out on Sunset Hill and keeps three servants, a man and his wife and a chambermaid. It did seem
as though she shouldn't begrudge Ella a window-box.

"It isn't the window-box," Mrs. Curtis denied ve-
hemently. "It's the principle of the thing. You no
sooner get a window-box than you have to get pink gera-
niums to go in it. And the upkeep! People don't seem
to realize that it costs anything to keep a place going—
they seem to think once they've bought it, that's all there
is to it. Why, look at our establishment—the upkeep
is something frightful. I said to Mr. Curtis just the
other day that much as I'd like to go up to the lake for
a couple of weeks this summer, I really didn't think we
ought to do it. None of the cottages there are big enough
for three servants and I couldn't enjoy myself a minute
to leave two of ours here and be paying their salaries for
doing nothing but eating me out of house and home."

Will thought buying the bungalow was crazy, too.
They were buying it on time, of course, but Will admitted
more houses were bought that way than any other.

"It isn't like the Bartells, buying things on time," I
defended Ella, "things they can't afford and, for all anybody knows, never really intend to pay for at all. Joe
can make the payments all right and you told him yourself that owning your home was good business."

"It isn't good business," said Will, "to sew yourself
up with payments that don't leave you any margin.
That's where the loose screw is, not buying on time. But
you know what Joe probably makes and you know that a
six-room bungalow is more than he can swing right now

without sailing pretty close to the wind." He paused a moment, then added, "Of course you can see how he'd like to give Ella a nice home—poor kid, she's never had anything before. And if everything breaks just right, he'll probably make the grade."

Most of the people in Montrose, however, didn't feel as kindly as Will. Every time anybody went over to Verblen, they came back with something new and foolish that Ella Crowninshield was doing. Mrs. Long, who is a malicious old gossip if ever one lived, even went so far as to go into the butcher's and grocer's and get into conversation with the cashier, just so she could ask if the young Millers kept their bills paid up. I think she was really kind of disappointed to find that they did.

Joe and Ella were buying furniture on the installment plan, too. The things they had had in the flat, of course, couldn't be stretched over six rooms. But they paid their installments right on the dot and I couldn't see that it was anybody's business. Everybody who'd ever known Ella, though—and that was about everybody in Montrose—made it their business. Fortunately for Ella, she'd made friends with a lot of Joe's friends and their wives over in Verblen and it didn't make any difference to her how all Montrose was bewailing that she didn't seem to have any sense. I kept defending her, trying to show people that she had as good a right as any other girl to have a little fun out of life, till actually I was on the defensive all the time. It got so that as soon as I'd hear Ella's name mentioned, I'd stiffen all up inside and get ready.

"Oh, you're silly about Ella," Mrs. Frank Kirsted said

one day when we were walking home from market together. When the Kirsteds had had their flivver, she had
used to drive down to market, but the new big car used
up so much gas and oil that they didn't take it out except
for state occasion. "She copies you all she can and it
flatters you."

It might be, I had to admit to myself, that there was
something in that. It was flattering to have Ella put her
davenport across the center of her new living room just
because that was the way I had mine, to have her buying
a bedroom set as near like ours as she could get, to have
her asking me if I'd mind if she made her pink and white
cotton broadcloth like my wash silk. And besides being
flattering, it made me feel especially near to Ella. I felt
it would be a personal blow to me if she and Joe came a
cropper, as everybody in Montrose prophesied they would.

"You mark my words," Mrs. Curtis was always saying, "the day will come when she'd be glad to have that
three-room flat over the garage again."

I really felt it would be as mortifying to me as it would
be to Ella if that time ever came. I'd sided in with Ella
against all Montrose so naturally I wanted to be able to
keep right on being proud of her.

I got a perfectly terrible shock the day I went to Betty
Bartell's luncheon for Marianna Martin Cox. There was
Ella Crowninshield waiting on the table.

"She offered to come," Betty told us in whispers in the
living room afterward. "I met her on Main Street over
in Verblen and she said she'd be glad to help me out any
time. She says she's all settled in her new house now and
that she doesn't have enough to do at home."

Everybody looked significantly at everybody else. It did sound kind of fishy. Mrs. Curtis nodded.

"I guess the shoe's beginning to pinch already," she said with considerable satisfaction. "I knew they were biting off more than they could chew."

Well, I worried about it almost constantly till I saw Ella the next time and after that I didn't feel any better about it. She said just the same thing to me, that any time I wanted her to come over and help me out, she'd be glad to. That she was all settled now and her housework didn't keep her busy. And she acted fussed and queer and pretended to be playing with the babies so she didn't have to look straight at me while she was saying it. Undoubtedly there was more in it than met the eye.

She looked so nice with her hair all soft and fluffy around her face and the candy-striped cotton broadcloth dress she'd make like mine and I was so proud of her and I thought of about all Montrose just waiting like a bunch of buzzards for her to come to grief just because she dared want nice things, the same as they all did, and was trying to get them. I thought of Mrs. Curtis with her big house and her three servants begrudging Ella a window-box and I determined I'd help Ella all I possibly could and stick by her through thick and thin.

It would have been easier, of course, if she had told me just how the land lay, but she didn't seem to want to say anything about it even to me so I had to blunder along and do what I could, working in the dark. I had her come over a few times to stay with the babies, though I really didn't feel I could afford it. I'd set my heart on a huge Chinese rug for the living room, and it was go-

ing to take every cent we could scrape together so that
twenty-five cents an hour counted. Still, it was one of
the few ways I could do anything to help Ella along so
I did it some. Goodness knows I'd never have taken a
whole day to go fishing with Will at twenty-five cents an
hour except for that, though we did have a perfectly
marvelous time.

Then I gave Ella what good advice I could, showed her
how to keep a budget and so on. She didn't seem to take
much interest in the budget, though; just said there wasn't
no budget made could make a dollar do the work of five.

It wasn't long before the news got around that Ella
Crowninshield could be got again to help out and of
course she had all the work she could possibly want.
Everybody began saying, Well, what could you expect?
and waiting to see what would happen next. Will and I,
however, were the only ones in Montrose who really knew
what did happen next. We'd had Ella and her husband
over for dinner several times and one Sunday night they
asked us over there for supper. Aunt Hattie was staying with me then so we could get away.

Their little house did certainly look like a million dollars. Joe had just mowed the lawn and it looked slick
as a pin. Ella was disappointed about her supper; she'd
been over to Montrose helping Mrs. Frank Kirsted who
was having Dr. Elincourt and his wife for dinner that
noon and Ella hadn't got home in time to make the popovers she'd planned to have. However, it was a lovely
supper just the same.

It was a cloudy evening, the kind that gets dark early,
and Ella had candles lighted on the table, just the way

they did in all the places she worked; she had parsley around the edge of her platter of sliced veal loaf and pimientos in her scalloped potatoes. Her hair and dress looked so pretty and Joe was so sweet to her—it was a domestic picture any one might be proud of having helped create.

But in spite of the candles and the salad forks, long before we'd reached the cocoanut layer cake, we knew there was something wrong. There was almost nothing you could put your finger on but there was something queer, like one of those heavy, sultry days when, even if the sun is shining, you know there's trouble brewing. When Will began to be especially talkative so that I knew he'd noticed it, too, I was sure that my imagination wasn't running in high. In spite of the salad forks, there was something wrong.

It was up to us to keep the conversation going, for one thing. Joe was terribly quiet and when you'd speak to him, he'd seem to come back suddenly with a start from somewhere he'd been. He kept watching Ella in a kind of nervous way. Ella was lively enough, but she couldn't have kept things going because while she rattled away, it wasn't any conversation—just rattling.

To keep things going a little, I asked Ella how her new Verblen friends were.

"I don't know," she said, "I hardly ever see them. I'm busy over in Montrose pretty near all the time and I don't get no time for them."

Joe frowned.

"I don't like her working her head off all the time and that's a fact," he said.

"I don't work my head off!" Ella retorted. You could tell by her kind of weary, patient accent that here was ground they'd been over lots of times before. "We couldn't have the Songola if I didn't do anything."

Merciful powers! They'd bought a Songola! It was the cabinet kind, too, the most expensive sort. What Montrose folks would say about that! I hung on to my platform just the same. Ella had just as much right to a little fun out of life as anybody else. I was determined to keep right on being proud of her.

As the evening went on, though, I kept feeling surer and surer that there was something wrong in that bungalow. We went back into the living room after supper. Ella wouldn't let us help with the dishes.

"It won't take I and Joe any time at all to get them done up after you're gone," she insisted.

We played the new Songola and all during the music you could see that both Ella and Joe were a long way off in some not any too pleasant place. They'd come back with a start just in time to change the records. Once Ella was kind of sharp with Joe when he got a scratchy needle. Oh, there was something wrong, something bleak and chilly, in that pretty homelike living room. There was candlelight and music but there wasn't any easy, jolly peace.

Was all Montrose right? With all their efforts, were they doomed to failure? I felt so sorry for Ella, putting up such a game fight and then not quite making it. And they weren't quite making it. Anybody with the least bit of sense could tell that, just by the spooky, cold feeling in the living room.

I guessed the reason just before Ella told me, which was when I was in the guest room putting on my hat. She was going to have a baby. I wondered that I hadn't tumbled to it before, the way Joe kept watching her, the fearful air they both had. In spite of Ella's fluffy hair and pretty dress and her not stooping so much any more, she looked five years older.

"Aren't you pleased?" I asked.

Ella hesitated.

"Oh, I'd like to have a baby all right," she said in a dull tone, as though that didn't have much to do with it.

I sat down on the guest-room chair that was so much like the one in our bedroom. Ella kept fixing the things on the dressing table, picking up a toilet water bottle and laying it down again, smoothing the cover over and over.

"It's going to cost something fierce to have a baby," she said at last.

As a mother of twins, I was the last person in the world who could deny this.

"Isn't Joe pleased?" I asked.

"Oh, he thinks it would be swell to have a kid," Ella admitted in that same kind of flat, almost hopeless, voice. "But where, he keeps saying, is the money coming from? He's taken on some of the night work in the garage already—a man can't do no more than work night and day."

Ella kept on fixing and unfixing the dresser cover. I knew just how she was feeling. She hated to say too much but she'd got to talk to somebody. Her mother

wouldn't understand or her two complaining slatternly
sisters. I was the only other person she felt well enough
acquainted with.

"If it could only of waited awhile!" she said.

I started to say what all of us have always said, that
you couldn't pick a time when it would be perfectly con-
venient to have a baby, so that it might as well be one
time as another, but I couldn't say it. I suddenly realized
the difference between Dulcie and Mrs. Frank Kirsted
and me on one side and Ella on the other. After all,
we all did have people back of us, somebody that we might
not want to turn to but that we could if worst came to
worst. Joe and Ella didn't have a living soul but just
themselves—just Joe working harder and harder in the
garage, Ella washing more and more dishes in Montrose.
And there's a limit to the money that can be made that
way. Just themselves—and a baby coming! No wonder
they were scared.

"It's kind of hard," said Ella, suddenly, as though she
wanted to get it out before she lost her nerve, "you don't
seem to have any fun any more, when there's a baby
coming. Joe tries to be nice, but he worries so much he's
an awful gloom around the house and I—I don't know—
I just can't seem to keep from getting cranky. I wish—
I wish we could keep right on having fun together."

Having fun together! I knew what Ella meant by
that. It was her way of saying she wanted to keep on
being in love with Joe and having him in love with her.
Of course she wished it—didn't we all? And for Ella—
why, having Joe in love with her was the only nice thing
that had ever happened to Ella. And she saw it slipping

away, saw herself working all the time, doing her very best and not being able to keep it.

Not wanting to look at Ella, I found myself looking at the bedspread she'd made for her bed and a sense of responsibility for her trouble just swept over me. The bedspread was almost exactly like mine. She'd copied me. I'd encouraged her right along—she didn't have another soul to turn to, all Montrose was just waiting to say, "I told you so!" and laugh at her. They shouldn't have a chance! I'd help her some way—I'd got to!

Of course I had the money I'd saved toward the Chinese rug, I could lend them that—but that wouldn't be enough to help such an awful lot—Ella wouldn't be able to work out so terribly long— For a second I had the queer feeling of being caught in a trap—why, that must be the feeling Ella was having right along! I'd got to do something to help her—*I'd got to!*

Going home in the flivver, Will told me something that was helping make Joe gloomy. While Ella'd been telling me about the baby, Joe had told Will that he'd had a chance to buy into the garage where he works. It would be a swell chance, he said. He knew, he'd seen it from the inside.

"He could get it for almost nothing, too," Will said. "Old Corley likes him and wants a young fellow in the business. All he's asking is cash enough to show that Joe'll stick. And Joe can't raise that. It's the chance of a lifetime and he can't take it. He's got every cent he can rake and scrape up sunk in that damn house. I told you he was making a mistake, sailing so close to the wind."

By Will's being so cross about it, so disgusted, I knew how sorry he was for Joe. It wasn't as though Joe and Ella had been spending their money on dissipation or anything that was wrong—just trying to get a home, something that everybody's entitled to. They paid their bills and worked hard and were honest and decent and doing their level best. It wasn't fair.

I worried about it constantly all the next two weeks. Mother and Father had been up to Minneapolis visiting Kathie and they said if I'd bring the twins up and come home with them, they'd pay my fare. But all the time I should have been enjoying the visit with my sister, I kept seeing Ella's scared thin little face. It made me anxious to get back and relieved when I did.

The very first day I got back, I left the twins with Rosie and drove over to see Ella, to tell her at least that I'd lend her my Chinese rug money, that whatever came she could count on me. But it was with a terrible feeling that I drove. I knew I wasn't enough to count on. Doing my level best, I couldn't keep things from going on about the same, any more than Joe and Ella could keep the sweetness of being in love in the face of what was ahead of them.

The first glimpse I got of their bungalow as I came along Picard Street I saw a great brand-new lawn swing out in the side yard. I just felt sick all over. Montrose was right—Ella just didn't have any sense. At a time like this to be buying a new lawn swing! What good would any little bit I could help do with her going right on and on, straight for the rocks?

As I drove up in front, my heart sank still further.

There were new curtains hanging at the windows. New curtains! Ella must be insane!

Not seeing her about, I rang the doorbell and was just going to whistle and walk right in when a strange woman came out of the living room.

"Where's El—Mrs. Miller?" I asked, surprised.

"Mrs. Miller doesn't live here any more," the woman said.

I fairly gasped. There was Ella's furniture—

"Wh-where is she living?" I managed to ask.

"Do you know where Corley's garage is?" the woman asked. I nodded. "Well, she's living in the flat above it."

For heaven's sake! The flat that she and Joe had started out in. Fairly aseethe with amazement, I drove down to Corley's garage, raced up to the three-room flat above. Had Ella given up already? Was she beaten so soon?

But the Ella who came to the door to meet me didn't look beaten, goodness knows. Her candy-striped dress was brand clean and she looked so pretty and she was grinning from ear to ear.

"For heaven's sake, what are you doing here?" I gasped.

"Living here," said Ella calmly.

I just stared, pie-eyed, around the living room. The only furniture in it was what they'd had when they first moved in.

"But what about your bungalow?"

"Sold it," said Ella. "The very day after you was over, a lady came in the afternoon, looking at the new one next door and felt terrible because it was sold. She got to talking to me and right out of a clear sky I asked her would she want to look at ours? She came in and was crazy about it. She brought her husband back that same evening when Joe was home and two days later they bought it."

"Well, for heaven's sake!" I had never heard anything so sudden in my life.

"And," said Ella triumphantly, "they paid down enough in cash so that Corley's willing to take it. Joe's gone in with him and part owns this garage."

"But all your lovely new furniture!" I asked limply.

"She took most of it," said Ella. "We wouldn't need it here, of course. It wasn't all paid for and we lost some on leaving her take it off our hands. Not a lot, though, and Joe says you gotta figure on losing something when you've bit off more'n you can chew and want to back out. He says he's satisfied a thousand percent."

I just sat down on the wicker davenport and stared at Ella. Back in the three-room flat over the garage, just as Mrs. Curtis said they'd be and glad enough to be there. At first I stared at Ella in admiring amazement. I'd never seen anybody put a better face on a bad business.

"Mr. Corley's going to finish up the little storeroom off the bedroom and throw it into our flat when the baby comes," Ella went on brightly, "so we'll be able to get along here grand. Say, do you want to see some cute things I'm making for the baby?"

While she was showing me the little slips and bands, Joe came up a minute from the garage. He was beaming from ear to ear, too. They were both as happy, kidding each other about whether it'd be little Joe or little Ella, or maybe they'd draw one of each the way we had. After awhile he spoke about the bungalow. He'd hated to give it up, he said, he wanted to give Ella a nice home. But someway in spite of what he said, his voice wasn't truly regretful; it was just as though he was doing his best to make it regretful on my account, as though way down underneath, both he and Ella knew everything was all right.

"This is a nice home," said Ella, looking about the flat. "And I got some peace to enjoy it with. We was working so hard all the time and worrying so much about the bungalow, we wasn't getting any fun out of it at all. Of course it was a swell place, but what's the use of a swell place in Verblen when you got to spend all your time in Montrose working for it? And what's the good of a guest room? We never had time for no guests." She looked around the living room of the flat, through the kitchen out onto the little back porch that Joe had screened. "This place is more like home than the bungalow ever was."

And it was. I thought of the last evening I'd spent in their bungalow, that queer, stiff, unhappy chill that had been in it. And then of this three-room flat, full of peace and security and laughing. Why, the bungalow might look more like a home, might have all the trimmings of a home. But this little three-room flat *was* home.

Ella wasn't bluffing, making the best of a bad business; she was honestly just what Mrs. Curtis said she'd be, back in her three-room flat and *glad* to be there.

"Not that we ain't going to get a home like that one

of these days," Joe assured me earnestly. "We're just going to wait till it'll be a little easier fitting."

Easy fitting—I suppose that was what Will meant by "not sailing too close to the wind," what the budget books mean by "a safe and comfortable margin between your overhead and your income." Lots of smarter, better-to-do people than Joe and Ella didn't do it. Look at Mrs. Curtis with her big house and three servants, feeling she couldn't afford to go to the lake for two weeks in the summer. Look at the Frank Kirsteds with a new car that looks as long as a locomotive and that they hardly ever ride in because it costs so much to run it. Look at—

"I suppose there's lots of people in Montrose'll be giving me the laugh," Ella was saying, "but I should worry."

To think I'd been afraid I couldn't go on being proud of Ella. Ella, who at nineteen had learned already that peace was worth more than candle fixtures in your living room, that one jolly guest for supper is better than an elegant guest room empty. Ella, who was able to put her finger on what was real for herself and her husband, and knowing that people were laughing at her for it, just say, "I should worry."

Suddenly I decided to forget that Chinese rug I'd been working toward. We didn't need a new rug at all, it wouldn't fit well with any of the furniture we'd already got, and it was cutting me out of an awful lot of fishing trips with Will and things like that to get it. And I wouldn't be one penny's worth happier after I got it. Why, just forgetting about that rug would leave us the grandest margin.

While I was deciding this inside, outside I was promising Ella I'd give her my list of what you really need to have for a baby.

"You've showed Ella an awful lot of things," Joe said gratefully.

"Well," I said, preparing to leave the jolly little three-room home, and then I said something that was true but that would have handed me an awful laugh six months ago: "As far as that goes, there are a few things Ella can show a lot of the rest of us, Joe."

IX

I FEEL pretty sure that if it hadn't been for Ben and Merribel Higgins Will and I would never have thought of going to Florida at all, and it's certain we would never have made a penny off Florida real estate for the main and simple reason that we'd never have dreamed of putting a penny into it. No, if it hadn't been for Ben and Merribel, we'd have been tickled pink and perfectly satisfied with clearing two thousand dollars on our Verblen land.

As a matter of fact, selling that Verblen land was plenty to get pepped up over. Father Horton and some of the other Town Council had been agitating another trolley line to Verblen for years and Will just figured out that it was due to come through before very long and that they'd be more likely to run it out the Pike than the east side they were talking about. So we put all the money we could save into land along the Pike and when the trolley really was put through, Will split the land up into building lots and we made two thousand dollars. We'd probably have sunk this in bonds for the time being and forgotten all about it if it hadn't been for Ben and Merribel's coming back to Montrose rich.

We'd all gone to high school with Merribel when she was Merribel Walsh and worked in "The Thread-and-

190

Needle Store" Saturdays and after school hours. Ben was delivering groceries for Nat and didn't have one nickel to rub against another. When Ben and Merribel eloped and got married even Father, who is usually mild-spoken, said he guessed two damn fools had met. They ran away to Chicago and nobody in Montrose heard from them for five years, when out of a clear sky, last spring, Father Horton got a letter from Ben asking him about the huge Wildron place at the lake. Ben wrote that he was thinking of buying it.

Father Horton thought it must be a joke, but, believe me, it wasn't. Ben had become actually wealthy out in California and he and Merribel were coming back to Montrose, supposedly to have a summer home, but really, as we all soon learned, to show off to all the rest of us.

If a sudden comet had landed and exploded on Main Street, it wouldn't have stirred up the Montrose young married couples as the Higginses' coming back did. Whenever any two or more of us got together, all we could talk about was Merribel and Ben.

"She's going to have a formal garden sloping down to the lake," Dulcie would say in an awed tone, "and take down the old Wildron summer gazebo." Dulcie would pause a moment and then say, "Heavens, I knew her when that gazebo was bigger than the house she lived in."

And—

"She's got four servants and just one baby," Rose-mary Merton, who had four babies and no servant at all, would gasp. "One of them's a French nurse. Merribel asked me if I didn't think it was a nice idea to have a child grow up speaking French. I told her I'd be satis-

fied if my two youngest ever learned to speak English.
Mercy, I knew her when she never had a dress that
wasn't made over from her cousin's!"

"I knew her when"— The boys got to making fun of
us girls because somebody was always saying that. As
a matter of fact, though, the Higginses upset the boys just
as much, only in different ways. Success had simply gone
to Ben's head. He'd tell everybody how they ought to
run their business. He'd tell Roger Lane that, in his
opinion, it was a dirty shame for Howard Merton to
plug along filling people's teeth and doing bridge work—
whoever heard of a dentist making any money? he'd say.
Then he'd tell Howard Merton that from his point of
view Roger Lane was making an awful mistake staying
in the bank—where's any future in a bank? he'd ask—
a ten-dollar-a-month raise once a year for spending your
life in an iron cage.

"In my opinion" and "from my point of view" Ben
was always saying.

"If he doesn't quit patronizing me," Howard said disgustedly, "one of these days I'll give him a crack that'll
separate his point of view from his opinions."

As for Will, Ben took every bit of pleasure Will would
have had out of his Verblen deal by telling about the
easy money he'd picked up here and there. He rather
thought he'd run down to Florida, he told Will. A friend
of his just cleared fifty thousand on a couple of acres of
land.

"You're a chump," he told Will frankly. "A fellow
with your brains sticking in a little one-horse town like

this. Why, there's more easy money to be picked up in real estate than any other line I know of. Why, I know a fellow out in California who got an option on some fruit country, picked it up for a song and—"

And so on. Everybody Ben knew was always picking up money—not any measly two thousand that it took three years to get, but tens of thousands made almost over night. By the time Will had actually got his two thousand, as he said, it looked like Tony, the bootblack's, savings.

It's funny how anything like that will get you if you just give it time. It took quite a little. For several weeks we all just either laughed or got mad at the Higginses, managed to ignore Merribel's New York clothes by remembering when she didn't have any winter coat but an old sweater of her aunt's, managed to stand Ben's patronizing ways by remembering how he used to be late with the groceries. I imagine, though, that we were just kidding ourselves all the time. There is something terribly upsetting in seeing your own successes suddenly as they look stacked up against the real thing. Roger Lane got his regular raise and Dulcie, who had planned to have a rarebit supper for us and the Mertons, to celebrate, didn't have the heart to have it.

"I hate to have Roger stick in that old bank," Dulcie confided to me. "Of course, I know Mr. Scoggins thinks an awful lot of Roger and all that, but after all when Peggy Scoggins gets married, there'll be another young man that Mr. Scoggins will be a lot more interested in pushing than Roger. And if you just depend on your regular salary—what's a ten-dollar raise? A hundred and twenty dollars a year! About what Ben Higgins pays for one suit."

And—

"I wish Howard had started to practice dentistry in Chicago," Rosemary said, wearily sticking her tiny new baby's bottle to heat in the bottom of the double boiler, as she took cereal for the other three out of the top. "It just makes me sick to think of the way Howard works for every cent he gets, when Merribel Higgins told me what she paid for some work she had done in New York. I'll bet Howard would do better in Chicago, even now. You can't charge any kind of prices here."

Howard and Rosie had both been awfully proud of having saved a thousand dollars since they'd been married, in spite of having had four babies in five years, but as Howard said, it had been like getting blood out of a turnip, the way they'd had to scrimp and worry to get it. And after all, what was a thousand dollars? Why, Ben Higgins knew a fellow who—

And so on.

For some time Will didn't get excited at all. He's quite a bit like Father Horton, pretty slow and cautious. When Roger Lane actually got out of the bank and went in with a Chicago bond house that was opening a branch here, Will thought he was crazy and he talked Rosie out of the idea of nagging Howard into pulling up stakes and heading for Chi.

"It's just up and down with fellows like Ben Higgins," Will would say. "One day they're sitting on top of the world and the next day they're begging the grocer to

let the bill run over till the first of March.   None of that
for mine, thank you."

Will talked a great deal like that.   There's something
about having a couple like the Higginses dropped down
in your crowd that seems to put you on the defensive half
the time.   You feel you have to keep sticking up for your
own way of doing.   And Will kept sticking up for his.
Slowly, though, in the midst of all his talking, a queer
idea came to me.   It suddenly dawned on me that Will
didn't know anything about what he was talking about.
He was just saying the sort of things he'd always heard
Father Horton say.   And did Father Horton himself
really know?

It's quite a shock to you the first time you realize that
people as old as Father Horton and that you've always
looked up to as knowing pretty near everything, might
have a few things to learn, themselves.   After all, Father
Horton had spent most of his life right in Montrose—
who was he to set himself up as knowing how everything all over the world was done?   I said something
of this sort to Will and though Will said he thought his
father had done pretty darn well by working along his
own line of reasoning, he was broadminded enough to
admit that there might be men who had done just as well
along their own lines, and that their lines might be something else again.

I guess Will must have got to thinking something along
the same lines I was because he began listening with
more respect to Ben when he talked about making money
in Florida real estate.   Ben wasn't just a blow-hard,
either.   He had plenty of proofs.   Men were making

fortunes over night, buying and selling land. You didn't even have to buy the land; you just bought a thirty-day option on it for ten per cent, and long before the thirty days were up, so was the price, and you sold your option for stacks more than you'd paid for it.

"For the two thou we made on that Verblen land," Will said to me one night, "We could get an option on a twenty-thousand-dollar piece of property. You know, there's real money to be made on a twenty-thousand-dollar deal."

At first, of course, it was just wild talk that Will was doing for the fun of it. But even the wild talk made his regular business seem terribly dinky. He finally sold the old Harrison place that has stood vacant for years and made what we would have used to call a nice piece of change out of it. Six months ago we'd have been delighted, but now Will got to figuring how many times he'd driven bum prospects out to that place and how many million times he'd pointed out the fine drive-well, the extra cistern, and raved about the heating plant, and as he said, when you figured out all the leg work you'd put in, anything you made out of real estate in Montrose was a long way from easy money.

And then, just to show that Ben's wasn't wild talk at all, Mr. Burris, who is one of the richest and certainly the best business man in Montrose, went down to Florida and cleaned up seventy-five thousand dollars in three weeks. If anything in the world could give a good substantial proof to any business, it was to have Mr. Burris go into it.

Will heard it the day that the sale of the Van Ness

block fell through. Will had been working like a dog on that sale and it was practically cinched. He'd gone over to Verblen in the worst blizzard we'd had in years to talk to the queer old geezer who's got a mortgage on it and to look up the old deed. Even the trolleys weren't running the snow was so deep, and our flivver sedan froze right up in the garage so Will had to drive over in an open car. He froze one cheek driving home, and when he got there he found the deal was off.

All through supper, he told me what he thought of the real estate business; how you worked your head off and froze your face and what did you make—even if you made it, which you probably wouldn't.

"What do you say, Dot," he said suddenly, "that we take the profits of the Harrison sale and take a trip to Florida?"

There was some faint hint of something in Will's voice that made me look up sharply and say:

"To buy land, you mean?"

"Oh, I'm not saying anything about buying any land," said Will. "But you've had a tough fall of it, both the kids sick at once—you need a rest. I know the folks would take Jill and I imagine your mother'd keep Jack for us, don't you?"

"Oh, sure," I said, still feeling that there was more in this than met the eye.

The trip alone was enough to get excited about. Florida in the winter—why, just being able to speak of it casually other winters would be worth all it would cost. But there was more than just the trip—I could tell that by just watching Will. When you've been married going on four years, a man doesn't have to hang out his thoughts like a license plate for you to know what he has in mind. Though Will wouldn't commit himself beyond saying there'd be no harm in taking along all the cash we had—which was the two thousand we'd made on the Verblen land—I knew he was figuring on buying land. Why, I knew so well what was going on in his mind that I could just tell what he was thinking about when he began to grumble about his father being so cautious. Father Horton is just like Will, only more so!

"Father is as full as a tick of all the old maxims he used to write in his copybook!" Will would grumble. " 'A penny saved is a penny earned' and 'Waste not, want not' and all those. He never even heard of 'Nothing venture, nothing have.' Say, it's too bad the fellow who invented the radio couldn't have talked it over with Dad first. Dad could have shown him it wouldn't work."

I didn't breathe a word of my suspicions to anybody, but Father Horton is pretty foxy. He thought our going South was kind of wild, but he and Mother Horton want to go to California all winter next year, so he didn't say much against it. Both they and Mother and Father were glad enough to take the babies for us. Nobody had breathed a word about real estate, but a few nights before we were to start, we were over there for supper and Father Horton looked up as sharp as could be.

"Don't go playing any wildcat schemes on land down there," he warned Will. "They say the whole state of Florida's gone crazy."

Will didn't have to get his father's permission to do what he wanted to with his own money so I kicked him under the table not to say nothing, and he didn't, except to say that Mr. Burris hadn't seemed to have done so bad at it. Father Horton just sniffed.

"A few fellows like Burris may get away with it," he admitted, "but let me tell you something—when that boom busts a lot of suckers are going to find themselves holding the bag." I don't think he really suspected a thing, but just to be dramatic, he added, "You fool any of your money away on that sort of thing and you needn't wire me for enough to get home with. 'S far as I'd be concerned you could stay right down there."

Going home, Will said he didn't see why we shouldn't invest in some real estate if we located a good buy.

It's funny, though, just going to Florida was enough. You didn't have to tell anybody. Everybody took it for granted you were going to buy real estate. And all the older men cautioned us against it. "You'll come back skinned, if you do," they'd all say. We heard that and heard it till it seemed to me I'd be the happiest person in the world if we could come home as rich as Ben Higgins and show them all. Will felt just the same.

"If we fliv it," he said, "all the town will be waiting to say I told you so." He grinned sheepishly. "It'd be fine, wouldn't it? to come back the way Mr. Burris did and when anybody asked you how you made out in Florida, just say, 'Oh, I picked up a little easy money down there.'"

Will and Howard Merton have been bosom chums ever since they were old enough to talk and Will must have told Howard the idea in the back of his mind. The night before we were to start, Howard came over and he and

Will went down to look at the furnace and stayed down there hours talking, while I pressed out the skirt of my fall suit that I'd shortened, and washed my hair and manicured my nails and did all the thrilling, last-minute things you do when you're going on a trip.

When at last we were getting ready for bed, Will told me that Howard had given him their thousand dollars to invest in land in case Will found anything he was willing to risk his own money on.

"I tried to talk him out of it," Will said. "They aren't in any position to take a chance, with four kids, but he just begged me to do it. He's tied hand and foot. As he says, if he knew they were picking thousand-dollar bills off the trees two hundred miles away, he wouldn't dare stop work long enough to go over and pick any. He says anything I'm willing to take a chance on with my money, he's willing to with his. So I finally told him if I bought anything for myself I'd put his thousand in. Gosh, if there's anybody in this world needs to pick up some money, it's poor old Mert!"

That trip was far and above the most exciting thing that had happened to me since the twins were born. Just starting out to go anywhere is thrilling; to be starting South in the winter is about the last word in elegance. We hadn't been aboard the Florida Special long enough to have found our berths before it seemed as though buying Florida real estate and getting rich at it was what everybody in the world was doing. It was too funny the first night in the diner. Every time the train slowed down so that you could suddenly hear what other people were saying, you'd hear:

"And he sold it for a thousand dollars a front foot!" or "And they'd bought tha land for fifty dollars an acre" or snatches like "—held it just six days—" "—under a foot of water but that didn't make any difference—"

It seemed as though everybody in the world was going to Florida to buy real estate. Will got into conversation with different men on the train and I listened in and the stories were simply amazing. Mercy, the sort Ben Higgins had told us were nursery rhymes compared with what was actually happening on all sides. I was certainly proud of Will; he was so manly and sensible in the way he talked to these people.

It wasn't just in the way he talked that Will was sensible, either. He acted even better than he talked. Long before we'd even left home, he had talked to several different men who knew Florida and had decided about what part would be the best bet. He'd picked a stretch of several miles along the Dixie Highway, but back from it. Long before we got there, I was so excited by listening to the talk on the train that it seemed to me Will ought to take his three thousand dollars and buy the nrst stretch of land he could get hold of before somebody else beat him to it. Will, though, was as calm and businesslike as though he'd been in land booms all his life. "Oh, Florida's a big state," he'd say carelessly. "There'll be land enough left for us all right, all right."

And when we got to Florence, a tiny little town near the part Will had picked on, he was as cool as a Marshmallow Delight. We had stopped the day before at Miami, and it had simply unhinged me. I never dreamed of a place so full of excitement. I had naturally planned on stopping at the best hotel so that I could write to Dulcie and Merribel Higgins and a few of the other girls on the stationery. But mercy, there was simply no chance to get into any hotel at all. We were lucky to get a room in a house that had a sign saying, "Tourists Accommodated." Will said it was no accommodation to him, at the prices they charged, but it was. We were lucky to get a room anywhere.

We went to a very spiffy hotel for breakfast though, and I stopped in the writing room and dropped a few notes home on the stationery, so it didn't make any difference. Then we walked out to see the sights. They were all real estate offices. I never saw so many in my life. Every inch of street space, to say nothing of the floors above, were full. And the real estate agents! Why, there must have been thousands of them. They were mostly young men, and they all wore golf knickers.

"I guess the knickers are like the secret grip in a lodge," said Will. "The agents can spot each other by 'em and not waste their time trying to sell land to each other.

I had broken my neck, getting a lot of smart-looking clothes together to wear South, but mercy, I might as well have saved my strength. Nobody noticed you at all; everybody was going somewhere so fast that all they asked of anybody else was not to get in their road. I might have worn a fireman's uniform for all the notice my clothes attracted. Even the women had the same look of being on the way somewhere that they couldn't possibly get to in time.

The next day we went out to Florence and Will began

scouting around for land. The first night when he came
back, he admitted that in spite of Florida's being a big
state, we hadn't got there any too soon. For there was
a huge residence development to be made almost in the
center of the district Will had picked out. It was to
be called Sea Gardens, though it was miles from the
sea and there certainly weren't any gardens yet. Just
weeds and underbrush, all marked out in streets and lots.
It gave you the queerest feeling to stand beside nothing
but a bunch of weeds and see by the sign that you were at
the corner of Coral Drive and South Third Street. We
saw the plans for a gorgeous big Casino and the place
where it was to be built.

"And do you know," Will demanded, "that every lot
in that whole blame development is sold already! A
syndicate handled most of it, but do you remember that
little fat fellow named Forstein who came down on the
train with us? Well, when he was down six months ago
he was on the inside of that syndicate deal and he got
hold of these acres just before the syndicate took it over.
They've all been cut up and sold in building lots and what
that little man made—say," observed Will cautiously, "if
he only made half what he said he did, they won't have
to get up any firemen's benefit for him!"

Will rented a rattly old flivver and we drove out to the
further edge of Sea Gardens. Even I, who don't claim
to have any business sense at all, could see the possibilities
of that land. There on one inch were the streets and
avenues of Sea Gardens, and on the very next inch was
just land, ordinary land that sells by the acre.

"Why, Will," I gasped, "this is almost as near the

Casino as the developed part—and with everything in Florida selling like hot-cakes—why, this part will go the very quickest of all! Don't you think so?"

But Will was figuring something or other on the back of an envelope, and didn't even answer me. We beat it right back in the flivver to Mr. Cluett's office. Mr. Cluett had the acres just outside Sea Gardens for sale. Mr. Cluett was a clean-cut, fine-looking, young fellow in knickerbockers.

"A thousand dollars an acre," he told Will, "and dirt cheap. You know what they're getting for fifty-foot lots not ten feet away."

Of course Will knew this, but he was very casual. He asked about some things that Mr. Cluett didn't know and then said he'd look them up, and that he wanted to go out to the property again before he made up his mind. He'd decide in a day or so, Will said. Mr. Cluett shrugged his shoulders and said that was up to Mr. Horton, of course, but that there was a gentleman from New York who was very much interested in the land, too, and of course he couldn't promise to hold it. Will wouldn't be hurried.

"I've worked that 'other fellow interested' too often myself," he confided to me when we were out on the sunny street again, "to be worried by it. Cluett's not going to rush me into buying a chunk of the State of Florida as though it were a spool of thread."

"Yes, but suppose it should be snapped up ahead of you!" I exclaimed uneasily.

"Well," Will admitted. "I suppose down here you do have to jump pretty quick. We'll beat it out to the place again and then I'll go back to the office this afternoon and sign right up."

So not three hours after we had been in the office before we went back and Will told Mr. Cluett we'd take the land.

"Sorry, Mr. Horton," said Mr. Cluett, "but the land's gone."

"Gone!" After Will's experience of the way sales hang fire in Montrose he just couldn't keep a certain dropped-jaw look from falling over his face.

"A Mr. Forstein from New York has just bought fifty acres. He signed up a half-hour after you were in the office."

Mr. Forstein was the fat little man on the train. It is perfectly awful how real estate brightens as it takes its flight, so to speak. I thought of Mr. Forstein, who had already made his fortune, swooping down like a hungry vulture to take ours away from us. It made me just sick with disappointment.

"What's on the other side of Sea Gardens?" Will demanded. "Toward Florence?"

"Splendid land!" said Mr. Cluett enthusiastically. "Beautiful country! Confidentially, if you're asking my opinion, I think it's a better buy than the land Mr. Forstein got. It's just as near the new Casino and then, too, it's nearer the ocean."

Will grinned at that.

"I'm a real estate agent, myself," he told Cluett. "Don't waste any sleight of hand on me. Once you get ten miles away from the ocean, I don't believe a half a mile nearer or farther cuts much figure."

Mr. Cluett grinned, too.

"Well, between brother thieves, then, there's the land. It's just as near the Casino as the other," he said, "and it looks to me like it's just as good a buy. Take it or leave it, though. Mr. Forstein's looking at that, too."

So we rattled out to the other side of Sea Gardens. Will hung on to an apparently calm manner by main force, but I could see that he was not so calm inside as he looked. As for me, I was on edge and when, just before we were ready to start back, we saw Mr. Forstein arriving in Mr. Cluett's nifty little sky-blue roadster, I was ready to jibber. It seemed to me that if he snatched this chance away from us, too, I'd never smile again.

Mr. Forstein didn't get that land, though. Will went right back to Mr. Cluett's office and by noon the next day everything was signed and settled. Will was the official owner of an option on thirty acres, just adjoining Sea Gardens where building lots were selling for heaven knows what, apiece!

It was a giddy feeling. The price of the land was a thousand dollars an acre and yet for a mere three thousand dollars we owned thirty acres for a month. A month! Why, in three days we could have made five thousand dollars.

It was just three days after we'd bought when Will met Mr. Forstein on the street.

"Well," said Mr. Forstein, "I hear you got stuck with that land next to Sea Gardens."

That, of course, was just Mr. Forstein's way of talking. Because before he finished, he offered Will eight thousand dollars for his option. Eight thousand—that meant a profit of five thousand dollars! Even Will got excited then.

"Five thousand dollars!" he said. "Just think of how long and hard plenty of men in Montrose work to make five thousand dollars."

Looked at from that point of view, of course, it seemed like a lot of money, but naturally, Will didn't consider accepting the offer. He knew it was merely a sign.

"I told Forstein not to make me laugh," he told me. "And then I just asked him what he made out of his acres inside Sea Gardens. And how much the fellow made who bought the stretch just east of Sea Gardens. Five thousand dollars. Don't make me laugh!"

We both laughed. Will sobered up then a little.

"Say," he said, "can't you see Mert's face when I hand him over the check for his share? After the way he's always worked for his money. Did I tell you that the night before we left, when he stopped at our house, he was just on his way home from the office? It was nine o'clock. Mrs. Long had telephoned that she'd broken off her tooth and had a raging toothache and Mert had gone back to the office after supper to take care of her. And he'd been on his feet since eight that morning. Just think of working thirteen hours a day for a living when money can be picked up like this!"

Oh, but it was an exciting time! Four days later Mr. Forstein sold his option on the land we had first wanted to buy. Nobody knew just how much he made on it because he didn't tell, himself, but the stories ranged anywhere from ten thousand to a hundred thousand dollars profit. Mr. Cluett admitted to Will that Forstein had picked up some easy money.

"He's a hard-boiled egg," Mr. Cluett said. "He'd take the pennies off a dead man's eyes."

I guess Mr. Forstein didn't know that we had heard about his sale because he came around again after it and made Will a still better offer for our property.

"You know," Will confessed to me, "I can see better now why Ben Higgins feels the way he does. To see things like this happening, to have had 'em happen to him and then to go back to a town where the only way people can make a few dollars is by working like dogs and men like Dad, who don't seem to know that money's ever made in any other way, go round shooting off their ideas all the time. I can see how it would sort of get his goat."

"Oh, so can I," I agreed. Why, all the hard-working, penny-pinching young married crowd at home seemed a million miles off and certainly to be pitied. Rosie, hating to throw away the beef after she's squeezed the juice out of it for the babies, because meat is so high. Dulcie cele-brating Roger's ten-dollar-a-month raise, Corinne pre-tending she'd rather cook on a coal range even in the summer, after the gas rate went up— And all the time money being made by the tens, the hundreds of thousands —*easy money!*

The property just east of Sea Gardens sold a second time—another huge sum was made. Oh, it was a breath-less sitting-on-the-world feeling! Will went around hum-ming under his breath, "Oh, it ain't gonna rain no mo', But how the heck can I wash my neck, if it ain't gonna rain no mo'?" which song always indicates a high state of suppressed excitement, I have learned during the period of our married life.

"We might get one of those new Sylvester eights," he suggested, "if we clean up right. And drive it home. How'd that be for a triumphant entrance?"

Mr. Forstein didn't make another offer right away, but Will would probably not have considered the offer even if he had. Will had decided to hold off till our last week. With prices leaping as they were on all sides of us we might as well hold off as long as we could and make all we could. As soon as we had cleaned up on this side, Will would buy an option on a place still bigger, and so on. Why, there was simply no limit.

The last half of our second week the agent told us that Mr. Forstein had gone back to New York. Will knew that was just Mr. Forstein's little dodge. "Playing 'possum," Will called it, not wanting us to realize how much interested he really was.

"Well, he's welcome to take a chance if he wants to," said Will, "but if I get an offer in the meantime that looks good enough to me, he's out. That's all."

But he didn't get an offer that looked good enough. In fact, through the third week he didn't get an offer at all. Scads of people looking all the time, rumors that the property east of Sea Gardens was to change hands again, but nobody made a definite bid on ours. That was all right, Will said comfortably, he wanted to hold out to as near the end as he could, anyway.

By the very end of the third week, though, Will began to be the least bit anxious. It gets to be nervous business when you've only a week left. He met Mr. Cluett on the street and asked him casually if Forstein had come back yet. Cluett said No, as far as he knew Mr. Forstein was through.

"Well," said Will to me, "if Forstein wants to lose his property, it's his funeral, of course."

But Will's voice, someway, wasn't quite as hearty and easy as it had been the last time he'd spoken about Mr. Forstein. The tenseness of the last week was getting on his nerves a little.

The fourth week there was more than tension to get on his nerves. There began to be uneasy rumors floating about. First, the reported sale of the property east of Sea Gardens was found to have been just a false alarm. There had been a buyer all ready to sign up when he was scared off by a crazy story that the development in Sea Gardens was being stopped.

At least Mr. Cluett said it was a crazy story. But it's simply frightful how a story like that will spread. We couldn't see that there was a grain of foundation for it except that the Casino, which was supposed to have been begun before now, wasn't getting started. Mr. Cluett insisted that it was just a delay; that everything was going on just as planned. It was a New York syndicate that owned it and of course it was hard to get definite information.

And in the meantime, the story spread. We began hearing it on all sides. Sea Gardens was dead, the rumor said. The plans had been given up. Or where the story wasn't quite as radical as that, it was that Sea Gardens was being delayed, there wouldn't be any development for a year, there was no need to hurry about getting hold of the land around it.

I had never seen a business rumor at work before, but it went just like gossip back home. You heard it everywhere; it blew like pollen. Mr. Cluett and all the other agents—every one who really knew anything about it—kept denying it, bringing out all sorts of proof, but it was like trying to put out a forest fire with a watering pot. All their denyings just made a faint sizzle. The story blazed right on.

"It'll run its course," Mr. Cluett told Will reassuringly, "and die out. Those stories always do. Nothing to be worried about."

Nothing to be worried about! With the last week of our option going day by day, day by day! Suppose the rumor did die out in a few weeks. What good would that do us? In the meantime nobody was making offers on land anywhere around Sea Gardens.

The end of our thirty-day option was on Saturday and by Tuesday Will was as jumpy as a cat. He got snappy at me, which is something Will never does. I didn't hold it against him, though, because I knew just how he was feeling. Wednesday and nothing happened. Everything around Sea Gardens as quiet as a graveyard on a sunny morning.

It was then that it began to get on my nerves. There was something so tense and frantic about it. Only two and a half more days left and nothing happening! I would think of the offer of Mr. Forstein's we'd turned down. Suppose we didn't get any other! To think we might have made that much and now might make nothing at all! I couldn't eat and I couldn't sleep Wednesday night. I'd get up and sit down, try to take a walk, try to read—I couldn't do anything.

Thursday morning Will faced the facts.

"There's no chance for us here," he said, "unless Forstein still wants to buy. I was a fool not to take him up on his last offer."

"Mr. Cluett says this slump can't possibly last," I said, trying to be as cheerful as possible.

"Neither can I," said Will grimly. "I last till Saturday at noon and that's all."

So Thursday morning he had Cluett wire Forstein to see if he still wished to buy at his last offer. We spent the day waiting for his answer. I had a raging headache. All day and no answer. Finally at eight o'clock it came. It was from Mr. Forstein's office. Mr. Forstein was out of town for a few days, the answer said; they would take it up with him when he came back.

Friday was one of those warm, regular gold days, one of the most beautiful days I have ever seen. But it didn't look beautiful to us. Because Friday was the time we finally realized that we weren't going to sell our land. Will had listed it with all the agencies that had a record for quick turn-overs, but no word had come from any of them. I had no idea there could be such torture in just nothing happening. Friday evening we suddenly faced the fact that nothing was going to happen.

"Six thousand dollars would give us another month," said Will with a frantic sort of bitterness. "And if it were any other kind of deal there are people I might be able to get it from. But the men at home that I'd go to,

I can't on a deal like this. It would make Dad's business look shaky. I couldn't even go to Mr. Burris, who cleaned up Heaven knows how much this same way."

"You—you don't think your father—" I began, hesitating and doubtfully.

"I do *not*!" Will snapped. "Not after what he said. Not your father either. If we're stuck on this, we'll take our medicine and shut up. If we've lost our money, we've lost it. That's all."

"Lost our money"—I repeated faintly.

Somehow, I hadn't thought of that at all. All I'd thought was that we might not make any. Not that we might lose what we'd had.

"Of course," said Will testily. "You didn't figure they were giving us a chance to clean up and then if we didn't, we'd get our money back, did you? Don't you know what buying an option means?"

I had known, of course, but someway I hadn't realized. I'd been so full of thoughts of making—whether we'd make three thousand or twenty thousand—the only kind of losing I'd thought about at all was the amount that we might possibly not make. But to lose our own money, all of it, our two thousand dollars—

Suddenly, I stopped seeing two thousand dollars as the mere trifle it looked in Florida and saw it again as it had looked in Montrose. The actual fact rose like a loose board you've stepped on, struck me in the face. We were going to lose *two thousand dollars!*

I said something in my sudden realization to Will. We were pretending to eat supper but neither of us could swallow much.

"That isn't the worst of it," said Will. "What gets me is Mert's thousand."

Mert's thousand! Will paid our supper check and we walked slowly back to our room. And the thought of Mert's thousand, of his and Rosie's saving it, walked along beside me like a ghost. Blood out of a turnip, Howard had called it. Blood money. Didn't I know it! Hadn't I seen Rosie actually blue because bacon had gone up two cents a pound? Seen her wear shoes that hurt her feet because she'd got to get the kind with an arch-supporter for little Howard and they cost so much?

"What gets me," said Will, "is the way Mert's worked for that money. He hasn't picked it up sitting around waiting for property to go up. Mert's made every penny of that thousand on his feet with that old drill of his." Will paused a moment. "Working eight to twelve hours a day six days a week and plenty of times Sundays, too!" Will sat down on the edge of the bed. "You know, Dot," he said awkwardly, "I've been thinking off and on all day about a talk Mert and I had once after their last baby came. I was kidding him because he wouldn't get into the golf tournament, going back to work Saturday afternoons when none of the other fellows do. He said, 'You know, Bill, it throws a scare into you to have a girl and her four babies with nobody in the world but you to look to.'"

Will stopped short, sat looking into the cocky mirror in our furnished room.

"Well, I've lost his thousand dollars for him," he said gruffly.

I knew what that gruff tone of Will's meant, because

I was feeling just the same. I knew that it wasn't our fault, that Howard had wanted to take a chance—I knew everything like that, too, but it didn't make any difference.

"Will," I said, "let's don't ever tell Howard what happened to the money. Let's just tell him that none of us have made anything and that it'll be tied up for some time, and then let's pay it back as fast as we can."

Will dug his hands deeper in his pockets.

"That's what I'd like to do," he admitted. "It don't seem fair to you, though. For me to lose all our own money for us and then obligate us for a thousand dollars besides. But you know, I—well, I just don't see how I could go on, knowing I'd lost all Mert had in the world for him."

"It's the only thing we can do," I said. "I want to just as much as you do."

There was a long silence.

"I've been a fool," Will said.

"No, you haven't," I defended him hastily. "You couldn't tell how things were coming out. Why, when Mr. Forstein—"

"I don't mean in turning his offer down," Will interrupted. "I've been a fool to get into this thing at all. It's not my game."

"I don't see why it isn't your game as much as anybody else's," I protested. "You're just as smart as anybody else."

"I'm smarter than I was thirty days ago," said Will. He was silent again for a while.

"How do you mean, this isn't your game?" I asked curiously. "Just because you lost this once?"

"It wouldn't have been my game even if I'd won out," said Will. "It's a long way from home; it's in circumstances I don't know anything about. If you make any money that way, it's just luck. And making money by luck isn't my game."

"Mr. Burris made money by luck," I said.

"No," Will denied. "It wasn't luck with Burris. It was business. He may have taken options, but he had the money to take 'em up if he'd had to. He could afford this kind of business."

"Mr. Forstein hadn't money enough to take up his options, I'll bet."

"I guess not," Will agreed. "He's another Ben Higgins. Making money by luck is his game. It isn't mine."

I sat quiet while Will talked on. And it did give me the queerest feeling. For Will was saying all the things he had said back in Montrose before he ever thought of getting rich buying Florida land. All the stuff about gambling not being his kind of game. And I remembered how when he'd said it then I'd had a strange sort of feeling that he didn't know what he was talking about. Somehow, I didn't have that feeling now.

I sat and thought a little while, too.

"If Mr. Forstein had made you a big enough offer so that you'd taken it and made a lot of money, wouldn't you be feeling different?" I asked.

"Sure I would," Will agreed. "And I'd have stuck it right back into land again and again, as long as I kept making easy money. But easy money is money made on luck and sometime luck would have turned, and whenever that happened I'd have felt just as I'm feeling now."

He paused. "Well, we might as well go to bed," he said. "There's nothing else to do."

We undressed in absolute silence. Just before we climbed into bed, Will said:

"I suppose I might have learned this sometime at a higher figure than three thousand." And after a minute, "Maybe it's just sour grapes, I don't know, but it seems to me that in the long run I'd rather have my job at home than Cluett's. He gets bigger commissions when he gets 'em. But when the boom breaks here, he'll have to move on to somewhere else where there's a boom of some kind. That life's all right while he's young enough to wear plus fours, but where'll he be by the time he's sixty-five? And his work doesn't amount to a hill of beans to anybody for anything, really, except to make a living for himself. Maybe I'm kidding myself, but when I sell a place at home and see that it's a fair deal all around, I'm helping somebody get what he wants and somebody else to sell something he's got to sell. And I'm figuring on maybe doing business with both of them again sometime and living right along in the town with 'em for some years ahead. What does the Casino in Sea Gardens mean to Cluett? Let 'em build it or not, he should worry. He's here to-day, gone to-morrow. What fun would I get out of the Kiwanis or the Boost Montrose Club if Montrose didn't mean any more to me than that?"

I finally got Will to stop talking and go to sleep. He certainly needed it. He looked like a rag, dark around the eyes and cross and jumpy. The last thing I thought before I went to sleep was that even if we'd made three thousand instead of losing it, and had put it back and kept

on making more and more, if it kept Will in such a con-
dition as this it wouldn't be all gravy.

It was while we were eating breakfast Saturday morning in the little restaurant where we'd had our discouraged
supper that, to our amazement, Mr. Forstein strolled in.
He sat down at the table with us and got to talking.

"Well," he said, "want to sell me your option for
thirty-three hundred?"

He may have meant this for a joke or he may have
learned that our option was up that day, or he may have
known that Sea Gardens would be going strong again in
a couple of weeks—I don't know a thing about it and
neither does Will. And, believe me, neither of us cared!
If Mr. Forstein did mean it for a joke, he stood by it
when Will snapped him up. By noon, when we had expected to be a thousand dollars in debt, we were free, out
of it all with three hundred dollars to the good. Mr.
Forstein went out looking like the cat that had eaten the
canary, but we didn't care.

"Want to take another option somewhere else and try
again?" I asked Will for fun.

Will just grinned.

I guess he told Howard Merton all about it after we
got back, but nobody else in Montrose has ever heard
the truth of it. When they press Will as to whether he
bought any real estate, he admits that he did and says
airily, oh, yes, he picked up a little change on the deal.

But ten days after we'd got back when Will sold the
Van Ness block, after having worked like a dog on it for
a dozen prospects that fell through, he got caught in the

worst rainstorm of the spring coming back in his father's little open car. Ben and Merribel Higgins happened to be calling when Will came dripping in. It was a cold March rain and he held his blue hands over the register to thaw them out, and shivered.

"Where you been, Billy boy?" Ben asked.

Will gave me a wink and, though it seems a strange description of a wink, it was just full of meaning and peace.

"Oh," said Will carelessly, "I've been over to Verblen, making a little Easy Money."

X

MADGE'S LAST CHANCE

When I invited Madge Edwards to come and visit us in June all our young married crowd agreed that I was doing my part in snatching a brand from the burning. If ever a girl was headed straight for being an old maid, it was Madge Edwards.

"The whole trouble with Madge," Dulcie had said, way back in our high school days, "is that she's too smart without being quite smart enough. She's just smart enough to help the boys with solid geometry and not smart enough *not* to do it."

And Dulcie had hit the nail on the head. All through high school, so far as I remember, Madge had never had a single beau. She was the only girl on the debating team and everybody knows what that will do to a girl. You can't prove in front of two hundred people that a boy is a lame brain about the League of Nations and then expect to have him holding your hand and whispering sweet nothings in your ear the next evening. There's no use pretending that boys and men aren't afraid of a girl who knows more than they do. Unless she also knows enough to keep it dark.

Madge went away to college terribly young, and made the four-year course in three years. Her last year, her father died and her mother moved down to Peoria to be nearer her sister. That was four years ago and Madge hadn't been back to Montrose in the meantime. Her father's money had been all tied up in the Van Ness block and when Will finally sold that in March, Madge wrote me that she thought she'd come back as soon as she graduated, and close up things for her mother.

"Graduated!" Rosemary Merton repeated blankly. "I thought she graduated from college about the time the rest of us did from high school."

"She did," I said, "and what do you suppose she's graduating from now?" It is always fun to spring a sensation.

"What on earth?" Dulcie demanded.

I paused to get all the dramatic effect I could out of it. Then "Medical college," I said simply.

Rosie looked at Dulcie and Dulcie looked at Rosie. Then Rosie asked whether she was going to be a trained nurse.

"You don't go through a medical college to be a trained nurse," I said. "She's going to be a doctor."

"A doctor!" Rosie and Dulcie looked at each other again.

"Wouldn't you have known it!" they both said together in a hopeless voice.

"Of course," I said, trying to be broadminded and modern, "of course, there are lots of women doctors."

Nobody paid any attention to this.

"I'll bet she'll wear a hat like a man's!" said Rosie.

"Of course she will," said Dulcie, "and shoes that bulge in the toes like a policeman's."

"She never did have any taste in clothes," I recalled.

We all sighed.

"Well, she'll never get married now, that's a cinch," said Rosie.

"She might better have been a trained nurse," said Dulcie. "Every now and then you hear of one of them marrying a patient. But whoever heard of a woman doctor marrying *anybody?*"

"Mrs. Doctor Powers in Verblen is married!" I suddenly recalled.

Mrs. Doctor Powers has iron gray hair and is about sixty.

"I'll bet she married Doctor Powers before she was one herself," Dulcie hazarded. None of us denied this. Mrs. Doctor Powers' getting married was way before our time.

"That's what Madge had better do," said Rosie. "If she doesn't get married before it's sure she never will afterward. Just imagine asking a man who he's going to marry and have him say 'Doctor Edwards'!"

We all giggled at that. But suddenly we turned serious.

"Maybe we could help Madge to do that very thing," I said. "When she's in Montrose this June. She says she's going to take the summer for a vacation and begin practicing in the fall. This summer is absolutely her last chance."

"I think we ought to do the very best we can," said Dulcie.

"So do I," said Rosemary.

I said I would invite Madge to stay with us while she was in Montrose.

"We'll all entertain and throw her with the right young men," said Dulcie.

There was a little pause. Then—

"But where are we going to find the right young men?" I asked faintly.

That was the sticker. As a matter of fact, there are precious few bachelors in Montrose, anyway. Most of the young fellows either go to Chicago or get married just as soon as they're making enough to. There were the Dower boys, of course, but we doubted that either of them was making enough to support a wife; they'd seemed to be kind of slow in taking hold. Then there was Sydney Hinckle, who travels for the Butterfly Silk house, but I wouldn't feel right in marrying any friend of mine off to him—he is said to drink and Heaven knows what when he's out on the road. There was John Duer, but he was so homely, and Bobby Martin, but Bobby had known Madge too well in high school.

In fact, by the time we had the possible young men talked over, we agreed that it would have to be Wells Prentice. That was unfortunate, because as we all agreed, Wells Prentice would be an awfully hard man to get. He was the catch of Montrose and he didn't want to get married. He often said so. He lived in the new hotel and kept a nifty little roadster and would run over to Chicago for week-ends whenever he felt like it. He'd said plenty of little things to intimate that he was glad he wasn't in the shoes of some of the men of our young married crowd, with rent and babies and such things to worry about.

Still, as the man at the Orpheum said, most young men

talk that way but we keep right on building schoolhouses just the same.

It was expecting an awful lot of Madge, though, even with all our help, to get a ripple out of Wells. He was nearly thirty and each new crop of young girls that had come along had tried their hand at him. He had become, as Will said, as gun-shy as a prairie chicken. He was a wonderful catch. He had a position in the bank and an independent income that his Uncle Harvey Clay had left him besides. He went a lot with the rich Harvester bunch. He was *very* good looking, too.

Madge alone, of course, wouldn't have had a ghost of a chance with Wells. But Madge, with all our young married crowd to help her! It was a challenge to all of us. I really believe that is why we all got so terribly interested. When you have been married anywhere from two to five years as we all have, you have reached the point where you realize that you understand men. And you watch the single girls stumbling and blundering along, making the most ridiculous, unnecessary mistakes, succeeding, when they do succeed, by mere flukes. You feel sure that if you wanted to put your mind to it, you could marry any man in the world.

Marrying off Madge would not be easy. We all realized this. In fact, I don't think any one of us would have dared tackle the job alone. But the difficulty only made the proposition more stimulating. In fact, while it was largely necessity that made us pick Wells Prentice, —there really didn't seem to be anybody else—I guess there was a certain element of pride in it, too. In Wells we had, so to speak, a foeman worthy of our steel.

Rosemary and Dulcie and I happened to meet in Nat's Grocery the Monday morning before Madge was due to arrive, and while we waited for Mrs. Curtis to give her mile-long order, we leaned against the counter and planned our opening guns.

"The thing to do, of course," said Rosie practically, "is to make sure that they meet casually. If Wells once got the idea Madge was setting her cap for him, he'd be off like a frightened doe."

"Her train gets in about noon, doesn't it?" Dulcie asked. "Well, Roger is in the bank nearly every day on his way home to dinner, and he and Wells usually walk up together. I'll tell Roger to drop around by the station to see Madge. I won't even mention Wells to him because once a man's trying to be subtle—good night! Wells will probably trail along, though."

I shook my head.

"No sale," I said firmly. "Don't let Wells see Madge till I've had a good look at her first. You know how she used to get herself up—she ought to be looking as pretty as possible on first meeting. First impressions are so important."

"How are you going to get her to fix herself up, though?" Rosie demanded practically. "You can't explain how necessary it is unless you come right out and tell her what you have in mind."

"Oh, that wouldn't do at all," said Dulcie. "It would make any girl so self-conscious she'd be a perfect handicap to us, and Madge of all girls! It might make her mad and so stubborn that she'd cut off her nose to spite her face and wouldn't even try. You'll have to do it subtly someway, Dot."

We decided that the best way to arrange a meeting would be to have a little bridge party. That would make asking Wells seem perfectly natural and impersonal.

"And we'll fix the tallies so that they'll play together,'' said Rosie.

Dulcie and I merely looked at her. For a girl who's lived with a man for five years Rosie seems to have learned the least!

"We'll fix the tallies," I said, "so they *won't* play together. We'll just introduce them and then see that they don't get together all evening."

Rosie looked baffled.

"Get him anxious to know her and then keep him from it," I explained patiently.

"How are you going to get him anxious, though?" Rosie persisted. "Tell him what a peach Madge is and how attractive and everything?"

Dulcie and I exchanged glances. It was plain to be seen that Rosie wasn't proving much of a help to us.

"I've been at work already," Dulcie explained to me. "I've told him that Dot is having a girl to visit her and that I'm so sorry it isn't Belinda Stevens, as I know he and Belinda would have taken to each other so."

I confess that for a minute I was dumb enough to try to think who Belinda Stevens was, but it didn't take me a moment to realize that, of course, there wasn't any such person.

"I merely told him Madge's name," Dulcie went on,

"and said I was awfully sorry Robert Dexter had moved to New York. Said we all wanted Madge to have a good time and intimated that Robert was the only man I could think of who might possibly interest her at all. You know Robert Dexter is the one person Wells has ever been jealous of. I could see him prick right up at the mere mention of his name."

That was all the start we'd made when Madge arrived at noon, Friday. Will and I were down to the train to meet her. The second I saw Madge down at the end of the platform I recognized her. Not because she looked the way I remembered her, but because she looked just the way I had been afraid she would.

It was a lovely warm spring day, but Madge had on a heavy dark blue suit. She had on a heavy, plain felt hat and heavy, square-toed shoes. She came swinging down the platform toward us, carrying her own suitcase.

"Hello, Dot, you old dear! Hello, Will!" She kissed me and gave Will a boyish handshake. "My, but it's great to see you both again!"

It was great to see Madge, too. I always did like Madge. She was so interested in everything we passed, going up home in the flivver, so crazy about our twins, so all around jolly that if I hadn't had it on my mind to get her married, I'd have just settled down to enjoy her visit.

But to one who had taken it upon her soul to marry Madge off, Madge was enough to make your heart sink. She had on a plain white shirtwaist with a high collar and tie. But I didn't know the worst till she took off her hat. Her hair was cut exactly like a man's. Short, shingled right up the back, every bit of her ears right out in the open, not so much as one feminine softening side-burn!

Of course we'd all seen that style in the movies and in the expensive fashion magazines, but nobody in Montrose had had the nerve to try it. And Madge, of all people! She certainly wasn't the one to carry it off.

My first impulse was to call up the girls and tell them our plan was off. It seemed so hopeless. But hope dies hard and I just couldn't bring myself to give up without trying. Besides, as the afternoon wore on, I found myself discovering what I'd sort of forgotten, how nice Madge really is in spite of being too smart and looking like a young man. I began to see that it was not only a stunt but my actual duty to do anything I possibly could for her.

But how much could I do? I could just see Wells Prentice taking one look and running for shelter. Still, if you try hard enough, it is amazing what bright ideas will come to you. In fact, the one which came to me was little short of an inspiration.

It had suddenly turned very warm and as Madge's trunk didn't come that afternoon, she borrowed a bungalow apron of me to put on for breakfast the next morning. It was an especially pretty apron, a bright, clear pink with crisp white rick-rack braid on it. I also lent her a pair of soft black mules instead of her heavy shoes. And seeing her standing in the sunshine at the kitchen window, I suddenly realized that, dressed right, in spite of her hair, Madge wasn't half bad looking. In fact, even her hair didn't look so bad. It was black and curly and, being so short, it did make her head look very small and attractive. Her eyes and nose and mouth weren't anything special, but that she had very black eye-lashes and such clear pink and white skin and such very white teeth that, standing there in bright pink and the sunshine, there was something very flashing looking about her.

She stretched her arms up in the warm June sunshine.

"My, but it feels good to get off that heavy suit!" she observed. "Thank goodness I've a lighter one in my trunk."

"Have you any light dresses?" I asked hopefully.

Madge shook her head.

"Your other suit," I began, dubiously, "is it about like the one you wore yesterday?"

Madge nodded carelessly, as though a suit that didn't fit right across the shoulders were a mere nothing.

"About the same," she said carelessly, "except that it's light weight."

My mind was working like chain lightning. Madge was almost my size. I had one or two dresses that she'd look really awfully well in. A yellow linen and a clear blue pique. If only— It was then I had my inspiration.

"I've got a little marketing to do for the party to-night," I said right after breakfast. "If you wouldn't mind staying here and keeping an eye on the babies, I'll run right down and do it before the Saturday crowd begins."

"Of course," said Madge heartily. "I'll do up the breakfast dishes while you're gone. Skip right along."

And I skipped! I stopped by for Dulcie, confided my

inspiration to her, and we dashed right down to the rail-road station. There was Madge's trunk, as big as life and twice as natural. Just full, as Dulcie said, of plain white shirtwaists and suits that didn't fit. We hunted up Seth, the baggage man. It was providential that Dulcie has stood in with Seth ever since she was a little tow-headed baby girl.

Of course, Dulcie didn't explain anything to Seth, just told him that we wanted to play a joke and wasn't there any way that trunk could be mislaid for a week or so? Seth scratched his head and at first wouldn't have any-thing to do with the idea. But Dulcie kept coaxing him; swore we'd see that he didn't get into any trouble. We could feel Seth weakening and finally he admitted that his helper had unloaded a trunk down in the shed once, just before he went on a vacation, and it stayed there a week before any one knew where it was. He said, of course, that could happen again. And so on. Dulcie and I went home simply triumphant.

When the trunk hadn't come by noon, Madge began to be anxious.

"Never mind," I said carelessly, "baggage gets held up at the Crossings once in a while. If it doesn't come by evening you can wear my pink—I think it would fit you."

By evening, of course, her trunk hadn't come and I got out my pink dress. That dress might have been made for Madge. It had always been a little too severe for me, but it was much more feminine than anything Madge ever wore. It was watermelon pink. I lent her my best flesh-colored chiffon stockings and my satin slippers. It left me with nothing but white linen pumps,

but what would any matchmaker care for that? And
Madge did look lovely. Dulcie, who came in early with
some of the dishes she was lending me for the party,
fairly gasped.

"Why, Dot," she said to me in the kitchen, "Dot, you
wouldn't know her!" Which was really considerable of
a compliment.

It was the truth, too. Madge didn't look like herself.
She had that same flashing look she'd had in the bungalow apron. She really looked lovely. And so different.
There was no girl in Montrose who looked anything even
faintly like her. She would stand out in any crowd.

From the moment that Wells Prentice was introduced,
you fairly heard him click. He's been run after so much
that he had an awfully indifferent attitude toward all
girls, a sort of "show *me*" air. I kept watching him sur-
reptitiously all evening. His table was well at the other
end of the living room from Madge's and actually he spent
the evening as near craning his neck as a man who rather
prides himself on being bored would allow himself to
come.

At refreshment time Dulcie and I had just slipped out
to the dining room when who should come strolling out
but Wells Prentice. He was evidently dummy at his
table.

"What's the idea of not progressing?" he asked.

We usually do progress from one table to another
every four hands, everybody finding it more sociable, but
now and then we just pivot. Dulcie and I exchanged
glances.

"Oh, the room is so crowded with four tables," I

explained carelessly. "We thought it would make less confusion for people to stay at the same tables."

"Aren't you going to change the tables for refreshments?" Wells asked.

"I thought we wouldn't," I said.

"Well, we're going to," said Wells in his rather masterful fashion, which, Peggy Scoggins has confessed, was what first gave her such a crush on him. "I'm not going to stick through refreshments with Julia Pettingill and Irma."

"Why, I thought you were rushing Julia," I exclaimed innocently. "Or is it Peggy Scoggins 1 should have asked for you?"

"You needn't have asked anybody 'for me,'" said Wells haughtily.

I smiled sideways at Dulcie.

"Why, of course, we'll shift the tables for refreshments," I agreed amiably. But when we had them all shifted, Wells was only one table nearer Madge. He didn't get to say two words to her the entire evening.

And the very next evening he came to call. I never dreamed of such a thing. The most popular bachelor in town doesn't waste his evenings paying party calls on married couples, for nothing. Of course, it was Madge. Our plan was working even better than we'd expected. We'd never planned on such quick action as that. In fact, I wasn't ready for it. Although it was Sunday evening, Madge had been out in the vegetable garden with Will and just had one of my old white middies on. We were sitting on the porch when Wells came strolling up the path.

"Oh, Madge," I gasped, "you must be cold!" And I dashed in and got my pink zephyr scarf and dropped it over her shoulders. Madge, instead of catching on as any other girl in the world would and shivering a little, to bear me out, merely looked amazed.

"Cold?" she exclaimed. "I'm melting." And calmly took the scarf off. However, she did let it lie across her lap where it was almost as becoming.

There was no doubt that Wells was interested. You could tell it, just the way he kept looking at Madge. I made an excuse to go out after a while and make some lemonade and shortly after I'd got out to the kitchen, I called Will to come and help me.

"What'll I do?" he asked, looking about at the plate I'd filled with cookies and the tray of glasses I had all ready to fill. "I can't see anything for me to do."

"Oh, just stick around for a few minutes and keep me company," I said, "while I wait for—for the sugar to dissolve."

Will obligingly leaned against the kitchen cabinet and watched me stir the lemonade. He didn't have a glimmer of suspicion, which was just as well. That's the only time you get any intelligent coöperation from a man on a subtle matter—when he doesn't know what he's doing.

When we went back to the porch, I could see at a glance that all was going better than I'd dared hope. Wells had got up out of his comfortable chair and was leaning against the railing, talking to Madge quite earnestly. I knew he was engrossed because he'd been smoking and the cigarette which he was still holding in his

hand had an ash an inch long which he hadn't thought
to knock off.

It seemed as though even nature was playing into our
hands, because the porch was just covered with honeysuckle and the fragrance was the most dreamy, roman-
tic— Oh, well, everybody knows what honeysuckle smells
like.

"I was just telling Miss Edwards I'd like to drive
her out by Grovelands," Wells said to me as we came out
with the lemonade. "She says she used to go to the old
Grove on picnics when she was a little girl. I think
Groveland Park would be quite a surprise to her."

"I'm sure it would," I agreed. "You'd be awfully interested, Madge."

"I'm sorry I can't take you and Will, too," said Wells,
"but unfortunately my boat is a two-some."

Will looked up, all interest.

"Why not take our flivver?" he said helpfully. "We
can all get into that, all right."

I looked at Will and if looks could kill he'd have been
a very sick man.

"Oh, we've seen Groveland," I said; "it wouldn't be
any treat to us. Let Wells take Madge out, his car is
much easier riding than the flivver."

I should have known better than to say that, but when
you have to grab so quick, you're likely to grab the wrong
thing. Will was on the defensive right away.

"I don't think there's a car in Montrose runs any easier
than the old flivver since I put on those new shock ab-
sorbers," he said. "Why not get the Lanes and the
Mertons and make it a good picnic?"

And while I was casting about frantically for some way to squelch Will without being too obvious about it, Madge chimed in in favor of the picnic.

"That would be a circus," she insisted. "The kind of picnic we used to have in high-school days. Have a fire and roast potatoes in the ashes and everything."

Well, there was nothing for me to do but to fall in, of course, as I told Dulcie and Rosemary the next morning.

"And the funny part is," I said, "that if Madge were clever that way and trying to play her cards just right, she couldn't have done better. Wells has been run after so much that the very fact that Madge didn't seem to appreciate his asking her alone was like kerosene on a slow fire. The man is simply wild with interest in her."

That fact—and it was a fact, all right—changed our entire technique. We had expected to have to do more of the matchmaking ourselves.

"Honestly," Rosie confessed, "I thought it was going to be just like the other night when we got a mouse in the dining room and shut the doors and all went after him with brooms and shovels. I imagined we'd have to chase Wells here and there, and cut off his retreats, and just throw Madge at him. Instead, here Madge is doing it every bit, herself."

Dulcie and I looked at her pityingly.

"The thing's a long way from done yet, Rosie,' Dulcie explained patiently. "Moreover, Madge isn't doing it at all. Madge may be smart but her brains don't run along that line. She just happened to like a picnic, that's all. And a man's asking a girl to go riding in his roadster is a long way from asking her to marry him. I'll admit that having Wells really interested is something I never figured on and it makes it a different problem altogether. But it keeps right on being a problem, just the samey."

"I should say it does," I agreed. "And it's a much more delicate problem than just throwing them together would have been. Why, it's as delicate as walking a railroad track with a pail of water on your head. They've got to be thrown together just enough, and left alone together just enough so that Wells will get worked up to the proposing point before Madge goes. But they can't be left too much alone or Madge will spoil things for herself just as sure as anything.

"Why, just last night," I went on, "my blood fairly ran cold. Something was said about medical college. Wells turned to Madge and laughed and said, 'Are you a doctor?' He just said it for the wildest sort of joke. Madge laughed, too, and said yes, a veterinary. Wells hasn't an idea that the whole thing was anything but a joke, but think what a narrow escape! Madge might just as easily have launched into a discussion of diagnostic clinics as she did to Will and me at the breakfast table this morning."

"But he's going to have to find out some time that she's a doctor," Rosemary said uneasily.

"I suppose so," Dulcie and I agreed resignedly. "But at least, the longer we can put it off, the better. If we can only keep things just right till he's completely in love —well, it's wonderful what a man who's completely in love will swallow."

Rosie is very conscientious.

"You know," she said in a troubled tone, "it doesn't seem as though we're being fair to Wells. To get him to fall in love with a girl who doesn't exist at all. Why, the girl he sees in Dot's clothes and in situations that we're all engineering for her, isn't the real Madge at all. There isn't any such person. What an awful thing if he should fall in love with this person and then find himself with nobody but Madge Edwards. It doesn't seem fair to Wells."

" 'All's fair in love and war,' " Dulcie and I assured her. "Besides, who can tell? Suppose he and Madge should actually get married. She wouldn't be a doctor then; she would never really have been one. So where would have been the deceit?"

But in spite of Dulcie's triumphant tone, Rosie insisted that it didn't seem as though we were being quite straightforward with Wells.

We didn't pay any attention to what Rosie said, however. At best, she was of very little help. Dulcie and I had the whole thing on our shoulders. We were certainly kept busy, part of the time arranging meetings and part of the time preventing them. The first part was easy enough. Wells was so much interested that he'd have arranged the meetings for himself all right if just let alone. It was preventing them that was enough to turn me into a jibbering maniac.

For instance, the day that Will took off to paint the garage and Madge insisted upon putting on an old pair of his overalls and helping him. In the midst of it, they got into an argument about homeopathy and were going it hot and heavy when Wells stopped by to invite Madge

to go canoeing. She looked a perfect sight, her hands
and face covered with brown paint and gesticulating to
Will with her dripping brush. Fortunately, Wells didn't
recognize her from the front of the house, and I took
the message and speeded him on his way, all unsuspecting.

It was like that all the time. Because, though we
laughed at Rosie for being worried by it, the truth of the
matter is that Wells never saw the real Madge at all.
We all managed by hook and crook to keep him from it.
We held off her trunk and kept her from buying anything
for herself from day to day, dressing her up in whatever
of our clothes we thought would be most becoming to
her. When I saw Wells coming I hid the terribly heavy
book she was reading, and dropped a popular novel in its
place; I stopped her a dozen times when I could see she
was on the very brink of starting some kind of discussion that would scare Wells off forever. I would be in
a perfect nervous state all the time Madge was alone with
him; there was no telling what she might be saying or
doing.

But day after day, Wells kept coming, kept interested.
We simply couldn't believe our luck. When we started,
we hadn't dared really hope to put it over, but now we
actually began to.

"We mustn't relax one bit, though," Dulcie cautioned
me. "One false step and it would be all over. Wells
has been awfully interested in other girls before and yet
it's fallen through." She was silent a moment. "I have
a splendid thought," she said suddenly, "something that
will cinch things if anything will. Dot, you tell Wells in

strict confidence that you're terribly worried, that you're afraid Will is falling in love with Madge."

"Well, of all things!" I said indignantly, "I'll do nothing of the kind!"

"I don't see why you won't," said Dulcie. "It would be bound to impress Wells if he should think that even a married man was crazy about her—"

"Well, you can tell him that you're afraid Roger is, then," I interrupted. "Roger is just as much married as Will."

"Oh, I shouldn't exactly like to do that," Dulcie said hastily. "It's a little different with Roger—"

So we compromised by telling Wells that we were terribly worried on Rosie's account, that we were afraid Howard seemed more interested than he should be in Madge. As neither Howard nor Rosie ever knew of this at all, it was perfectly all right.

Things were going along amazingly well, Wells actually telephoning every day and sometimes oftener than that. It was just like walking along in the dark, though, not knowing when you're coming to a step down. I never knew when Madge was going to make a false step and spill the beans altogether.

When, after a week, she announced that she would have to go home next Monday, I realized how critical it was. If she didn't become actually engaged to Wells before she left, she never would be. I was sure of that. Of course, he might easily go to Peoria to see her. But then he'd see her in her own clothes, against her own background; she'd be herself, without any of us to hide her worst points and bring out her good ones for her. And all our work and scheming would be wasted.

We all redoubled our efforts when we heard that. I did the best I could but there was so much I couldn't manage. I couldn't get Wells to see Madge when she was truly at her best. For instance, she insisted on bathing the twins for me every morning and no man could have seen her with those two babies without asking her to marry him on the spot. She wore my pink bungalow apron and she was so *sweet,* no more like a brainy woman doctor than Dulcie. Even the fake person we had built up for Wells' benefit was no sweeter than Madge was then. And the day that she spent with an old friend of her mother's who is going blind, told her funny stories that, it appears, happen in medical colleges just like any other colleges till Mrs. Keane was in stitches. Then spent the afternoon getting Mrs. Keane all interested in learning to read by the Braille method so that she'd be prepared that much. And all of it done with such tact as nobody, seeing Madge arguing with a likely suitor, would have believed she could possibly have.

But Wells never saw her these times. And Madge was going home Monday. It was I who had the idea of taking her and Wells up to the cottage at the lake for their last week-end. The cottage is a ramshackle old place up at Winneposockett, with nothing but kerosene lamps and a gasoline stove that's going to blow somebody up some day. But it is in the most beautiful woods, on a hill looking out over the lake, and is the loveliest place.

Will always loves to go up there so I didn't have to tell him any of my secret reasons. Our mothers would keep the twins for us. As I said to the girls that week-end would be the climax of our scheme. The wild roses were in bloom, the moon was full—I was right on hand to keep Madge from doing anything foolish. If Wells didn't propose by Sunday— But he would! All day Saturday I felt surer and surer of it. As evening approached I began trying to figure out some tactful way for Will and me to vamoose and leave Wells and Madge alone. I felt that things had reached the pass where that was all that was necessary. And then didn't Will insist on playing Five Hundred. Madge agreed, too; she seemed to have no idea of the momentousness of the hour.

Wells was so disappointed at having to play cards with Will and me that he positively sulked all evening, was actually almost rude. Not that I minded that—I knew too well what was back of it. To-morrow night! I thought triumphantly. Not once during the entire evening did the famous saying "Strike while the iron is hot" occur to me in warning. I never even stopped to think that it might rain Sunday.

It did. When we woke up it was pouring sheets, rattling on the tin roof over the porch. At ten o'clock, Father Horton telephoned. He was laid up with rheumatism in his feet, he said, and a man to see the Simmons place was to be in town. There was nothing for it; Will would have to go in that afternoon.

All the afternoon it poured. At first, I thought I'd take a nap and leave Madge and Wells alone. But then I was afraid to. For along with the rain, a mood of perverse black mischief seemed to have come over Madge. She seemed determined at this, practically the moment

of triumph, to ruin everything for herself. She started
to argue with Wells about religion, of all things. She
and Will really like to argue and neither of them ever
gets mad, but to argue with Wells! A girl with any
sense at all could tell that Wells is the kind of man who
can't bear to have anybody disagree with him. I could
see how this was affecting him, and by an almost superhuman effort of tact, I managed to steer Madge off. And
not ten minutes later when I happened to have left them
alone a few minutes, I came back to hear Madge saying
scornfully, "*What* great statesman ever said that?" Merciful powers! She was off on politics!

I narrowly averted catastrophe again, but I was worried. There seemed to be something about being cooped
in like this in the rain that made Madge rambunctious.
There was no hope of its clearing off by evening, anyway, so I decided to call up Will and tell him we'd be
ready to come home if he'd just drive out after us.
Madge seemed more tractable someway in Montrose.

But nature, which had been playing along with me in
honeysuckles and moonlight, had apparently turned
against me. Though we hadn't even noticed any lightning, the telephone was out of kilter, completely dead.
I couldn't get Will, there was nothing to do but to stay
right there and wait for him to come.

The afternoon dragged along with me hurling my tact
into one breach after another and Madge seeming more
perversely determined to kill her own chances with every
slow, rainy hour. By six, it seemed to me I should go
crazy if Will didn't come. It had turned cold along with
the rain and I barely kept Madge from putting on a dis-

reputable old khaki sweater of Will's over my very becoming blue pique. Seven, and still Will hadn't come. It was the most uncongenial threesome, and yet I actually didn't dare leave Wells and Madge alone, with her in her present mood.

Half-past seven. Still pouring and no Will.

Suddenly, above the swish-swish of the rain, we heard footsteps hurrying over the wood porch floor. There was a sharp, anxious-sounding rap at the door. Wells went to open it, and we heard a strange voice, a man's.

"Have you got a telephone that's working here? Or a car of any kind?"

I heard Wells say No, and Madge and I went to the door curiously. There was a young fellow, drenched to the skin, and with the most scared frantic-looking face I've ever seen. Wells was about to close the door when I interrupted:

"What's the trouble?"

"My wife's having a baby," he said in a shaky voice, "and I'm after a doctor. Doctor Hessey said he'd come out from Verblen, but all the telephones out our way are off. I started off in the car and the gas tank sprang a leak back a ways on the wood road and I can't run another foot. What's the next nearest house?"

"Tollheimers," I said, "but they're all away in their car; they drove past here this morning. And it's two miles to the Browns. Is it your wife's first baby?"

But I needn't have asked, the sheer terror on his face would have told anybody it was. And his wife was on the old Harley farm, five miles away. Will might be along any minute in the car, but it might be hours before he came—it would take two hours to drive into Verblen, anyway, two more hours back with the doctor, even if there wasn't a minute's delay— I felt myself sharing the terror in the young husband's face. There was just a young girl out there with his wife—no wonder he was scared!

I turned frantically to Wells.

"We've got to get a doctor," I said. "What can we do?"

But before Wells could answer, Madge said:

"Can we make that old wreck of a flivver in the shed run?"

"I don't know," I gasped. "And I don't know of a doctor nearer than Verblen—"

Madge turned sharply to Wells.

"See if you can get that old flivver started," she ordered. "Dot, where did you put that little black bag of mine?"

For a dazed second I wondered what on earth Madge wanted of the little black bag she'd insisted on bringing. Why stop for a bag when you've got to get a doctor. Then suddenly the truth flared into my mind. *Madge was a doctor.*

Wells had suddenly seemed to realize that he was the only man in the crowd—the poor scared young husband didn't count.

"Now don't let's lose our heads," he said in his masterful way. And to the young man, "The thing to do is for you to beat it right on to the next house—that old flivver won't run and—"

"How do you know it won't?" Madge interrupted.

Wells glanced at her with the irritated air of a man who is interrupted while he's being masterful.

"For one thing, there's no gasoline in it," he said patiently.

"There's gas in the tank of the stove, isn't there?" Madge demanded. I nodded.

"The tires are all flat," said Wells.

"Ride 'em flat," said Madge.

She snatched up Will's awful khaki sweater, stuck an old hat of his on her head, and grabbed her black kit.

"Come along," she ordered.

The young husband followed us blindly through the cottage, out the back door, into the dark shed.

Wells climbed up and looked into the wreck of an old flivver.

"There, I told you," he said triumphantly. "There isn't even a self-starter." Madge slipped on the wet shed floor and Wells put his arm around her to steady her, a masculine, protective gesture. Madge shook it off.

"Get the gas in the tank, quick," she said.

With shaking hands, the young husband and I emptied the kitchen stove tank, poured the gasoline into the flivver.

"Crank the car," said Madge to Wells.

Wells started to obey the order automatically, it was so sharp and authoritative. He gave the crank two or three turns. Then—

"I told you this car wouldn't run," he said. "And if you're wise—"

But Madge didn't even hear him. She brushed him aside as though he were a mosquito.

"Give me that crank," she said.

Wells just stood looking on as Madge cranked the car. Of course, cranking a flivver is more a knack than a matter of strength. I was thinking of that poor young wife away up in the Harley farm and I could hear my own heart thumping while I waited. Madge turned the crank once more. The engine gave a couple of thumping sounds and then actually started. A cough—a few back fires, but it ran!

"Got my bag?" Madge asked. "All right. Get in."

Silently, swiftly, we all climbed in. There seemed nothing to do but to obey Madge. I had the queerest feeling of trust. She didn't seem like Madge Edwards at all; there in the old khaki sweater and a man's hat she was a doctor. Wells had never driven a car as cheap as a flivver, the young husband didn't know how, either. So Madge took the wheel. The engine coughed and the emergency brake squeaked as she took it off. But the car started. We drove out into the driving rain, headed her toward the wood road. It was almost dark, and of course we had no lights.

How Madge did drive! The old car flopped and bumped along on its flat tires, the wheels slewed in the slimy mud, the steering wheel shook and shivered.

"It's stark crazy to drive a car like this," Wells said to me on the back seat, "over wet roads."

"We've got to get there," I explained tensely, "before it gets too dark to see the road."

The foot brake didn't hold, I could feel that on the first down hill, knew Madge must be using the reverse instead, by the way the engine kept dying. We drove along in tight silence through the half dark and the driving rain. Only once again on the whole trip did any one speak. That was as we skidded and half turned around on Soap Hill.

"There's no use killing us all," said Wells.

Madge didn't turn her eyes an instant from the road ahead.

"Get out and walk back if you want to," she said.

"I'll go with you, of course," said Wells, with great dignity, "but there's no need for such an insane rush as this."

Madge made the only other comment of the entire trip. Curt, scornful:

"Tell that to the stork," she said.

It all seems like a queer dream, the wild ride through the rain, the lights of the little farm house suddenly appearing. Then the still queerer dream. The scared young neighbor girl posted home by Madge, the dazed willing young husband blindly doing what Madge told him, myself following Madge's orders as fast as I could, Wells humped up in the empty parlor, waiting. Water boiling, the sickish scent of chloroform—our shadows flickering big and black in the lamplight—a sudden sinking of sheer panic with Madge right there, firm and steady as Gibraltar.

Then out of the wild dream and the panic the sudden, faint, sharp sound of a baby's cry.

.   .   .   .

At two o'clock the next morning I was still too jibbery with excitement to have even thought of our ruined matchmaking schemes. The telephones had started work-

ing again before eleven and Will had come after us all
and we'd driven back to Montrose. We'd had hot
coffee in our kitchen and Wells had gone home and
Madge, yawning and beginning to relax, had gone up to
bed. It was coming upstairs and seeing her through the
crack in the door in my old rose-colored crêpe kimono, her
black hair curled tight with the rain, her cheeks pinker
than her gown, that made me suddenly remember Wells,
not as the rather weak member of a rescue party that he
had certainly been last night, but as the ardent suitor
he had been until then. The suitor lost forever. For
while maybe some lovers might have weathered Madge
in her man's hat, cranking the car, ordering everybody
about, proving herself far and away the best man in
the bunch, I knew well enough that Wells wouldn't. Our
scheming had come to naught. It couldn't have been
helped, of course, but there was no dodging the truth.
As a lover, Madge had lost Wells Prentice forever.

I paused a moment at the crack of her door to say
goodnight. Madge yawned comfortably.

"Well, I guess to-night squelched Wells Prentice for
good," she observed.

I fairly gasped. Had Madge then known what had
been going on all along? I was so amazed I could only
falter:

"Why, did you—has he—"

"Has he!" Madge interrupted. "I guess this is the
first day since I've been in Montrose that he hasn't pro-
posed to me."

I just stood in the doorway, utterly speechless, completely dashed. All this week, while we'd been scheming

our heads off trying to work him up to the proposing point!

"I suppose I oughtn't to repeat it," Madge admitted, dropping back lazily onto her pillow, "but it's tit for tat. He's the kind who'd kiss and tell, himself. He hasn't spared me one of the girls who have been running after him."

"And he asked you to marry him?" I finally managed to get out.

"Heavens, yes! A half a dozen times," Madge yawned.

"And you—you refused?"

Madge didn't even bother to straighten up.

"Refused!" she echoed. "Well, naturally. You don't suppose I'd even dream of being tied up to that selfish, opinionated, incompetent, conceited pinhead of a man, do you?"

I merely stared.

"I'm engaged, anyway," Madge went on carelessly.

"I'm going to marry the best doctor in the state of Illinois. Or at least, he's going to be the best. We aren't saying anything about it because he's got another year in the hospital yet, and we're going to wait till we've both built up a practice. So don't tell any of the girls."

I said faintly that I wouldn't and that I hoped she'd be very happy. At least I guess I said that. I was so dazed I'm not quite sure. The excitement of the chase, so to speak, being suddenly over, I suddenly realized how it had been blinding me to the truth. Pictures came flashing through my mind like cut-backs in a movie. Madge bathing the twins in the pink bungalow apron,

Madge cheering up poor, half-blind Mrs. Keane with a tender tact that would bring tears to your eyes, Madge slewing and bumping that old wreck of a car through the rain and the dark, Madge smiling down at the tiny scrap of the new-born baby in the crook of her arm—Madge as brave and ready as any man, as sweet and true as any woman. And we'd dared think of Wells Prentince for her!

I leaned over and kissed Madge. I couldn't say what I was thinking, that sort of thing is said so much it doesn't have any meaning when you put it into words. But what I was hoping, humbly and honestly, was that the best doctor in the state of Illinois was as deserving as he was lucky.

XI

"IT's the first baby," observed Rosemary, tucking a khaki-colored blanket about her fourth, "who gets the shell-pink sweaters."

We all knew that she was talking about Dulcie, just as you can usually tell by the tone when any of our mothers' generation are talking about Miss Prescott. It is seldom even necessary to mention names.

"It certainly is," Corinne agreed. "She"—we all knew, of course, that "she" meant Dulcie—"she washes a sweater every single day for little Dulcie and puts on two clean dresses a day, a hand-embroidered one for afternoon. She says that she thinks it's very important to instill an appreciation of daintiness and beauty in a child's mind."

"A child of ten months has got precious little mind to instill anything in, if you ask me," said Mrs. Frank Kirsted. "Frankie, come away from those eggs." We had met, as some of the crowd nearly always does meet, at the Busy Bee Grocery, doing our daily marketing.

"Dulcie makes me sick, anyhow," said Rosemary feelingly. "She's so everlastingly pleased with herself. She told me yesterday that it was a girl's duty to keep just as young and fresh looking after her babies comes as she did before. She said"—Rosie paused for effect—"that she

251

made a special point of lying flat on the sofa and relaxing every afternoon while she puts little Dulcie on a comfort on the floor beside her for her daily rollic."

We all just looked at each other, words failing us. Rosie recovered speech first.

"When my four go in for a 'rollic,' " she said, "is not the time I pick for relaxing. I sit tight and only pray they won't jar the filling out of my back teeth."

"I don't wish anybody any ill luck," I said feelingly, "but I hope Dulcie's next baby is twins."

At this moment I missed one of my own twins. Just a second before, it seemed to me, they had been staggering around under my eyes, and beyond keeping an eye on the oil can faucet which was just within their reach, I had felt very comfortable about them.

"Where's Jill?" I gasped.

The other girls looked around.

"She didn't go out the door, I know," said Mrs. Kirsted, "because I've been watching it."

I hurried to the back of the store. There, among the boxes all packed up with the day's orders, ready for delivery, was Jill, her little blonde curl standing straight up, wobbling around among the boxes, taking a can of baking powder out of this order and putting it in that, lugging a head of lettuce or a bag of bananas half across the store to put it in some other box.

Horrified, I tried to undo the damage she had done, hoping Nat wouldn't come back till I was through, but the order slips in the boxes were carbons and not so very plain and, though I did the best I could, I finally left with the feeling that some people were going to be sur-

prised at the groceries they got that day.   Talking about
Dulcie always makes us all forget everything else.

There is nothing that makes me feel as well acquainted
with people as old as Mother and Mother Horton as realizing that every generation seems to have its Dulcie.   And
Miss Prescott is the Dulcie for Mother and Father's
bunch.   Not that she was ever as pretty as Dulcie or as
good at taking other girls' beaux away from them which
was the way Dulcie used to keep all our crowd nervous
most of the time before we were married, but Miss Prescott had something almost as important as beauty.   Even
when she was just a young girl in Montrose, she was
rich.   Not terribly rich like the Scoggins and the Burrises, but plenty rich enough for a single woman.

Plenty of the Montrose men who were young at the
time she was wouldn't have minded marrying a girl with
money of her own.   Mr. Pettibone used to court her,
Mother told me, and even funny, grouchy old Mr. Long.
It gives you an awfully funny feeling to hear about anybody like that ever having courted anybody but their own
wives; it always seems as though they must have been
born married.   And I must say, looking at the men who
courted Miss Prescott, after twenty-five or thirty years,
it didn't look as though she'd passed up much.

Staying single, though, and being independently off,
Miss Prescott had a chance to be a pest to people of her
own age in a way that, naturally, would never even have
occurred to Dulcie.   When it became very clear that she
wasn't going to get married, Miss Prescott had taken to
clubs.

Not but what clubs are all right in their way; Mother

and Mother Horton belong to the Ossili and everybody in town who amounts to anything belongs to the Women's Club. Clubs, as Father says, are all right for women who can take 'em or leave 'em alone, but Miss Prescott wasn't one of those women. Clubs had got her, Father said, the way drink gets some men. Father, of course, was prejudiced against her and her clubs because she was the first one in town to get the idea that women's clubs ought to do good work for the community, not just furnish pleasure for their members. And Father was one of those who got caught in this first good done to the community.

"I don't know anything about doing the community good," said Father disgustedly, "but she's certainly done the merchants and done them *good*." Father who always uses excellent grammar except when he doesn't on purpose, meant, of course, that Miss Prescott had done the merchants *well*.

It was about closing the store on Saturday night. All the stores used to keep open till ten o'clock and often till midnight. Saturday night was the big shopping time of the week for everybody who didn't live right in town. All the farmers drove in right after supper and if you went down town after seven o'clock, it was as much as your life was worth to get across Main Street. The curbs of all the side streets were lined with flivvers till you couldn't have found a place to park a kiddy car.

Everybody took this for granted, of course. It's the same in Verblen and even in Berrytown, but Miss Prescott who has been to London and Paris and goes to the state capital all the time, said that all the stores in the bigger places closed at six o'clock on Saturday, like any

other day, and that it wasn't fair to the salespeople to
make them work a thirteen-hour day once a week.

At first nobody paid any attention to this; the merchants just saying that if the salespeople didn't kick, why
should Miss Prescott? and when would the farmers shop?
The president of the Women's Club whose husband owns
the biggest hardware store in town, appointed a committee and made Miss Prescott chairman, which allowed the
president to appear progressive and still pass the buck.

Mrs. Scoggins announced that she wished to entertain
the club at a garden tea and in this excitement Miss Prescott's idea was generally forgotten. The first thing anybody knew about it, one of the committee called on Father
and told him that the owner of the Emporium said he
would shut up Saturday night if Father would. How
anybody ever got old Spinney to promise that, nobody
ever knew. At first Father hemmed and hawed around,
but Mrs. Holder kept right after him, and it began to be
rumored that the furniture store was going to close and
Wells, the jeweler. Father held out for quite a while,
but when Mother came home from Women's Club, all
worked up about it and said Father was purposely making
her life hard for her, he just gave up. He said there'd
been dirty work at the crossroads somehow, but nobody
knew just what had happened, except that Miss Prescott
had started it all.

That was only the beginning. She just wore the
Women's Club out, sicking them onto first one thing and
then another. Nobody liked to stand out against being
progressive; the club took up one reform after another
that were all good enough in their way but that nobody

would ever have worried about if it hadn't been for Miss
Prescott.   She got the dangerous road out on Soap Hill
changed and got the old Jefferson school building con-
demned—goodness knows it was a fire-trap!—and plenty
of other things that were good for the town, of course,
but stirred people up and made lots of trouble.   It had
got so that the older people called Miss Prescott "she"
about as our young bunch called Dulcie, and wished to
goodness that she had got married and had had something besides reforming everything to think about.

And then she organized the Mothers' Club.

"Wouldn't you *know* she'd have done it?" the older
people said, in the very words our young bunch used when
Dulcie enameled the inside of their flivver French gray
and made rose-colored slip covers for it.

It really did seem like quite a sketch for an old maid
to be getting up a Mothers' Club.   All our young crowd
joined, though, partly, I must confess, because she said
we could have our meetings out in her new house and
we were all crazy to see the place.   That was the reason,
of course, that Mrs. Long joined.   None of the older
crowd did except her, because, as Mother Horton said,
while she supposes she is still a mother, goodness knows
she's stopped working at it.   Mrs. Long's daughter is
married and gone and it seemed the silliest thing in the
world for her to join a Mothers' Club except that it did
give her a chance to tell around town that Miss Prescott
had electric light fixtures that, to her taste, just ruined the
whole house.   Mrs. Long is a sharp-tongued, gossipy old
cat if ever one lived.

All the rest of the members were our young crowd and

two or three of the girls in the Harvester bunch and a
couple from the Church Street crowd. It was a jolly
bunch and we looked forward to having quite a lot of fun
out of the club and not to let Miss Prescott put anything
over on us. We'd heard so much about her from the old
people that we were well on our guard. She might be
able to run the Women's Club, but an old maid would
be out of her line trying to run a mothers' club.

"Wait till she's put on three mustard plasters four
times a day and then let her talk to me about being a
mother," said Rosie, whose entire family was down with
bronchial colds at once.

"I suppose she'll want us to go in for psychology,"
hazarded Mrs. Frank Kirsted, "but she needn't think
that's anything new to us. I've done my best to bring up
Frankie according to the modern methods and not let
him get any inhibitions or anything."

The rest of us glanced at each other at that, Frankie
Kirsted being the worst spoiled little pest in Montrose.

"The best method for Frankie would be to tie him
up in a sack and drop him off a high bridge," said Dulcie
in a low voice to me. There's always been a little edge
between Dulcie and Mrs. Frank Kirsted—they're the two
prettiest girls in town and I suppose it's only natural, and
then one time Dulcie found Frankie trying to feed little
Dulcie poison ivy and that prejudiced her still more.

Miss Prescott, however, didn't try to tell any of us how
we ought to bring up our babies. She really wasn't bossy
a bit and, to everybody's surprise, we all found that we
liked her. Of course, she introduced a lot more good
works into the club than we'd figured on. We had elected

her president out of compliment, on account of her having organized the club, and she kept bringing up one thing after another that she said, as mothers, of course we were interested in. Like seeing that the health inspector kept after old Van Holderen about his cows, though wo all took our milk from the Harrises, so Van Holderen's cows were nothing to us one way or the other. And getting up a subscription for a visiting nurse to tell the Hunky mothers down by the tracks not to give their babies coffee, and calling on the school board to protest about the lighting in the primary rooms, though none of our children were old enough to go to school.

I had to hand it to her, the slick way she got us all to work; having been chairman of the Alumnæ bazaar myself, once, and having seen the way everybody left everything for me to do. We would probably have left everything to Miss Prescott in just the same way, but she would appoint a committee and then call on the chairman for reports in a way that would be embarrassing if you didn't have anything to report. In fact, it became so strenuous that there were times when we felt about the way our mothers did about her.

"If she were a real mother instead of just president of a mothers' club," said Corinne, "she'd find she didn't have so much time for all this reforming, either."

That, of course, was one reason we didn't get antagonized at Miss Prescott, the way our mothers did. Ours being a mothers' club, we had a real advantage over her. She might be richer and older and smarter and everything else, but on that one point we had her. She was the only one in the club who wasn't a real mother.

It was a bit of a rest at that when she went away for two months in the summer. I must admit that we relaxed considerably on the good works. As we didn't have her big living room to meet in then, Mrs. Long said that if the club would like to fix it up we could use one floor of her warehouse for a regular meeting room. The warehouse was vacant right now, but it had been rented and the new people wouldn't be using the top floor. We were tickled to death, of course—having your own club-room makes any club seem so much more important. There was a very exciting meeting while plans were made for furnishing our club-room. Father had said that he would give us three wicker chairs and several of the other merchants were going to give us things, too.

I didn't happen to be at that meeting on account of a rather peculiar job I had at home. I had had everything arranged to go, America was to be at the house washing that day and would keep an eye on the children. Will had got little Ben Brace to come and paint the trim on the garage, having decided that, what with the garden and everything, he'd never get around to it, himself, and Ben could be got for only seventy-five cents a day. But Ben was a faithful hard-working little fellow and I wouldn't need to be on hand to watch him. I just strolled out once, about two o'clock, just as I was ready to leave for the club, to see how he was getting along.

"Hello, Ben," I said, "how does it go?"

I could see without asking that it was going all right. Over half the job was already done, but I wanted to be pleasant. Ben had been to work for us before and he was such a sturdy, dependable kid that I had taken quite

a fancy to him. I guess the real reason for my taking a
fancy, though, wasn't because he was hard-working and
dependable, but because he looked like my little Jack.
He had the same kind of blue eyes and sort of sandy hair
and he wrinkled his nose when he smiled, just as my
baby does. I couldn't help thinking of my little Jack at
ten or twelve having to paint garages for seventy-five
cents a day and it made me feel kind of friendly and unhappy about Ben, both at once. I always made it a point
to have a specially good dinner the days he came to work
and I usually had him stop and have a glass of root beer
and a doughnut or a cookie in the middle of the afternoon.

To-day when I went out to speak to him, though, he
wasn't friendly and nice as he always had been before.
He answered my question with a "A'right, I guess" and
didn't look at me, just went on painting.

"What's the matter, Ben?" I asked. "Don't you feel
well?"

"Sure, I'm all right," he said.

Of course, it wasn't really any of my business how Ben
acted, so long as he went on painting the garage trim, but
I kind of hated to go off and leave him. I had a hunch
that he wasn't just being surly; it struck me that something
was wrong, that if he had been a girl he'd have been crying, but being a little boy he was being rude, instead. So,
though he let me see plain enough that he didn't want
me, I kept hanging around. And finally, without his
really telling me, I found out what was the trouble.

A bunch of boys had come by and tried to get him
to go swimming with them.

Well, I knew just how he felt. It was a hot day and it isn't much fun to stay and paint garages while all the other boys are going swimming. Still, Ben was earning seventy-five cents, I reminded him. And then I learned that he didn't get one cent of it himself. The man he'd been living with since his mother died just farmed him out summers and Saturdays and after school hours. To pay for boarding him, the man said.

That did seem awful, a boy only twelve years old just isn't built to go to school and work all the time with no fun. I hated to go on to club meeting. I knew I shouldn't enjoy a minute of it for thinking of Ben at home painting the garage and just crazy to go swimming.

"Maybe you can go before supper time, after you get through?" I said.

"Nope," said Ben. "Gotta go home and do chores."

I meant to hesitate just a minute longer but in that minute I found out that Ben hadn't been swimming one single time all summer.

That was too much. I just couldn't stand it. I thought of my little Jack standing there in those blue overalls, painting somebody's garage while all the other boys were swimming, day after day after day. I took off the new rajah coat I'd put on for club meeting.

"Cut along, Ben," I said, "and catch up with the other boys. I'll finish up this painting."

At first Ben couldn't believe it, but it doesn't take long for a twelve-year-old boy to take in anything like that. With a look at me as though he didn't dare tarry for fear he'd wake up, he was off.

So I had to get out of my new dress and white kid

shoes and into an old gingham I kept for rough work. I felt it really was up to me to do the painting because I had a feeling that while Will might think it was a darn shame for a kid not to get to swimming all summer, he'd feel that it wasn't very businesslike to pay him seventy-five cents a day for going.

So I didn't get to that meeting of the Mothers' Club.

I didn't get there the next week, either. America couldn't come to wash till Thursday and I couldn't find anybody to stay with the babies. I put in the afternoon painting the window-boxes and the backs of the front porch steps—painting the garage had got me started and you know how it is once you get started painting. The painting got me to thinking about Ben Brace and I couldn't put him out of my head, a twelve-year-old boy who looked like my baby and never got a chance to go swimming. All the time I was painting I kept thinking about him and my little Jack. Jack and Jill were playing out inside their chicken wire, every now and then bringing something over to show me; Jack always opened his eyes wide and looked so surprised at everything he found and said, "O-o-oh! 'tick!" when he'd show me a stick. And as I painted along, I couldn't keep from thinking—suppose it were Jack, all alone in the world with nobody but a man who would farm him out every minute and never let him have any fun.

Dulcie stopped by on her way home from Mothers' Club meeting to tell me the news. Mrs. Kirsted had brought Frankie and it being so hot Mrs. Vanter had taken off her hat and while the meeting was going on, nobody remembered Frankie and he had taken off all the trimming and was filling the hat with dirt, to plant the trimming in, he said. Also, the Emporium had given the club a wicker divan.

"We're going to see if the electrical fixture store won't give us some plain fixtures," Dulcie went on with the news. "And Mrs. Long is simply furious. Some boys broke into the warehouse one day last week and broke a lot of windows and pulled some of the electric wiring loose and did some other damage, I guess. She found out who they were, some of the Hunkies down by the tracks and she's had them arrested. She's simply wild; she's going over to Verblen Friday to appear against them."

Also Miss Prescott was coming back the end of the week and Betty Bartell wanted to join the club though her baby wasn't due till fall. And so on, Dulcie certainly had a lot of news.

Thursday afternoon I took the twins up to Mother's and used her electric sewing machine all the afternoon. When I got back, America, who had been at my house washing, said a woman had been to see me, a "Mrs. Rzwqtrvs," it sounded like when America tried to say the name and I couldn't imagine who it was. America said she said something about the Mothers' Club, but I couldn't place any member with a name that sounded like that and I finally gave it up.

Will wasn't going to be home that night; he and Father Horton had gone out to Berrytown to appraise some farms and were going to stay overnight and go on the next day to look at some property on beyond. Dulcie's house being so close, I wasn't a bit afraid to stay alone

with the babies, but when I heard a knock at the back
door after dark, it did give me a bit of a start. However, to my relief, I saw that it was just Ben Brace. He'd
come to get his sweater, a poor, ratty, little, old thing
that he'd left in the garage.

"Come on in, Ben, and have a piece of chocolate cake,"
I said. The poor kid always looked so spindly I had
a feeling he didn't get such terribly good board in spite
of working hard for it. So I gave him a glass of milk
and a veal loaf sandwich and a peach, too, and sat out
on the kitchen stool watching him eat.

"I got 'rested the other day," he suddenly said between
bites:

"Arrested, Ben!" I gasped. "When? What for?"

"The day you let me go swimmin'," he said. "For
playing in a empty building. We stopped on the way
back from the Hole."

My heart sank. He must have been with those Hunkies
when they got into Mrs. Long's warehouse.

"Oh, Ben," I said, "you all did a lot of damage."

"Yes'm," said Ben. "We didn't plan to do no damage—we just got to fooling and we broke some windows
and wires 'n things." He paused a moment. "It was
an empty building," he said hopefully.

"And you have to appear before Judge Corson?"

"Yes'm, to-morrow."

"Is your—the man you live with going with you?"

"Yes'm," said Ben.

You could see, just mentioning this man, that Ben was
afraid of him. He'd given Ben a terrible whipping for
getting arrested. Someway, Ben, sitting there on the

other kitchen stool eating a piece of chocolate cake as
though he'd never had a piece in his life before, looking
so little and spindly and kiddy, made things seem different. It had seemed natural enough for Mrs. Long
to have a gang of boys who'd broken into her warehouse
arrested—it never occurred to me that they weren't regular young criminals, out deliberately breaking windows
and wires and everything. But Ben, sitting there eating
chocolate cake, didn't look any more like a criminal than
my little Jack asleep upstairs.

"It was an *empty* building," he repeated.

An empty building—I could remember when we were
youngsters how we always used to play in the old canning
factory. And Will and the other boys were always getting into empty houses if they could. Of course, it used
to make the owners mad, but nobody ever dreamed of its
being criminal. I cut Ben another piece of cake—that
poor kid wasn't any more criminal than I was, myself.
He'd just got into bad company.

It worried me all night. I knew Judge Corson had the
reputation of being pretty hard on people and Mrs. Long,
of course, is always mean as vinegar anyway. I felt
awfully sorry for Ben. Dulcie ran in first thing in the
morning to see that I was all right, having been alone
in the house.

"Did you see Mrs. Rapotowski last night?" she asked.

"Mrs. who?"

"Mrs. Rapotowski. One of the Hunky women down
by the tracks. She's been around trying to see the members of the Mothers' Club."

That must have been the woman America told me about.

"What does she want of the Mothers' Club?" I asked, puzzled.

Dulcie shrugged her shoulders.

"She seemed to think the Mothers' Club would do something about her boy that Mrs. Long had arrested, you know, for breaking into the warehouse. I said, 'Goodness, Mrs. Rapotowski, the Mothers' Club is a funny place for you to come with anything like that. Our club-room is in the warehouse, you know, and suffered as much as the other floors.'" Dulcie picked up the orange I'd been squeezing for the babies and nibbled at the inside that was left. "Bunch of young criminals!" she added.

I thought of little Ben Brace.

"Ben Brace is no criminal," I said. "There's nothing criminal in a boy breaking into an empty building and you know it. I'll bet your own husband used to do it."

"Well, don't jump on me about it," said Dulcie. "It isn't my warehouse. Go tell Mrs. Long you bet her husband used to, too."

Mrs. Long's husband has just got a divorce and Dulcie laughed good-naturedly at the idea.

"Mrs. Rapotowski was all worked up about it," she added. "She's afraid they'll send her precious Nick to the reform school. You ought to have seen her hat. Somebody'd given it to her when willow plumes were still in style."

Honestly, when Dulcie said that, it seemed as though the sunshine pouring over my kitchen table had suddenly

gone gray. If the Hunkies were sent to the reform
school Ben would be, too!

The reform school! Why, it's almost like a prison
record for a man! The only boy I'd ever heard of who
had to go never had lived it down. At the very best it
would be a terrible handicap for years. As though Ben
didn't have handicaps enough! I would see that kid face
of his— "It was an *empty* building"—he hadn't meant
a thing in the world but maybe a little mischief. The
reform school for Ben Brace!

After Dulcie had gone I just stood staring at the table
for several minutes. Then I stopped and pulled myself
together. This just couldn't be let happen. Something
had got to be done. If Will were only home! I looked
at the kitchen clock, eight o'clock. No use to telephone
Will at the Berrytown hotel; he'd said they were going
to be up and off by seven. I had no idea where I could
get him before night. And the hearing was in Verblen
at three that afternoon.

If I could only have got Father Horton. He has a
lot of influence with all the politicians and takes lots of
interest in getting young people started right. Mother
Horton always says she expects to see him come home
some day with a bead band around his head and telling
her he's joined the Campfire Girls. Surely he could have
done something about Ben. But both Will and Father
Horton were as far out of reach as the moon.

I pushed some breakfast down the twins, fastened them
into the back seat of the flivver with their safety straps,
so they couldn't climb out and dashed down to the store
to find Father. He wouldn't have been as good as Father

Horton even at his best and this day was his very worst.
He prides himself on taking inventory in the store during the dull time in August instead of doing it the last
of the year, like the Emporium, when the clerks are all
in after the Christmas rush. So Father was hard at the
inventory when I got there, trying to get all they possibly could done before customers began coming in. At
first, I couldn't even make him realize that I was talking to him. When he did, he looked up from under a
counter where he was trying to find something or other
and asked:

"Are you or the babies sick or hurt or anything?"

"No, but—" I began.

"Then don't talk to me now," he said. "Come over
to the house to-night."

"I can't—to-night will be too late—"

"That must be fourteen, not nineteen," said Father
to Miss MacAllister, paying no more attention to me
than as though I'd been a breeze blowing in at the door.
Certainly there was no help there.

Then I dashed up to see Mother. She'd just had a
letter from Kathie asking her if she'd make some rompers
like the pattern she was sending and Mother was trying
the pattern out on a piece of pink chambray she'd had in
the house.

"If I piece the sleeves all under the arm, I can get four
out," she said. "What's the trouble, Dotty?" She didn't
know little Ben Brace and wouldn't take her mind off the
rompers. She listened to me in a vague way and I knew
she was calculating on the pieced sleeves all the time.
"Oh, I wouldn't worry about it," she said absently. "The

judge isn't going to send any boy to reform school who hasn't done anything."

Then I went to Mother Horton's. She paid attention to what I said, but she said that the reform school was the place for boys who went around breaking into warehouses.

"It was an *empty* warehouse, Mother Horton," I said. "Why, you know, Will used to break into empty houses, himself."

"He never broke into a warehouse. I'm sure of that!" said Mother Horton.

"That was because there wasn't any warehouse in Montrose then," I said. "He might have if there had been."

"Well," said Mother Horton neatly, "nobody was ever sent to the reform school for something he might have done."

And as far as she was concerned, that closed the subject. I climbed back into the car, beginning to feel desperate. Something had simply got to be done. Then I happened to think of Mrs. Rapotowski thinking the Mothers' Club might do something about it and it struck me that that mightn't be such a silly idea and drove to Rosemary's.

Rosie was sympathetic enough, but not helpful. She hoped Ben wouldn't get sent to the reform school, but that was as far as it went. Of course, no house where there are four children under six years old is any place to go for help in the morning. I drove from there up to Mrs. Frank Kirsted's. That was a million times worse. Frankie had been exposed to measles and Mrs. Kirsted was frantic and had been taking his temperature every half hour all morning to see if he'd caught them and the last time Frankie had got mad and bitten the end off the thermometer and I had to stay till the doctor got there.

Corinne didn't know Ben Brace and said she didn't see what the Mothers' Club could possibly do about it, anyway. She didn't believe they'd send a boy to reform school for just that and had I forgotten that this was the afternoon of Dulcie's baby party for little Dulcie's first birthday? I actually had forgotten but as soon as I remembered I realized that it would be useless to tackle Dulcie.

That was the way it went everywhere. The twins got tired and cross, being strapped into the flivver so long, and both yelled blue murder, their voices floating after like streamers as I drove from place to place. When I finally got home at noon, I had tried everybody I could think of and there wasn't a soul who would do anything.

As I fed the children and got them down for their naps, I made up my mind that, though I didn't see what on earth I could do, I should have to go over to Verblen by myself that afternoon. Someway, watching little Jack eating spinach, his funny fat little hand grabbing the spoon like a shovel, I knew that, though it was a cinch I couldn't do anything to help, at least I'd got to go.

I called up Mother and she said she'd got the rompers all cut and stitched up and that she'd bring them down to finish by hand and watch the twins, so once more I started out in the flivver.

I shall never forget the scared gloomy feeling I had

riding off down Main Street. I had a feeling of something terrible about to happen that I'd got to stop and
couldn't. It was a terrible, frantic, miserable feeling.
Mrs. Pomeroy, one of the Harvester crowd members of
the club that I'd seen that morning, said I mustn't get sentimental, that her husband said that was why women were
no good outside their own homes, they were always
getting sentimental.

Probably I was sentimental, but I couldn't help it. I
couldn't think of Ben chasing off for his first swim without the tears coming to my eyes. And now he'd have to
go to reform school! And I should be right there to see
it happen and wouldn't be able to do a thing to stop it!
It was a lonesome, gloomy feeling.

As I drove past Father's store I slowed up with the
desperate idea of making one more try at him, but when
I saw how many people were going into the store, I realized it would be useless. Besides, I didn't have an awful
lot of time to waste. Judge Corson's office is on the
farther side of Verblen.

I was driving along, feeling more and more miserable
every minute. At the station, Number Six was just in
and people were getting off the train. Somebody bowed
to me in a friendly way and I recognized Miss Prescott.
For a moment I just stared at her slick gray traveling
suit and small black hat. And then suddenly it was as
though the sun had come out from behind the clouds.

"Oh, Miss Prescott, Miss Prescott! Can you wait
just a minute?"

She came over to the flivver and desperately I told her
what I'd been telling all over Montrose all morning. But

how different it was. Miss Prescott listened and paid attention and understood. She'd never seen Ben, but she thought it was awful, even for the Hunkies. She put her suitcase in the back of the sedan and climbed into the front seat beside me. I drove along, feeling as different from the way I'd started as day from night. Someway, I felt as though I'd been starting alone and now had the whole U. S. army and navy back of me.

Judge Corson's office was little and stuffy, and there was a bunch of black-eyed boys, all scrubbed up within an inch of their lives and looking scared to death. Their mothers were there, too, shabby, worried-looking women; Mrs. Rapotowski in her drooping willow plumes. I saw Ben Brace there with the meanest, sneakiest-looking man. And Mrs. Long, her mouth set on that hard, tight line. Send a boy to reform school—she'd send one to the electric chair if she could, for injuring any of her property! I looked at the black-eyed boys and their shabby, scared-looking mothers, and it suddenly dawned on me that if Ben hadn't thought of doing anything criminal, neither had they. After all, breaking into an empty building wasn't any worse, just because it was some of the bunch down by the tracks that did it. After all, they might be Hunkies, but they were boys. I saw Mrs. Rapotowski looking at her Nick from under her willow plumes. Could it be that Nick looked to her just the way little Jack with his pudgy hand around the spinach spoon did to me?

Judge Corson had just finished sending a boy to the reform school, not one of this crowd but a seventeen-year-old from Verblen, a shifty-eyed, filthy fellow who'd been arrested twice before for stealing. The idea of little Ben

Brace being thrown in with older boys like that just made me sick all over. I didn't even want Mrs. Rapotowski's Nick to be.

Then Judge Corson called on Mrs. Long. You could tell that he was tired and hot and cross. After all, I suppose even judges are human and Judge Corson has the reputation of being terribly hard on all the boys who come up before him. Mrs. Long had an itemized account of all the damage that had been done; she reeled it off. Then the judge heard the policemen who had arrested the boys.

"This seems to be a perfectly clear case," he said. He turned to the shabby mothers and asked if any of them had anything to say. Three leaped up and all began to talk at once, each one trying to talk the loudest and glare the other two down and none of them making themselves understood. It was plain to be seen that this was making Judge Corson all the crosser. He pounded on his desk and said, "One at a time," pointing to the first one. She was so excited you couldn't understand what she said except that Nicolletti was good boy—never no trouble— The other two women jumped again.

Judge Corson rapped sharply for them all to sit down. Mrs. Long smiled that mean I-told-you-so smile of hers.

"Judge Corson, will you allow me to say just one word, please?"

After all the babble Miss Prescott's voice sounded as sweet and cool as a drink of water. Judge Corson nodded to her to go ahead. It was a most courteous, respectful nod. Miss Prescott looked so slim and smart and competent in her well-fitting, quiet clothes. And then, of course, as Judge Corson knew as well as anybody else, right back of Miss Prescott towered the Prescott Building on Main Street and stretched away acre after acre of rich farm land.

For years I'd heard about how Miss Prescott had got the merchants to do this and the Women's Club to do that, I'd seen the clever way she handled our Mothers' Club committees. But I'd never really seen her at work before.

It was a revelation. Quietly she talked, in that soft, well-bred voice of hers. As president of the Mothers' Club she told the judge she was speaking for the mothers who weren't quite intelligible when they spoke for themselves. Her smile was subtly flattering, it was as though it established a sort of understanding between her and the judge. She went on to speak of what a very clean record the district down by the tracks had always had, as far as law-breaking was concerned: she spoke of the warehouse affair which Mrs. Long had said was done out of spite and malice and sheer criminality as a bit of "most unfortunate boy mischief."

It was the strangest thing to see the judge's crossness melting away under that cool, pleasant voice. Just the right touch of flattery here and there—so subtle you could hardly call it flattery, but it worked just like it. You could see Judge Corson fairly purring under it. She felt quite safe in promising, she went on, that the boys' families could be depended upon to see that nothing of the sort happened again. Mrs. Long leaped to her feet.

"What about my warehouse?" she demanded. "That's

already happened. What about what it will cost me to put it back in shape?"

One of the mothers jumped and began to jabber something and the judge pounded.

Miss Prescott did not even look at angry Mrs. Long.

"If your Honor will be good enough to urge Mrs. Long to drop her charge," she said, "I feel sure the parents of the offenders will see that the damage is repaired. If they are not able to do so, I will assume the responsibility, myself."

There was a pause while the judge looked from Miss Prescott to Mrs. Long. It was a queer sort of silence. I never knew before that you could actually feel things, like power or hate in the air. While Miss Prescott had been talking I had thought it must be something in her voice that made you so aware, in spite of her suave, flattering courtesy, of the iron hand inside the velvet glove. But the same feeling was in the very air after she stopped talking. Just as you could actually feel Mrs. Long's hate sizzling, you could feel that quiet, purposeful force. Maybe, of course, it was just Miss Prescott's fame as a reformer, the reputation she's got for always putting things over. I can't be sure.

But I am sure of one thing. Mrs. Long rather sulkily withdrew her charge, and each scared, black-eyed boy was given into the custody of his own mother. All until the judge got to Ben Brace. Judge Corson knew the man Ben was living with and evidently didn't think much of him. He hemmed around, asked the man if he'd ever taken out formal guardianship of Ben? The man never had and the judge asked Ben if he had any relatives. Ben said no. The judge said Ben would be better off in the reform school than with this man.

I had relaxed all over in relief, but when I heard him saying this, everything tightened up again. After all I'd gone through would Ben have to go to the reform school? Unconsciously I clutched Miss Prescott's arm. She was looking at Ben Brace, little and spindly and over-worked. I thought of little Jack at home, and suddenly I knew there was nothing now I could do. Inside me I began praying desperately, asking the Lord to help me. I'd done all I could—couldn't He take care of Ben Brace?

Suddenly I heard Miss Prescott's voice.

"If your Honor approves," she said, "I should like to take the responsibility for this boy, myself."

I could hardly believe I was hearing straight. But I was. It was like a miracle. My prayer was answered. I listened just enough to realize that his Honor did approve, most decidedly, to hear something or other about arrangements. But I only listened absently. Inside, in a sort of daze, I was still praying:

"Oh, thank you, Lord, thank you, thank you—"

I didn't have to say anything more about His looking out for Ben Brace. I knew Miss Prescott could do it just as well.

.   .   .   .

When, three months later, Miss Prescott actually legally adopted Ben, the town had something to talk about for weeks. In spite of the prejudice against the idea of an old maid having a boy to bring up, most people admitted she'd do well by Ben. And a good thing, it would be, plenty of people said. It would give her something to do besides going around town looking for something to improve. It was an awful blow, of course, when the first thing she did after adopting Ben was to get our Mothers' Club to work for a special children's judge and probation officers to be appointed in Verblen.

"You'd think she'd have enough to do at home now, bringing up Ben," said Mrs. Frank Kirsted to me, "without going into politics. But then, of course, you couldn't expect her to take a real mother's interest in a boy she'd just adopted."

A real mother—I thought suddenly of Miss Prescott flying over to Verblen all a-fire to save some boys she had never even seen. And of all the rest of us "real mothers" safely, contentedly looking out for our own children and too busy to lift a hand to help some other woman's. If little Ben Brace, who happened to look like my own baby, hadn't been in the scrape, too, I'd have listened as carelessly as Dulcie when Mrs. Rapotowski begged us to help her Nick.

A real mother. I could remember the very moment when I thought I had become one, that scary moment up in my old sewing room when I heard Jack's faint, quavery little new-baby cry and felt that he and Jill were all alone in the world except for me. But now, standing right on the corner of Main and Water Street talking to Mrs. Frank Kirsted, my own babies over two years old, I had the strangest sense of never having known before what a real mother was. A real mother who could never turn a deaf ear toward the faint quavery cry of anything that was young and helpless and in trouble.

Naturally, I didn't go into this to Mrs. Frank Kirsted. She was too occupied keeping Frankie from getting run over and I wouldn't have, anyway. I merely said mildly that Miss Prescott would never neglect Ben any. Mrs. Kirsted would just have thought I had gone crazy if I had tried to explain to her what I was suddenly thinking. For I was hoping truly and solemnly that having two babies of my own wouldn't keep me from becoming a mother.

THE END